THE HEART OF
FAMILY

A
SAGAS FROM THE SHORES
NOVEL

RENEE FIELD

Heart of Family
Copyright © 2023 Renee Field

All rights reserved. Without limiting the rights under copyright reserved above, no part of this publication may be reproduced, storied in or introduced into a retrieval system, or transmitted, in any form, or by any means (electronic, mechanical, photocopying, recording, or otherwise) without the prior written permission of the copyright owner.

This is a work of fiction. Names, characters, places, brands, media and incidents are either the product of the author's imagination or are used fictitiously. The author acknowledges the trademarked status and trademark owners of various products referenced in this work of fiction, which has been used without permission. The publication/use of these trademarks is not authorized, associated with, or sponsored by the trademark owners.

I would like to dedicate this novel to my own mother, Diane Pace, who took the time to encourage me to pursue my writing passion. Over the years, I've come to appreciate you even more and as we both learn how best to navigate your dementia journey I am relearning how dear you were to me in my fundamental years. You taught me to laugh, dance in the kitchen, savour reading books and love with all my heart. You held me when I cried, always saying things would get better. Now, I'm the one holding your hand. I feel blessed to have you as a mother and while this journey has and is difficult, we are each coping the best way we know how; usually with lots of laughter and yes, tears.
To all the women out there who are struggling to find their voice, identity and love while juggling the demands of motherhood and caregiving this story is for you.

Chapter 1

Fern

"The muffins are burning."

Fern leapt out of the chair, grabbed a dish towel and yanked out the hot muffin tray, burning her thumb in the process. Slamming the tray onto the cutting board, she turned on the cold water for her blistering appendage. "You could have given me a five-minute warning."

Lily rolled her eyes. "You're the baker in the family."

"I'm busy and have a lot on my mind."

"Such as?"

"Stuff," said Fern, sucking her thumb to alleviate the pulsing from the burn. The gesture was childish, but it did make her feel better.

"You're heading to the cottage."

Fern realized this was why Lily was visiting her. She should have expected it, but the visitations were always unexpected. A thrill she never tired of but when Lily left, and she always did as unexpected as she came, the sense of loss often left Fern feeling like she'd walked through a polar vortex to another world where joy got frozen in crystal clear bubbles of memories, slicing through her later like shards of glass.

"It's our time of year," said Fern. "Rose and I need this."

Lily didn't say anything for a full minute.

"What about Willow?"

"I told you about Willow."

"She's family," said Lily, giving Fern one of her famous 'get over it' stares.

"I'm not sure what family means anymore."

Lily laughed. "It's not complicated. You're making it so."

Lily always simplified things but Fern realized her sister was right. She'd had the exact same thought circling in her brain like a repeating fog horn, blaring to her that family was family and to get-over it. Too bad Rose would never agree.

Fern's thumb wasn't throbbing anymore, but she'd have a nice size blister for her carelessness which said next time, put the timer on.

"Everyone deserves a second chance," said Lily.

"Now you sound like Mom."

Lily tilted her head to the side as she leaned against the hutch, looking ageless. How Fern envied her.

"I think that's the nicest thing you've said to me."

Fern grinned, feeling the words Lily said and totally grasping the warmth of their meaning. She turned back to the muffins and started to place them on the cooling rack.

"Mom hasn't been doing so great," said Fern, while thinking she might chuck the muffins into the green bin as they truly did look burnt, which was pathetic.

When Lily didn't respond, Fern looked to where she'd been standing and grimaced. Gone. One minute crashing into her life and then next disappearing without even a goodbye. That more than anything always hurt.

Chapter 2
Rose

Rose craved a cigarette so badly her eyes burned. She hadn't had a cig in six months, but the itch ate at her. This morning it felt like a bug had crawled under her skin and every fibre of her being said walk those two blocks to the corner store and buy a pack. Last night she'd dreamt of Lily, which always made her sad. Lily was the reason why she'd started smoking anyway. Or more to the fact, Lily dying drove her to start smoking. Yup, all Lily's fault. Rose wiped away a tear. She would not cry or give into her craving. Instead, she drank a fifth cup of black coffee and swallowed an aspirin. The sound of Harold snoring rolled through the small townhouse like a broken foghorn.

How could a person go from loving someone so much to loathing them intensely sometimes? Rose recognized now she had never loved her first husband, but he'd been nice, and it had seemed exotic he had been a navy guy. She'd only discovered he liked to play the field after their second child had been born. The knowledge had hurt but it hadn't buckled her. She had done what had to be done–gotten divorced. Thankfully, he had been okay with it and while he paid his child support payments, he certainly didn't cough up anything else for his kids. Take for instance splitting the cost of any sport teams the kids played on. Nope. It was a concept out of his realm of thinking. Adding her planned getaway with her sister this coming week meant shutting her mouth and being more polite than usual when dealing with him. It had been grating. The one week out of the entire year she and Fern escaped. To get him to agree to have his kids for the entire freaking week, she had to agree to have them for three weeks so he could take his new twenty-something lover to Costa Rica. Sad, Rose had said yes instantly.

To top it off, last week she'd discovered Harold had added a password to his cell. Nothing wrong with being safe, but for Harold to go out of his way to set it up screamed something she didn't want to examine. Something her first husband had gifted her–mistrust.

Rose thought to ask Toby, her eldest, if he'd set it up for Harold but Toby was like an unwanted house guest. He blew in, made a mess, and was best left alone. When pressed, Toby could be a firecracker so Rose didn't ask the question pressing on her subconscious.

This morning could have been another shouting match, but for once she'd kept silent. Plus, Harold wouldn't do that to her, she told herself for the umpteenth time. Harold had his own problems but those involved the bottle and his need to pretend he'd made it big, when he realized deep down they were barely holding on to what they had. Harold didn't screw around. He loved her. Harold had loved her for two years before she'd even dared a date with him and then it had been six months before she'd let him into her bed. He had been patient, letting her set the pace. She would disregard the nagging doubt seeping into her marriage like a leaky faucet. And leaky faucets were Harold's specialty. He was a plumber who worked with the city, but it seemed everyone in the city wanted a plumber to visit off-hours or the weekend, so his weekend time meant side projects for cash.

Eleven years later, Rose felt they were no closer to achieving their goals and it irked her. Where did the money go? Well, groceries ate more than half her pay. Eating healthy wasn't cheap, but Rose, like Fern, would never let her kids go hungry. She knew from first-hand experience what it felt like and she'd rather work two or three jobs to ensure it never happened to her family. Harold wanted Toby to pay rent and earn his keep, but Rose couldn't do it. At twenty, he worked the night shift for Costco. It wasn't a life plan, but Rose didn't think Toby would ever have a plan. Her ex wanted Toby to enlist. Said it would make a man out of him. Never going to happen. Toby took after her father's Siteman side of the family with his view of life. At five foot-eight, Toby would have towered over Rose's father, who had been five foot-five, but her son, like her father, expected life to fall into line for him. Since it hadn't once worked for her father, Rose prayed Toby soon got his act together. Toby had been the kid she'd pushed to finish high school, but getting him to go beyond, even to a trade school, seemed out of reach, at the moment. Rose hoped the monotony of his current job would wear thin after a few years and he'd see the value in learning a trade. What trade he'd pick, she had no idea. Rose worried about him, but she wasn't sure what he excelled at, except making a mess and playing videogames.

Rose turned on the shower. She had to wait two minutes for the water to heat up. She prayed they didn't need a new water heater. Harold had promised a week ago to look at it. That hadn't happened.

A chirping sound from her phone alerted her to a text from Tyler. Unlike his brother, he didn't need any help with life goals. A member of the naval reserves, he practically worshipped his father. His plan—and yes, he would succeed—was to enlist and get his university degree paid for by the military. Tyler hadn't needed her since the age of fifteen. It had been a relief not to worry about him.

Rose read the text, grimacing from all the short syntax. "Not hme tnight. At Steve's. Early game. Alset."

"K," she typed back, playing his game.

She stepped into the shower and almost slipped on the girls' loofahs. One purple, the other yellow. They were off limits, like the expensive body soaps the girls had recently bought at the mall. Rose sniffed one, savouring the smell of roses with a hint of orange. Ignoring her conscience, she grabbed the yellow loofah and poured a large dose of body soap on it and scrubbed up. Ignorance was bliss for the girls.

The girls, truly a gift, came from Harold. They were now eight and ten and thick as thieves. The girls loved their brothers, but they didn't really know them. Toby had claimed the basement and sometimes an entire week went by before Rose set eyes on her first-born. Tyler, busy with the reserves, high school, and his sport teams, basically already lived by his own schedule. He had saved up enough money from his reserve work to buy a two-thousand-dollar car, which had surprised them all by making it through the first winter without breaking down.

Rose showered quickly, making sure to drop the loofahs back where they had been and grabbed her work clothes. Harold drooled on his pillow. The sight disgusted her. She eyed Harold like one of her clients. At fifty, he looked to be in his mid-sixties. A decade ago, he hadn't had a pot belly, but the years of drink were quickly making him round in the face and rounder in the stomach. He looked like her when she'd been pregnant. Rose had worked those pounds off with determination.

She grabbed a yogourt from the fridge. She eyed the pile of dishes in the sink. If the dishwasher worked, they'd be sitting in it for days. Harold had promised to fix the machine a month ago and Rose wasn't, on principle, going to bring it up again. Her phone chirped again. The sound annoyed her. Mentally she made a note to change the chirp to something else.

"For you, darlin'. Have a great girls' weekend!"

The text, followed with a picture of a box of chocolates from Blair, her co-worker, made her heart speed up. Blair, ten years her junior, liked to cook, make homemade wine, and talk about the cooking shows he watched on his off time. Rose smiled. Blair always commented on her new haircut, her perfume, and how gorgeous she looked after four kids. Rose darted back upstairs to the washroom off her bedroom. With care, she applied her make-up and made sure to spray on Chanel No. 5. Blair said the scent drove him mad.

Harold farted loudly in his sleep. Rose rolled her eyes and resisted the urge to throw something at him. On her break, she'd tell Blair all about Harold's latest episode, as she referred to them, and he'd offer her comfort. She liked what he had to say about Harold, who he viewed as a first-class loser while saying she deserved better. What Rose deserved was someone like Blair, who liked to run marathons and plan a meal all would enjoy. Her reality? She had Harold.

Rose held her breath when she re-entered the bedroom to shut the window, not wanting Harold to catch a chill. The humid summer temperature had broken overnight, and it had brought an instant cooling to the morning, a sure sign fall coasted around the corner on the East Coast. The last thing she needed to hear was Harold whine like he did when he got a cold. He acted like he was dying and made them all in the house miserable. Dying would set her free, but it wouldn't help. She'd be left with two devastated girls and no co-parent. Rose was starting to dislike her husband, but he was a good father. She threw an extra blanket on Harold's dead-to-the-world form and finally took a breath of non-rancid air once she was in the hallway.

Chapter 3

Craig

Craig O'Leary had a headache and a pain in the middle of his chest. He gulped down two aspirin with his Tim Horton's double-double. This morning, his wife barely spoke to him. Her silence had become routine. Something was off. At first, he'd chalked it up to that time of the month, but two months later he wasn't so sure. He looked at the pile of papers in his inbox and groaned. He could have sworn he'd cleared out most of the stuff yesterday. He picked up the first in the pile and realized his secretary had been in early. The pile consisted of new work, but something had felt tense lately at the firm. He hadn't had his weekly meeting with his boss and in the last twenty years, he couldn't remember never having a meeting. Since one other big insurance firm had recently been acquired by an Ontario company, Craig's sense of stability had decreased.

He took a sip of the hot coffee and turned on his computer. Three years away from retirement didn't seem long, but there was talk–big talk–that Midlife, the largest insurance company in the Atlantic Region, would contract out their IT. They'd probably contract it out to some nineteen-year-old kid from India and ask Craig to train him. If it happened, he'd be up the creek. With his pay and five kids, they were barely making it, not like he'd let on to Fern. Fern thought their finances were great. Why shouldn't she? He handled the money, and she handled the kids. It had been their unwritten arrangement when they'd moved back East, and Fern stayed home to raise the children. Fern had kept up her end of the bargain, but Craig had slipped over the years. Slipped in ways his wife knew nothing about.

They lived modestly, mostly because Fern hated to eat out. She claimed it was stressful with the kids, which was true, but she also picked apart the food, saying if she could cook it at home why pay for it? Fern also hated airplanes, which made a vacation a close to home affair. The one time he'd begged for the kids' sake to go to Disney World in Florida had been a disaster.

He had whispered in the stewardess' ear as he'd boarded how nervous his wife was of flying. Bless the woman, who had handed his wife a nice cold glass of white wine the minute the seatbelt sign had gone off. His wife had an anti-anxiety pill and Fern had knocked back the drug with the wine. Fifteen minutes later, she'd closed her eyes and he'd handled the rowdy kids, who were super excited to be in the air. The same stewardess had handed out colouring kits to his kids who then had been twelve, ten, and nine, with six-year-old twins. It had surprised Craig to see Dale, his eldest, colour away like it was the coolest thing in the world. When they'd landed, he had a hard time rousing Fern, but once they disembarked, her instincts had kicked in and she'd handled the kids in her motherly, bossy way. Getting her back on the plane for the ride home wasn't so smooth. Fern refused the wine, saying it gave her a headache for two days in Florida and he'd practically begged her to take the drug, but she insisted she was okay when she wasn't. Halfway home, the plane hit turbulence. Instantly, Fern thought the plane was going down. She screamed, upsetting the kids and other passengers, and embarrassed him. It took the not-so-nice male steward speaking sternly to her for Fern to stay quiet. He'd held her hand for the rest of the flight, whispering words of comfort, but she had zoned out. When they landed, she threw up all over his shoes. It had been the last flight he had taken with Fern or the kids.

Today, pay day. He'd take a thousand out of his credit line and pay off the loan shark and all would be okay. He'd take on some side IT jobs. Wasn't Harold telling him the other day about all the side jobs he did on the weekend to make ends meet? Craig also recalled how Harold had mentioned a client who lived out by the new subdivision called The Lakes who was looking for someone to install his IT system, as he worked from home. A month ago, Craig had laughed and said he was busy enough, but a month ago he hadn't gambled six thousand dollars of his savings down the drain. Craig called Rose and Harold's house. He'd casually ask about Harold's client. The phone rang and rang. If it went to the machine, he'd have to hang up, but he didn't have Harold's cell and he couldn't ask Fern for it because she'd think it weird. Craig barely tolerated Harold and he'd made no secret of his feelings over the years.

"Yup," answered Harold, who sounded like he'd just woken up. Craig checked his Rolex. It was 11 a.m.

"Harold. It's Craig."

"Yup," repeated Harold, who then proceeded to belch to the side of the phone.

"Ah, yeah, listen you had mentioned a client who needed some IT help. I might be interested."

A long period of silence on the other end greeted him. Craig thought for a second maybe Harold had hung up.

"What client?" asked Harold.

This was why Craig didn't like Harold. Harold was an idiot. If Craig knew the name of the client, he'd never have had to call Harold in the first place.

"Harold, you mentioned some guy you were working for who had a new house being built at The Lakes. I think you were installing a hot tub."

Harold laughed. "Ah yeah, he's loaded. Sure, I've got his number. I'll send it to you. By the way, what time is it?"

"Thank you. It's 11 a.m."

Harold spoke loudly into the phone. "Sorry man, I've got to go."

"So, you'll text me his number," repeated Craig, needing reassurance Harold would do as instructed.

"On it. Talk later, man," said Harold.

"Thanks," said Craig, hanging up.

Craig buzzed his secretary. He had to see the boss. "Can you check to see if Jim's in?"

"On it, boss," said Sherry.

Craig smiled. Sherry with her pretty smile and friendly voice would woo Jim into meeting with him. At lunch, he'd withdraw a thousand and hand it over to Rob, who would then stop breathing down his neck. He'd work the IT job and put the money back in the savings account and Fern wouldn't know a thing. All would be good as gold in his world once again.

Chapter 4

Harold

Harold needed to piss. The phone call from Craig had jostled his brain. He didn't remember much about last night except vodka had been involved. Drinking sucked.

Harold ambled slowly to the bathroom. He noticed the leaky faucet, something he'd promised to fix a good six months ago. He lifted the seat and took a long leak, reflecting on how he'd made it home from his binge. The last job of the day had been the one to send him over the edge. He'd finished putting in the third large tub for a guy building a new house in Chester. The guy had come home and insisted on inspecting his work, which Harold had found insulting. Harold had assumed he'd hate the client, but the second the guy had walked in, Harold knew his assumption had been wrong. Turns out Dave Gray, the client, was a singer/carpenter. This build was his dream house that he was personally crafting into a home. He was a guy who also liked to get his hands dirty. He might be a big hot shot in Nashville, but originally from the South Shore, he wanted this house to be his family's summer home. Dave had said it was a cliché and Harold had laughed, but he'd got it. As far as people moved away, sometimes their blood brought them back home where they could be themselves. Dave had loved Harold's work and respected how clean he liked to keep his workspace. When Dave had invited him to join him at the bar downtown, Harold should have said a polite thank you and driven home. Instead, he had joined him. Thus, his downfall.

He remembered driving home something he should not have done. He also vividly recalled texting his two co-workers, Bill and Ned, who had joined him at the Spit, the bar in Downtown Halifax his crew liked to go to on a Friday night or weekend. Harold became the life of the party when he drank. It's what his co-workers told him.

Harold had a quick and efficient shower. He dressed in his city work clothes and ate three Tums to settle his queasy stomach. Thankfully, his car was miraculously parked in the driveway without a scratch. He drove to the nearest Tim's for a dark coffee and twenty minutes later pulled into the parking lot of the warehouse where the rest of the crew would be, unless they were working off-site on a job.

"Nice of you to join us," said Bob Taylor.

Harold ground his back molars and kept his head down. Bob, his supervisor, a fact he lauded time and time again, was on his heels. Harold stuffed his hands in his pocket and made his way to his workstation.

Bob had been a terrible plumber and worse supervisor. Every single time Harold had been paired with Bob in the early years, Bob had either broken something or doubled their hours of service to simply install a toilet. Thankfully, Bob was now all admin and didn't go near any three-quarter wrenches. Harold detested the fact Bob made ten thousand more in pay for his incompetence. However, that was how life worked in a union.

"Heard you had a late night," said Bob, waiting for Harold to respond.

Jim Steele walked in and thankfully saved Harold. "Great job on The Corner's 6C, Harold. Toby said you'd already installed the toilet and all he had to do was the sink. Saved us big time."

Harold nodded, unsure what to say. He'd installed the toilet in The Corner's 6C Friday afternoon, not this morning.

"So, he was on the job site this morning?" asked Bob to Jim.

Jim took a sip of his hot coffee and nodded. "Yup. Check with Toby."

Bob didn't look pleased. "I will, Jim. I certainly will."

Harold didn't say anything. Instead, he followed Jim to the supply room. "Thanks, man. I owe you."

"Not to worry. We've got your back. Toby didn't file a report you'd installed the toilet on Friday and when he heard you and a few of the guys had been out drinking, he figured you might walk in sort of late," said Jim, with a gruff laugh.

"Yeah, sorry. Won't happen again."

"Well, good. Hate to keep bailing you out. You might want to thank Toby though and be warned, I heard he's looking for some help with a cottage he's building on the shore. Isn't he from your way?"

Toby Baker belonged to the Baker clan, whose family practically colonized the Eastern Shore and Harold had known a lot of them growing up. They were nice folks who relied more on trade then cash to get things done. Owing them a favour, however, meant a debt for life and it sucked. When Toby came knocking for some help, Harold wouldn't be able to say no, and it would set Rose off. Rose didn't like the Bakers. He wasn't sure why, but she wouldn't talk about it. Harold felt certain something must have happened in high school, but getting Rose to open up wasn't easy. Rose was like her name, beautiful and bright but often prickly and thorny. More and more, Harold found himself tiptoeing around her. Their lives were busy with the kids and work, and they were often two ships passing in the night. Still though, Harold knew she had managed to tuck him into bed sometime last night. For her efforts he'd get her flowers. Rose liked flowers but not roses. That was too cliché. No, he'd get those exotic flowers she always raved about.

"Thanks again, Jim. I'll pop by and thank Toby personally. He supposed to be at The Corner all day?"

The Corner was the public housing facility in the north end of Halifax. It was the main place of work for the city maintenance staff.

"Yeah, he's working the sixth floor all day and it's not pretty.

You're on seven, and I'd skip lunch and get to it before Bob comes at you again."

Jim quickly grabbed his gear and left the supply room. A few minutes later, Harold followed him with his supply bag loaded with gear. He took a city van and once at The Corner, used Google to find a florist in Dartmouth to place his order.

Harold popped two more Tums and smiled, thinking he'd made Rose's day with his surprise. Mentally, he made a note to ensure she never saw the bill. If Rose knew he'd spent over a hundred dollars on flowers, which in days would end up in the green organic bin, she'd kill him. First, she'd rant about how useless flowers were. Then she'd go on about how the money could have been used to buy the girls new sneakers, which she swore cost a freaking fortune. For a minute, Harold debated cancelling the order. It's what he should do, but playing his cards right with a surprise might score him sex.

Harold grinned as he exited the van. Today might be his lucky day after all.

Chapter 5

Fern

"Mom, the brakes. Hit the brakes!"

Fern hit the brakes and the van came to a screeching halt. She immediately turned her head to look at her eldest. "You okay?"

"Yes, what the heck were they thinking?" shouted Dale.

"Dale, it's okay. He's okay. I braked. All is good."

"He just went from the road into the crosswalk on his bike like a moron," said Dale, running an aggravated hand through his long hair.

"Good thing you saw him and shouted. I didn't see him."

"He should have a light on his bike and decide if he wants to be a bicyclists or walker; not both. He could have got hit. We could have hit him."

Fern slowly pushed down on the gas. Accident diverted, her

heart still hadn't gone back to its normal rhythm, but she took a calming breath and proceeded home.

"I'm glad you decided to come home for the weekend," said Fern, lightly.

Dale had been living with a few friends while studying at the local university and even though Fern still had a full house of children, she missed having her eldest home.

"Yeah, I can only stay for supper. Dad said he'd drive me back later."

"Oh, okay," said Fern, annoyed. Once again her and Craig weren't on the same page. They had talked about Dale coming for supper and she wanted him to stay home for the night so they could talk but again Craig hadn't listened to her.

Fern pulled on to their street. Dale was immersed in a text conversation with someone which annoyed her. She knew it was the norm for everyone these days but Fern hated it. If she wanted to have a conversation with someone, she called them.

"David will be home in a few minutes. He was hoping you'd look at his physics project," said Fern as she parked in the driveway.

"Sure, yeah, no problem," said Dale, while his fingers continued texting.

"Who are you texting?" asked Fern.

"No one," replied Dale, defensively.

Fern dropped it. She couldn't pry. He was a young adult, living on his own and tonight she was happy at least he'd come for supper. "I'm making homemade pizza."

"With cheese in the crusts?" asked Dale.

"Sure."

"Perfect. I'm going to hop in the shower before supper," said Dale, jumping out of the van to haul his two bags into the house.

"Want me to put your wash on?"

"Nay, I'm good," said Dale, as he made his way up to his room.

Even though he'd left the house, Fern had kept his room the same for this reason; she wanted her son to feel like he could come home anytime. Craig thought it was a waste of space and was urging her to convert it into a bedroom for one of the twins. The twins, still in elementary, were inseparable. It had taken over a year before they had adjusted to sleeping in single beds in the same room and Fern knew at the moment giving them each a room would be useless. That didn't mean she wasn't thinking about it but it wasn't something she wanted to tackle this year.

Her cell chimed, altering her she's missed a phone call.

Fern, still sitting in the driver's seat, listened to the call and instantly her stomach churned. Thankfully Dale was already in the house when she cursed. Debating for a few minutes if she should return the personal care worker's call until after supper was prepped, she knew it was only putting off the inevitable. She hit redial and as luck would have it the worker picked up the phone.

Five minutes later, Fern had dumped her groceries inside the kitchen and was back in the driver's seat. This time her excitement to head downtown was void. Being called into her mother's assistant living facility was never fun. Hopefully, Fern prayed, her visit would calm her mother down enough to allow the personal care worker to do her job and bathe her mother. Fern fought not to cry. She'd shed enough tears lately. Dealing with the dementia slowly destroying her once strong mother who had shaped her life had almost become routine. Almost but not quite. Never in a thousand years would Fern get used to seeing the changes taking shape in her mother and deep down she thought that was a good thing.

She once had said to a fellow mother on the school grounds while they were waiting for their children, she felt as if she was grieving her mother in pieces and her friend had snapped at her saying, "at least your mother is still alive". While correct, it felt like an inaccurate statement, and made her realize no one could understand how she felt as her mother decayed before her eyes. The mother Fern knew corroded daily into someone else, and the stress of dealing with her mother, the demands of her own family and her personal health were clashing more and more. Fern felt like she couldn't breathe, and she was starting to miss parts of herself, and her identity. The other night she'd snapped at her husband for no good reason and even while they had argued over something so trivial, which she couldn't recall, she had wanted him to feel like she felt; pressed and squeezed all day with someone always wanting something from her. Later she'd apologized and Craig had brushed it off and even that irritated her.

By the time Fern returned home, the homemade pizza was discarded. Craig had texted he'd ordered some cardboard version of pizza, which she hated and Dale had gone to a friend's house. Fern was sad, annoyed and angry by the time she pulled back into the driveway. Doing what she'd been doing for months, no, she thought years now, she plastered on her smile and opened the door to the chaos of her house, once again pretending all was okay when it was far from such. More than anything it felt to Fern getting her breath to get through the days hurt her heart and soul in a way she couldn't describe to anyone, which was the saddest thought to filter through her brain all day.

Fern doesn't want to wake up. She tossed all night and fragments of the dream hang like clothes on a line being buffeted by the wind; there but slightly out of her peripheral vision. Reality intrudes and she opens her eyes. The dream is a vivid reminder of the day a small tornado touched down on the Eastern Shore. Roofs were torn off and sheds ripped from their concrete moorings. The phenomenon made national news. At the tender age of twelve it had been the first time the *touch*, as her grandmother referred to it, had been mentioned, but certainly not the last time Fern had a sixth sense of things to come.

Fern shivered under the covers. She knew something was coming her way, and it terrified her. Some would call her instinct laughable. But Fern was the type of person who could take one whiff of the weather and confidently declare a big one was on the way. She'd call people and say "Get your stuff off your deck. There's a big one coming." Other people might check their iPhones for weather alerts, but the people Fern called, like her sister Rose, her friends and a few cousins who lived on the Eastern Shore, did as instructed without batting an eye. If Fern called you and said a big one was coming, she did you a favour.

At forty-seven, Fern should have been happy. She'd successfully raised five children, and those busy years of constantly interrupted sleep had passed. Even her children's afterschool curriculum frenzy to eat a homemade supper quickly and dash out the door for soccer, football, or piano lessons had faded. Fern recognized this as a new turn in her life, much like the change of the seasons, but an itch all was not right made her want to stay under the covers.

It was an unusually hot mid-October. Fall had marked the calendar a few weeks ago. Fern savoured the season. She loved how the light got crisp and clear, how the morning air had a distinct cool smell with the scent of evergreens blowing on the wind and how dusk settled with a calmer feel to the night. She loved taking the children for the hour drive to the Valley to pick apples. She especially got a thrill out of watching the crazy but marvellous people who carved out large pumpkins to race, like dories, across the river in Windsor. And most importantly, she loved to make jams, jellies, and pickles. Rose said she should have been born a hundred years ago when women were content to stay at home and take care of the family. As nostalgic as the idea was, it wasn't her.

Fern slowly moved from her bedroom through the house.

She eyed the kitchen floor. It could use a mopping, but what did it matter? Her cellphone chimed and she ignored it. Instead, she poured herself another cup of tea and turned on her computer.

She looked around her house, letting the silence settle. The house at one time had been cramped, but now it felt like a baggy pair of jeans–not fitting her anymore. Maybe it was time to downsize. The thought of tackling that made her instantly nauseous. As with most things in her life she'd have to lead the change. She'd be responsible for getting the house ready for the market while dragging Craig out to look at new homes. He'd say it was up to her, but when it came to large financial decisions, it wasn't the case.

The silence irritated her. A vacant sense of loss overwhelmed her. She turned on Facebook, half-heartedly reading the posts from friends. The word didn't aptly describe the people who followed Fern. Acquaintances yes, but friends not so much. Fern had friends, but the number had dwindled over the years. A friend was a person you confided in and most certainly anyone on Facebook didn't fit the category. No way would Fern rant about how she felt for all the world to read. Blithely, she posted something quirky and meaningless.

Her cell chimed again. Why couldn't people use the house phone?

"Are we still on for Sunday?"

It took Fern a moment to discern the voice. It was Rose, her sister, but some days her voice sounded so much like their youngest sister, Willow, it caused her heart to beat madly.

Thinking of Willow made her instantly think of Lily, Willow's twin, and sadness sat heavy in her heart. Since neither Rose nor Fern had talked to their youngest sister in over two years, you'd think Fern could easily recognize Rose's voice. Then again, Rose and Willow had always had the same gravelly voice and half the time if she wasn't paying attention, she couldn't tell them apart; not that she had let on to her sister. She wondered if her boys felt the same about their twin sisters? She hoped not.

"Oh, yes. Sorry, I've got my list ready and we're all good."

Rose sighed. Since Fern had accidentally clicked the speaker button, or as her daughters teased and said she'd cheek-butted the button on her outdated iPhone, the sigh made Fern pay closer attention to her sister.

"Everything okay?" she asked, reaching for a pad of paper and pen to start making her daily list.

"Nope."

Fern took a sip of her now tepid tea. Drama followed Rose like a salmon trying desperately to fight its way upstream to lay eggs.

"He didn't come home until 3 a.m. this morning."

Fern didn't need to ask who. Rose's second husband, Howard, had a binge drinking problem. One he didn't think he had, but one which took hold of him once in a while. It was the main problem in their relationship from the beginning.

"I found him on the back patio before the kids got up. I got them off to school and dealt with him, as usual."

What could Fern say? She'd said it all before. They'd talked about her leaving him, but Rose worked casual hours as a bank clerk and didn't earn enough to support her four children. A month ago, Rose had even scored a second job, working as a receptionist for a hair salon in the mall, but still it seemed the money evaporated into thin air.

"Oh honey, I'm so sorry. Is he sleeping it off?"

"Yup. Like usual. I'm so looking forward to getting away. You still good to get me on Sunday for our yearly escape? Need me to pick up anything?"

"I can't wait. The break will do us both good. Why don't you drop off Ava and Paige Saturday after work so they can be with the girls on Sunday, and I'll swing by and get you early? We'll hit the Starbucks and the new pastry shop on the waterfront in Dartmouth. I read they have great croissants."

"Sounds perfect. You sure it's okay if the girls stay at your place?"

"Are you kidding me? The twins have lined up a bunch of movies and junk food. Don't be surprised when you reclaim your kids that they're wired. It's only a week. Duncan will drop off the girls at their school in the morning and pick them up after school. He's thrilled to have the car all week."

"I don't know Fern. It sounds like I'm putting a lot of work on your family."

She was, but Fern would die before admitting it. The only way Duncan had agreed to be his cousins' chauffeur was because Fern had offered to pay him a hundred dollars for the week, which of course Craig knew nothing about. If he discovered, the shit would hit the fan in her house. Fern wasn't worried. Craig had been oblivious to what happened at home for years.

There had been a time when the tradition had been a week away with all her sisters. It had started when three of them had young children and were desperate for a break. Lily came along the few times she'd been home in the summer because she claimed she liked to catch up on the gossip. The fact she had remained single and childless made her the envy of the group. Fern missed the closeness they'd had as sisters. Tears sprang to her eyes. She would not let them fall. She'd cried enough years ago for the what ifs of life and the hope of reconciliation with Willow.

"Seriously, Rose. My kids are older, and they're used to being on their own. Is it all set up with the boys?"

"Okay, yes. The ex has agreed to take Tyler and Toby's staying with friends for the weekend. Tyler's pissed he can't drive his car because it didn't pass the vehicle inspection. Blast it, I need to drop him at his father's place on Sunday morning and Howard's got another job lined up for this weekend, so he'll be off early with the car."

"Not a problem. When I swing by and get you, we'll drop him first and then get our treats and hit the road. I already picked up some new craft beer we can try."

Rose laughed. Fern smiled. Rose laughing was the best drug ever, thought Fern. When Rose was happy, the world became a bright warm place.

"A co-worker gave me two bottles of his homemade wine."

Fern groaned. She hated homemade wine. "If it's anything like the homemade wine Lily made, I'll pass!"

Rose choked on a laugh. "I miss her, and I forgot about that horrible incident. Wasn't that the night we were also drinking homemade beer Willow had brought?

"Yeah, you're right. I forgot about the beer. It was awful."

"I have to say to this day I've never been so sick in my life. I'm sure Blair's wine will be perfect," said Rose.

"Willow couldn't stop vomiting and I ended up throwing up in the kitchen sink. What a horrible memory to retain," said Fern, smiling.

"Lily ended up getting sick off the porch and the next day, all you smelled when you opened the door had been a horrid sour vomit smell, making you gag," said Rose, with a small chuckle.

Fern felt her throat constrict. "It's hard to believe next month it will be eight years since she died."

Rose gave a hurtful chuckle. "At least she missed all the family drama."

"Okay, enough of this. Going away will be fun and we deserve it. However, I'm sticking with my local beer, and you can claim the wine," said Fern, twisting the pen in her hand.

Rose laughed again. "Good plan. I've got to go and get ready for work. Got called to take an extra shift for today and tomorrow. Listen, I hate to spring this on you, but with Harold snoring like a seal and this shift, I'm not going to be able to take Mom to her appointment tomorrow. I can call and reschedule for later, but you know what a hassle it is."

Fern did what was expected. "Not a problem, I'll give her a call tomorrow and take her in. See you in a few days."

The lies Fern told to herself were mounting. Dealing with her mother today hadn't been on her agenda. Resentment and instant guilt made her tense her shoulders. The dull ache in her lower back started to protest.

Something most certainly was coming her way, but what?

Chapter 6

Rose

"You are such a doll," said Rose to Blair on their break, as he handed her the wine he'd made for her weekend getaway. "You shouldn't have." But she felt happy he had.

"I'd die to see this place. The way you talk about it all the time makes me envious."

Rose smiled. Grand did not describe the cottage, but to her and Fern it encompassed their special world.

"Maybe I'll drive up and surprise you."

Blair winked at her. Rose's heart did a fluttery thing she thought had died years ago. "Well, you can drive up but you need a boat to get to us."

"Maybe I'll swim across the lake."

"Knowing you, you could probably do it, but don't. This is our one week to escape and do I need it."

Rose launched into Harold's latest episode. Blair nodded sympathetically and even grabbed her hand. Rose felt the contact straight to her toes. She should remove her hand, but no other person sat in the break room, so why not. She wasn't doing anything wrong.

After work, Rose dashed home and assembled the pile of leftovers on the counter to see what she could salvage for supper. She had two hours until her second job and a list of chores for her eldest.

The doorbell rang, surprising her.

"Come in," she yelled, assuming one of her needy neighbours wanted something. To her right, Angie Smythe, who always ran out of milk, sugar, and tea and in that order. Roberta Kulawinski lived in the beige house to her left, and she tended to drop over when they sat down to supper. She usually wanted to bum a cigarette off Rose or make herself at home for a good fifteen minutes.

The bell rang again.

Cursing, Rose rushed to the door.

"You Rose Siteman?"

Rose loved hearing her name. It had cost her five hundred dollars to reclaim her maiden name; worth every penny. "Yes."

"These are for you," said the flower delivery man, indicating where to sign on the electronic key pad for her bundle of joy.

Rose quickly scribbled her name. She thanked him and then with her heart beating like a drum, she opened the flowers and smiled. They were exotic. The type she pictured from Blair. Only after she cut the purple azalea, along with two birds of paradise, four tiger lilies, and breathed in the flora scent from the delicate blue delphinium did Rose look for the card. She didn't see one and felt a moment of regret. Placing the flowers in a large vase filled with water, she smiled. Of course, Blair wouldn't leave a card, because anyone could accept the flowers, and what would have happened if Harold had been home? In a dream, she walked back into the kitchen after placing the flowers smack-dab in the middle of the dining room table to start dishing out leftover supper for the second day straight.

Chapter 7

Fern

The suitcase jammed with stuff sat next to the front door. Fern prided herself on having only one piece of luggage for her week-long excursion with her sister. Hauling her stuff from the wharf to the cottage was a royal pain. She'd learned over the years jeans and yoga pants and casual sweaters were all she'd wear all week anyway. Lily had always showed up with a backpack and a bag of liquor while Willow had packed enough for two weeks. As twins, their taste in clothing was as different as night and day and as cooks, their tastes were equally vast.

Why am I thinking of them? Because missing your sisters is natural even when you're mad at both of them for different reasons. Fern turned her focus to the task at hand as she eyed the other big bag holding her supplies. This week they were making bread and butter pickles, cranberry jelly, their grandmother's favourite quick and easy refrigerator pickles, hot pepper jelly and if the apples were ready, apple jelly. This is what they planned to do for good chunks of the day. Plus, Rose would bake up a storm in her usual easy manner, amazing Fern. Their getaway had become their time together for the things they liked, while chatting, laughing and sometimes crying. They had done a lot of crying in the house over the years. A summer of laughter was long overdue.

The cottage, filled with history, love and family memories, soothed Fern's soul. It had been where her grandparents escaped to every summer from the bustle of city life. *The cottage is truly an escape house where magical things can happen.* Her grandmother's family secret recipes were kept bundled in a cedar chest, written down in a scrapbook in her long loopy cursive hand writing. These were guarded and while Fern had a few close neighbours vying for her favourite Siteman squares and melt-in-your-mouth fudge, sharing was not an option.

The kitchen was the heart of the place. *Isn't it true of any loving home?* Fern looked around her house. It felt too quiet. The girls and their cousins were secluded upstairs watching something on YouTube and Craig sat downstairs in the TV room, flicking channels. The house smelled lemony and clean, but it felt fake. Fern longed for the smell of a wood fire, bubbling tea and homemade buttermilk biscuits with fresh strawberry jam. It's what a home filled with love smelled like. In their childhood, the cottage scents smelled exactly like that during this time of year.

The four of them had run wild around the island and spent chunks of time searching for treasures along the shore, going fishing and baking with their grandmother. The four of them. Fern gulped. A flashback to the time Willow had almost drowned washed over her. Rose had been tasked with keeping an eye on her, but Fern had felt something was off. She had raced through the woods to search along the shore, only to spot Willow far out in the lake. Fern had dived straight in and swum hard to reach her sister, who by then had been floundering. Fern flipped her over to her back and with heavy arms somehow managed to bring them both back to shore. It had been a struggle and she'd prayed the entire time for help. On shore, they'd clung to each other, panting with exhaustion. Fern had rubbed her little sister's back saying, "I've got you," over and over again.

For the second time in a few days, she wondered how her youngest sister coped. Who had her back now since she'd shunned anyone who had been part of her family, including her own children?

"You ready?" Craig shouted, coming up the stairs.

Fern wiped away a loose tear. Memories of childhood were best kept locked away. She looked at Craig, who wore loose sweats and his favourite Patriots hoodie, his normal football season attire. Fern smiled. He itched to have the game all to himself. She got it.

However, the dull ache in her lower back had started again. Fern pulled her hair into a ponytail. She had to put her happy face on. It had become a mask she'd gotten used to wearing lately. The reality was that she and Rose needed this time together.

"Don't forget I put the list on the fridge and if you need us, call Kelly and she'll get word to us."

"Oh, for the love of mercy, Fern, we've got it. You showed me everything twice last night. You go away every year and not once have we had to force someone to get in a boat to get you. Have fun and I'm looking forward to the rewards when you get home," said Craig, coming into the kitchen to give her an awkward stiff hug.

Fern cast her eyes around the kitchen one last time. It looked the same and still smelled of the cleaner she'd used to mop the floor one last time this morning, but she couldn't shake the feeling something felt off. "Remind Duncan about dropping the girls off at school and seriously, don't feed them junk all week." Fern pushed her arms into her light fall jacket.

Craig, armed with a beer in his hand and a bag of chips, returned to the TV room. "Go, Fern, and stop your nattering. We're good," he yelled up from the stairs.

She ventured halfway down the stairs and looked at him. He had plopped down on the sofa and the bag of chips sat ready to be consumed. Craig didn't often indulge in junk food. Maybe her getting away allowed him time to himself and the kids.

"Okay, I'm outta here," said Fern.

"Dad down there?" asked David, when she got into the kitchen.

David, at fifteen, had finally started his growth spurt. He ate like a starved child, always eager for more. Fern noticed the stubble on his chin and barely resisted reaching out to touch it. Like his brothers, he teetered at the age where showing affection to your mother was frowned upon. It hurt in ways Fern couldn't tell her children, but she also understood their slow movement to break the parental bond and enter into the world of adulthood.

"He's got the chips and he's waiting for you," said Fern to David.

David grabbed a soda from the fridge. "Great."

"I'll be back in a week, so be good for him."

David looked over at the bags of food by the door and her luggage. "That time of year again."

Fern nodded.

"Have fun, Mom," said David, shocking her. "Bring back some of those squares auntie knows I like."

Fern grinned. David liked anything Rose made. "Will do. Be good with your sisters also."

He mumbled something as he ran down the stairs to watch the game with Craig.

Fern grabbed her rubber boots by the door and started loading up the car. The temptation to turn around and run inside for more hugs from her children was a hard ache to ignore. The girls were playing with their cousins and at last peek, they were doing make-up. It had looked more like they were getting ready for a clown make-off. Fern had been secretly pleased they sucked at it. Even then, Fern knew she had already evaporated from their minds. Duncan had left early for work so she hadn't managed to squeeze in a hug, not that he was the hugging type of teen. Dale, her eldest, would have given her two hugs and joked with her about the movies they had mapped out to watch all week. He was back at his place and hadn't responded to her last text; a normal thing for him now. Fern felt another moment of worry as a gust of wind hit her while loading up the car. She stilled and looked around. Goosebumps formed on her skin.

She ran back inside and shouted to Craig. "Will you call Dale and touch base with him later. He's not responding to my text?"

"Dale's fine. Stop worrying. Get. Rose is going to get worried," said Craig.

Craig nailed it. If she didn't get going, Rose would call and give her heck. Fern nodded, chastising herself. Leaving shouldn't be hard, but cutting the chains keeping her anchored to her family often felt too weighted. Her heart fluttered and for a minute, Fern wondered if a panic attack would halt her plans.

She looked at her house one more time. She tried to ignore a nagging feeling she was missing something. The crisp air would make for a perfect drive and the weather forecast for the week sounded great. Why then did she feel she couldn't catch her breath?

Once behind the wheel with the radio cranked to her favourite singer, Enya, Fern breathed easier.

Thirty minutes later, she pulled into Rose's driveway. Her sister sat waiting with Tyler on the top step of their house. Tyler scrambled into the car. "Hello, Auntie Fern." Never would Fern tire hearing him call her auntie. Only after Tyler darted from their car to spend the week with Rose's ex-husband did Fern feel like the peace and magic of the weekend was within grasp. It was key for the weekend.

"Turn left up ahead."

Rose played her usual role as back seat driver. Fern did as instructed and they drove through the Starbucks for their coffees and then stopped at the new café for their croissants.

"We are not worrying about calories this weekend." Rose laughed.

They each bought two croissants.

Fern wasn't about to argue such sound logic and they ate their sinful, messy breakfast on the road driving to their destination. Fern would clean the car when they returned. Already Rose's messiness resided in the back seat with her open bags and thrown in clothing. Last minute packing was Rose's habitual forté.

At the end of Upper Lakeville, they parked at the campsite. Kelly Weaver, the owner of the campsite, stood on the deck of the small store. The Weavers had owned the family campsite for four generations and it held the pride of Upper Lakeville.

Kelly, a five-foot-three blonde, scared the living crap out of anyone who crossed her. Generous to a fault, she swore like a sailor and could outdrink them both. After giving them each a fierce hug, she said, "George will help get you loaded into the boat."

Kelly had gone to school with Fern and Rose and knew them inside and out. She had been a closer friend during high school with Rose because of their ages. Their two families had remained close. When Kelly found out what their youngest sister, Willow, had done, she had taken a stand. It had been hard sharing the family drama with Kelly, but Rose and Fern had needed shoulders to cry on. Willow had made their mother, who had dementia by then, deed a large piece of family homestead to her for not a penny. Kelly called it like it was. Willow stole land from her own mother. The Weavers forced Willow's family to find another wharf for their boat. It was a small act, but in tiny rural communities, those had large ramifications. It had meant the world to both Rose and Fern. Kelly had a key to the cottage. When not used by either of them, Kelly's family kept an eye on the property and people in the community knew this, which is probably why it had never been vandalized over the years. Eyes and ears in small rural communities had a way of seeing mischief when others thought naught.

Fern watched George load the boat with the luggage and boxes of goods. George, in his late twenties, was Kelly's oldest child and named after his grandfather, and the only one who still lived in Canada. Kelly's two other children lived abroad – one in Scotland and the other in Australia. The thought that could someday be Fern if her children chose such a course made her cringe.

"George took me up to the place a few days ago and I aired

it out as much as I could and added the groceries you wanted, Fern."

"Thanks so much, Kelly. You didn't have to do all that work, but we appreciate it," said Fern, opening her wallet to offer Kelly some cash.

As usual, Kelly made her close her wallet. "Square up at the end of your stay. You know I'd do anything for you two."

Rose hugged Kelly and Fern did the same. It had been a morning of hugs. Normally, this pleased Fern, but again, something made her skittish. Ignoring the feeling, she smiled and laughed when Kelly tried to tuck two large blueberry muffins into their hands. They thanked George for lugging their stuff to the motorboat and then sat down for the ride.

It was hard to talk with the loud motor, so Rose and Fern simply nodded when George spoke. They thanked him again when he dropped them off at the wharf. Years ago, Rose and Fern always arrived a day ahead of the twins. Willow's family had a boat and she and Lily always arrived giggling with loads of groceries. Lily would drop the bags and within five minutes, she and Rose were usually arguing over which recipes they would be making. Willow and Fern, armed with a glass of wine each, escaped to the front porch to chat about the kids and life.

"You sure I can't help you carry up something?" asked George.

"We're good," said Fern, shaking off the memories. Thinking of how things used to be felt like it had happened to another person.

George chuckled at them. As usual, they wouldn't let him

help them get their gear into the old farm house. Fern wondered what he told Kelly. He probably thought they were crazy old ladies. Not far from the truth. Some would say hauling gear was a chore, but not to Rose or Fern. To them, stepping up the windy path lined with granite slabs and rose bushes the likes of Centifolia, with their bright pink petals now long gone, only to showcase their orange bulbous rosebuds, and lush Indian ferns all around them, made the trek to the cottage like stepping back in time.

"That window could use some new paint," said Rose, after dropping her two suitcases by the front door.

Fern unlocked the door. "You said the same thing last summer and we never got to it." The door opened with a loud creak. "And I think I said we needed to oil the hinges of the door."

They both laughed.

Fern hauled her bags inside and immediately claimed her bedroom. "We're awful. What would Gram say?"

Shouting down the hallway, Rose shouted, "She'd say pour me a stiff one."

Fern giggled, moving her stuff into her bedroom. The place still smelled damp. She opened her window. Her bedroom, the first off the kitchen and the largest, with two small twin beds and dressers, had two large windows. Rose's room, located at the end of the hall, had one large double bed, a dresser and only one window. Rose loved the double bed and Fern loved the crisp morning light. About thirty years ago, when they used to spend weeks with their grandmother, they had different rooms.

Back then, Willow and Lily shared the bedroom with the double bed and Rose and Fern had the room with the twin beds.

After Lily died, nothing felt the same. Willow had come up with them for two summers, but she'd been different, and who could blame her? When things progressed with their mother, the gulf between Fern, Rose and Willow had grown to the size of the Grand Canyon. It had been a relief when Fern and Rose claimed the cottage on their own. Willow's toxic attitude wasn't something they understood.

Fern sneezed. Dust and cobwebs marred the ceilings. She'd clean them tomorrow. In many ways, nothing in the cottage had changed over the years, when in fact so much in their lives had. Fern missed the late night talks she used to have with Willow as they shared stories about their children while ranting sometimes about life and their husbands. All of their shared history had evaporated. Willow had left her husband and now shunned her family.

Fern turned her mind to the task of unpacking her clothes and hung up her sweaters in the small closet. The smell of mothballs hit her nose. Immediately, she wished she'd brought air freshener. Once the wood stove caught, the place would start to smell more like home.

Rose wouldn't unpack. She lived out of her suitcases. Bless her sister though, she'd start putting away the groceries and uncork the wine.

Fern walked into the kitchen, noticing the pile of wood by the old stove and the small pile of kindling. *Thank you, Kelly.*

The small things do matter. She walked over to the old black transistor radio which relied on batteries and smiled when CBC radio's crackly station came in clear.

"We are not listening to it all weekend," said Rose. A favourite Lily saying.

Fern pulled the elastic out of her hair and used her fingers to loosen it. "Only while we get things organized." She looked out the large kitchen window to the lake. She would never tire of watching the water on the lake.

Rose came up and put her arms around Fern's middle. "We are blessed."

"Coming from, you that's rich."

Rose pinched Fern's butt. Fern swatted her sister's hand. They were being childish. The magical charm of the cottage had settled into their bones.

Rose pulled a bottle of wine out of one of her bags and uncorked it. "Don't judge. I might not go to church, but it doesn't mean I can't feel blessed."

Ain't it the truth. "You know what I mean."

"Sadly, I do. Have you heard from her?" asked Rose, pouring them each a glass of wine.

Fern choked on a harsh laugh. "No. Have you?"

"No. I wondered." Rose took a big sip of wine and then set about getting a fire going in the old stove. Rose, a natural wood-stove expert, enjoyed her role. Fern, quick to acknowledge it, moved into the kitchen.

Rose rolled up a few old newspapers to stuff into the stove

and made a teepee-like thing with the kindling. "It's this place. Makes me remember when things were different."

Fern cut up some cheese and an apple for them to go with the wine. "There are days I still can't believe this has happened to us." She finally admitted something she'd longed to voice. "We truly are a dysfunctional family."

"We didn't do this, Fern. Willow is the villain in our family drama. What she did to our mother, to you. Thinking about it has my blood boiling."

Fern sipped her wine, thinking it was good. She turned the bottle around to see the label and smiled. "Avondale. You brought local wine and it's surprisingly good."

"I've been telling you that for a while. You're a wine snob. And you're trying to change the subject." Rose gave her a crafty smile and lit a match.

Fern watched the fire roar to life. She *was* trying to change the subject. "I try hard to not think about it."

"Me too, but it's always there like a low-grade headache."

Rose's analysis was keenly astute.

"I did hear something," said Rose.

"What?"

Rose shut the stove door, and opened two vents. "They've been working on the land."

They would be her latest boy-toy. *The land?* The way she could say 'the land' like it had meant nothing when the mere mention of it had Fern's heart accelerating astounded her.

Rose reclaimed her wine. "I think we should go take a look."

They talked about this yearly, but not once had the conversation amounted to anything more actionable.

If they used the old but sturdy rowboat, which sat turtle-like upside down by the wharf, it would take them an hour of rowing to go further up the lake to the spot where an old logging road existed. The ATV club kept the logging road in good condition, but it would be a solid hour of hiking before they'd set foot on their ancestral land. It was doable. It had been the scenario they'd envisioned for the past two years, but they never did it. They wondered how the old homestead fared but each felt too raw and hurt to be able to do more than talk about it.

Fern put on her sweater she'd draped over a kitchen chair. The place still damp smelled better. "Maybe." She downed the rest of her wine, which was pleasantly good. "So, what's the game plan today?" She hoped her sister got the hint. The conversation had to end. Their fun weekend could not be a long walk down a painful memory road.

Rose ate the rest of the cheese and said, "Let's get the cucumbers sliced. They have to sit for a day and it's my least favourite part."

"I hate canning them."

"Who doesn't?" Rose switched the classical music station to a fun upbeat one. "They're playing ABBA's Dancing Queen."

The song, both their favourite, beat into their marrow of their bones.

Rose cranked up the radio and shimmied across the worn wooden kitchen floor to get out the supplies they needed to slice two large tubs of cucumbers into thin pieces, perfect for pickle making.

Together, they belted out the words to the song and swayed their hips to the music. Already Fern felt her limbs loosen and her heart felt lighter. The magic of the cottage finally flared to life.

Chapter 8

Sean

Sean Slaunwhite sauntered into Kelly's canteen. At forty-eight, and a seasoned RCMP sergeant, he'd seen a lot over the years. In two years, he'd retire and the thought always robbed him of breath. He'd rather face a junked-up bank robber than retire. The mere thought of no routine and doing nothing all day might seem idyllic for some. The scenario wasn't in Sean's blood, and he viewed it as a looming nightmare coming closer every day.

"You missed them," said Kelly, as keen as a cat with nine lives.

"Now, Kelly, you know I'm only here for your muffins." He smiled as he turned down the volume on his walkie-talkie and snatched a big blueberry muffin from the basket by the coffee urn.

"It's what they all say," she said, flirting back at him with a knowing grin. "Well, in case you were wondering, George's back. The girls are out there cooking up their usual gifts and if you time it right next Sunday afternoon, you might get a treat."

"I'm patrolling like I normally do."

"Well, Jim Patterson did say he worried about a black bear close to them. If you want to take the boat up for a run sometime to do a quick check, I'm sure the girls would appreciate the gesture."

Sean smiled. "Thanks Kelly, but Jim's always seeing black bears. I swung by for my usual. See you later." He paid for his stuff and exited the warm canteen to head back to his squad car.

Only when Sean settled in his RCMP car did he eye the boat. Every part of him longed to see Fern, especially after last summer when he'd surprised the girls with a quick visit only to discover George had picked up Rose early and it had been only Fern spending the last night at the cottage. His visit had turned into a 3 a.m. excursion, a walk down memory lane and all Sean had done for the past year was think of those stolen moments. He'd told her more things about his divorce than he'd disclosed to his therapist. More importantly, being with Fern felt natural and comfortable. He wasn't the man in the uniform with her. She'd known him his entire life.

At first, they'd kept to the safe topics like their kids, then they had reminisced about high school when they'd dated for two years. They'd even laughed about their first time doing it, which both admitted had been a terribly clumsily affair. Two glasses of wine later, they started talking about their lives. He knew there had been some family trouble, but last summer when Fern leaned her head-on his shoulder and cried, telling him quietly what had happened with her twin sisters, Lily and Willow, and the progression of dementia for her mother, he'd held her tight. In return, he'd opened up about his ex-wife, who he'd kept quiet about until Fern's confession. No one knew his ex-had been screwing around on him because he'd lived a life with her in Calgary and he'd kept his mouth shut. When the divorce went through and an opening back home came up, Sean had jumped at the fresh start. In doing so though, he missed his girls. They came up for visits over Christmas and in the summer, but at the ages of seventeen and sixteen, they were getting to the stage when their social lives took precedence over his needs.

That night, holding Fern close to him had awoken something in Sean. Try as he had over the months to ignore it, he couldn't. They hadn't done anything except cuddle on the old sofa, but Fern, like she had in high school, had wrapped herself around his heart. He could have sought out a kiss and pushed things, but Fern had been vulnerable. Sean would never take what she wouldn't freely offer. He knew her marriage had troubles, but he didn't dare add to them.

A call came over the system. Sean put his muffin wrapped in cellophane on the seat next to him. He might drop-in on Fern later, but for the moment, he had to get his head in the game. Fern had to remain off limits. She was a married woman. What they had in their shared past had to stay there.

Chapter 9

Rose

A morning chill clung to the walls and floors in the cottage. Rose tiptoed out to the kitchen, past her sister's closed bedroom door and quickly lit the kitchen stove. The smell of the cucumbers sitting in the brine, and cinnamon from the two loaves she'd baked yesterday, permeated the cottage. She loved it. She missed Wi-Fi and deeply longed to text Blair, but that was a no-no. They had vowed early on no talking to outsiders on their week away. She did wonder what he had planned. Like her, he was an early riser. She pictured Blair getting ready for work as she put the kettle on the stove. Fern would want tea, but Rose needed strong black coffee, especially after they'd polished off two bottles of red wine last night.

Fern's bed creaked, a sure sign her sister was about to

emerge from her bedroom. Rose heard her sister in the bathroom. A minute later, she emerged looking the worse for wear.

"Please tell me you're making tea."

Fern pulled her purple bathrobe tighter. Her long brown hair had knots in it. "No wine tonight."

Rose pointed to the sign on the fridge. "Wine...not whining." A tacky magnet Rose had picked up years ago had become their motto for their getaway week. She handed a hot cup of tea with milk to her sister, who couldn't quite make eye contact. Rose grinned.

"Your age is catching up with you, sis," said Rose, with a chuckle.

"Buzz off."

Her sister grinned and then took a sip of the tea. "You going fishing this morning?"

Rose put her short brown hair in a bandana. "Yup. First I'm going to get the biscotti going and you're in charge of baking it."

Rose pulled the large mixing bowl down from the top shelf and watched Fern nod. Too content drinking tea to answer, Rose knew Fern regretted the wine she drank last night. *Best medicine in the world for hangovers was caffeine.*

Rose set about getting the ingredients for the biscotti laid out on the tabletop. The recipe always reminded her of Lily. They'd talked about her last night and of course Rose's mind was full of her dead sister this morning. People always thought the twins did the same things and liked the same things, but it hadn't been the case. Willow hated baking and Lily loved it.

The biscotti recipe had come from an Italian lover and Lily hadn't been joking. Rose smiled. Lily had loved life to the fullest. While the rest of them had married and started having babies, Lily had finished high school and spent a gap year hiking across Australia, then later Europe and Italy. She'd come back and within no time, it was like she'd never left. Rose still couldn't believe in a month her sister would be dead for eight years. If she spent time thinking about it, she couldn't get out of bed and Lily would not want her to wallow.

Fern tucked herself into the old heavy-as-a-Ford-truck sofa with a book in hand. By the time she was done her second cup of tea, Rose was itching to get her rubber boots on and head out to fish. She left written instructions for her sister, who laughed at her. Rose reminded her what had happened last year. Fern had burned the biscotti. Today, she didn't want to leave them to chance.

Together they turned the old aluminum rowboat over. Once Rose had on her usual bright pink life vest, Fern gave the ancient vessel a good shove from the wharf. Rose never went far from the shore. Fishing this far up the lake was prime real estate. She rowed around the bend, and out of sight of her sister's ever-watchful eyes. She took a few selfies she'd delight in showing to Blair when she got back to work. She prayed her ex remembered Tyler had track and field tryouts early at the school. She thought about giving him a call, but then thought better of it. Her time mattered. With skill, she slid a wiggling worm on her hook and within ten minutes had her first bite of the day.

About an hour later, four good-sized fresh water perch had

a home in her bucket. Two others she put back in the lake. Fern knew she'd be gone for a good chunk of the day so Rose put away her fishing gear and set about for a good row to the destination she had in mind. If Fern knew her clandestine plan, or the fact she had done it last summer, her sister would be angry. Rose, however, desperately needed to see the old family homestead.

Last year she'd gone on her excursion without thinking of Fern. The need to see the place had been a calling. She reminded herself, she had the right to be on the land. It had been her ancestral homestead and the fact Willow had stolen it still made her angry. *What sort of person steals from their mother?* Worse, the family held a meeting to talk about the land because they'd had an offer and their mother needed money. At the meeting, they had decided if their sister offered the same cash, about fifty thousand for the one hundred and twenty-five acres, which had been the current offer on the table, it would be acceptable. Instead, their sister and her conniving husband at the time took their mother to a lawyer behind Rose and Fern's back, and convinced their mother to gift the land to them. Their mother didn't get a penny from the transaction. In fact, it ended up costing her money in capital gains the next year.

Thankfully Fern had hired a lawyer to ensure no other assets from their mother's estate were stolen. Looking back, Rose realized she should have seen it coming. Willow, the baby of the family, had entitlement issues. She felt her parents loved her more and thus the land belonged to her. Rose wondered if she'd have done what she did if Lily had been alive. Lately that strange thought poked at her subconscious. Lily had a way of making Willow see sense. Fern was the more forgiving kind, but Rose felt to the marrow of her bones after Lily's death that Willow's behaviour had become more narcissistic. She firmly believed her sister needed professional help. But neither of them could speak to their sister. Too much turbulent water under a decaying bridge.

Rose remembered trying to make Lily understand they too had lots of years and memories of their own as teenagers and newly married couples at the old homestead. None of it had mattered to Willow. It never had. She always played the poor me act with their parents, who then bent over backward to give her whatever she wanted. Case in point: getting pregnant at sixteen to a guy the entire family knew was a bad apple. Willow of course kept the baby, then got pregnant a year later with baby number two and then insisted their father pay for a wedding. Their marriage barely lasted three years. Rose, who had seen the bruises on her sister's face and arms, had been glad when Willow finally saw the light. At least Rose's ex hadn't been abusive, but Willow's guy realized early on he could get away with a few punches. However, when Willow came crawling home with two babies in tow, she convinced her parents she needed a house, and voilà, within a few weeks she had a town house. Willow paid rent but often late, and it certainly hadn't been a regular landlord-tenant relationship. A year later, when Rose's marriage ended and she'd come home with two babies, her parents gave her a week to get on her feet without a dime of support. Rose would never have asked for financial help, but the offer would have bolstered her spirits. Willow expected it from their parents and often demanded it. It was a trait which separated Willow from both Fern and Rose. It certainly hadn't characterized Lily.

Lily, from the moment she learned to walk at ten months, was off running. It had taken Willow two more months before she dared to take a step. Lily had started working at the drug store when she was fifteen and finished high school with honours, while Willow was into drama, drugs and sex. She'd saved enough money to head off to Australia on a gap year and from there, she came home and took a hair dressing course, saying she could travel the world and make a living simply by cutting people's hair. She'd worked five years and then took off first to travel through Europe and then she was working at a winery in Italy for a number of years. Thinking about all the places she'd been often made Rose envious. Lily never worried about money because she was a planner, which certainly didn't describe Willow. While Lily was in Australia, Willow was having baby number two. Rose wondered if they remained close, but doubted it. Did the divide, beside the span of a continent, start in high school? She wasn't sure because when Lily did come home, the two of them acted like they'd never been separated.

The morning smelled of evergreens and fresh fish, but a hint of rain dotted the horizon. Sweat dripped down Rose's back by the time she judged she still had a twenty-minute walk from the old logging road. An osprey dropped down close to her, probably eyeing his own mid-morning snack.

A motor boat bounced on the lake as it came her way. She wondered for a second if it might be George or Kelly. As the boat got closer, she realized Sean, Fern's old high school flame, was waving at her. He slowed until he idled alongside her row boat. Rose prayed all was okay. Dressed casually and not in his RCMP uniform she started to relax.

"Hi Rose. Kelly mentioned you and Fern were at the cottage."

"Hi Sean. Nice to see you. Yeah, we came yesterday. You should drop by and say hi. I know Fern would love to see you." Rose didn't know that but she also didn't want Sean asking where she was going. Her excursion had to remain a secret.

"You sure she won't mind me popping by? I know this is your girls' week away," he said, giving her a devilish grin.

Sean, like Fern, was almost fifty. A good-looking man, who obviously kept fit; aging suited him. He had a head full of light brown wavy hair and with his six-foot-three frame, he'd kept in good shape over the years. There were more wrinkles around those baby blue eyes of his but when Sean looked at you, you had his full attention. She remembered when he used to drive an old navy-blue Pontiac without a back bumper. He'd swing by the house to pick up Fern, and Rose longed to be the one going on those beach rides with him. Rose knew he had two girls out West somewhere and an ex who had taken him to the cleaners. Sean had been the one Fern had walked away from. They had been the cliché high school couple everyone thought would get married and settle down. Even Rose had thought it, but two months before graduation, Fern had ended things.

Rose and Fern never talked about what had happened. Some secrets were hard to pry from her sister.

Fern wasn't happy. The heart-to-heart she'd had with her sister last night had been an eye-opener. Fern felt useless in her family. She'd confessed the longing to be intimate with Craig had withered to an assignment she did once a month. Of course, by then Fern had been crying, so Rose had plied her with more wine. She said Craig didn't understand her need for something more than being home with the children or how taking care of their mother had become a stifling chore for Fern. Rose got it. What mother didn't? However, what advice could Rose offer? Fern had to sort out her own life, and having Rose say get a job, leave Craig, wouldn't help, so Rose held her tongue, drank her wine and hugged her sister as she cried into her shoulder.

Rose held up her bucket with the fish. "Actually, I'm going to fish more up river. Would you mind taking these to Fern and ask her to clean them? It's our supper tonight." Rose displayed her catch to Sean.

"Wow, you did great. Sure. I'll drop those off to her for you."

"Tell Fern I'll be home close to supper. I'm going to row to the Falls and try my hand at some casting."

"I didn't know you liked to fly fish."

Rose chuckled and swatted at the flies landing in her boat. "Well, I've never done it before, but I googled it so I'm trying it. Fern even picked me up a few flies. She says I'll love it."

"I didn't know Fern fished."

This time Rose gave a hearty laugh. "Fern fish? Oh my, funny man. Fern can't fish. The minute she steps into the rowboat, the fish sense her and leave. I've never caught a fish with Fern and it's why I do this solo. Grandpa used to take Fern fly fishing up by the Falls and while she says she knows how to cast in all the years we've been coming to the cottage not once have I been able to convince her to come with me. Honestly, I think she feels bad for the fish."

Sean took the bucket from Rose. "Now that sounds like Fern. Didn't Lily fish?"

Rose smiled. "Oh yeah, Lily most certainly did. She could sit in a boat all day and fish, but you'd never get to eat them. She always let them go, which truthfully pissed me off."

"I remember her being sort of a pacifist. I have this old memory of a large spider Fern was trying to kill in the house and Lily scooping it up in a tissue to let it go outside."

"Yup, that would have been Lily. You know when she became a vegan in her late teens, none of us were surprised. I think she made Willow try it but the notion certainly hadn't stuck."

"Fern told me last summer things between Willow and the two of you had taken a nasty turn."

"It's sad you know, and true," said Rose. "You off today?"

Sean grinned, like he knew her steering the conversation to another topic had been deliberate.

"I'm off now until Friday. Lucky me, I get the weekend shift. It's when it's usually a little louder down here."

"Yeah, I can imagine. Still dealing with the drunk teenagers down by the old mill?"

"Some things never change. First I deal with the seventy-year-old men trying to pick fights at the Legion and then I deal with the fifteen-year-olds puking up peach schnapps and Red Bull at the mill."

"Oh, those happy memories. Listen, why don't you join Fern and me for supper tonight if you're not busy?"

"Oh, Rose, thanks, but I don't want to impose. This is your time with her. Plus, Fern might not like it."

"Sean, get real. This is Fern we're talking about. Plus, if you don't join us, I'll end up watching The Princess Bride tonight and I can't handle that movie again."

Sean adjusted his ball cap. "Still Fern's favourite, isn't it?"

"You know it. I'm pretty certain tonight's Magic Mike will steal the show. She hasn't seen it, but I've brought it and we are so watching it. But like I said, some things never change. Join us. Better yet, clean the fish for Fern and she'll insist you stay."

Sean grinned. "Now, that I can do. A man does like to earn his keep."

"Yeah, I hear you, but don't forget who caught the meal," said Rose, winking at him.

"I wouldn't dare, Sergeant Pepper," said Sean.

Rose laughed so hard she had to grab the side of the row boat to steady herself. "I can't believe you remembered."

"I might be old but I'm not dead. I called you that for years."

"It was a nickname to annoy me. Then again, I do recall being a pest."

"You weren't a pest. Fern had come up with it."

"What?" Rose was stunned by the revelation.

"She was the one who came up with the nickname. She knew it would annoy you. She said you listened to your father's Beatles album, Sergeant Pepper, day and night, so the name suited you."

"I liked my father's music. All Fern listened to was Madonna."

This time, Sean laughed. "I had forgotten how much she loved Material Girl."

"Back then, the classics were my thing and she went with the in-crowd. Funny how things change. I suspect when you drop off the fish, she's listening to that boring CBC station again with its sleepy classical music. I don't know how she convinces herself she likes it."

Sean eyed the fish. "Guess I should get going. You sure about the dinner?"

"Yes. We'd love it. Tell Fern I insisted you join us, but my gut says she'll be inviting you before you can say anything."

"Well, as long as I'm not imposing."

"Actually, you're doing me a favour but I should warn you, my plan is to watch Magic Mike tonight, so I'll understand if you want to skedaddle after dessert, which by the way is your favourite."

"Lemon meringue pie?"

Rose found the note of longing in Sean's voice almost comical. He had become in every sense of the word a bachelor. A home-cooked meal would do him good and hopefully make Fern smile. "Fern was planning on making it today along with old-fashioned maple fudge."

"Okay, what man can say no to all that? And thanks for the heads up on the movie. Not sure I need to see it, but it certainly would be nice to join you gals for supper. See you later." Sean slowly pushed away from her boat before starting the motorboat.

Rose waved goodbye and started rowing in earnest. She had time to make up if she wanted to complete her secret mission without getting caught too late on the lake. She hoped Fern wouldn't be angry she had sent Sean her way, and secretly prayed her sister would be a little wild for a change. But this was Fern she was thinking about and while wild might have been a part of Fern's adolescence, it certainly had become dormant in her almost fifty-year-old sister. Rose wished her sister would have a mini midlife crisis and do something a little unscheduled in her life? Seeing Fern smile again would make Rose's day.

Chapter 10

Craig

Craig was shitting bricks. His hands were clammy and he could barely breathe. The memo on clean crisp white paper lying on his desk made him see red and for a second he thought he might be suffering an actual heart attack.

Monday. He'd been fired on a Monday. A sad cliché. Well, technically he hadn't been fired because the company had closed his entire department. All the IT for the company would be contracted out. It was a cost-effective measure, said the memo. *What did it even mean?*

Craig tried logging into his computer, but they'd been smart. All passwords had been disabled. They had followed the number one thing on the list when firing anyone but still it pissed him off.

"Craig, what is this?" asked John Carrie, who hadn't bothered to knock. John with his hooked nose and eyes spaced too close together had always reminded Craig of a crow. Crows were smart; John not so much. Craig noticed he held a letter in his hand.

"Looks to me like we're fired." Craig sounded cool when his insides burned and his stomach made noises like explosive diarrhea would have him sitting on the toilet for half an hour. His mouth already had two canker sores thanks to a weekend of candy indulgence since his wife's excursion. He reached into his desk drawer and poured out two Rolaids.

John walked over to his desk and held out his hand. Craig handed him the bottle. John sat in the chair across from Craig and both men ate their antacids in silence.

"Can they do this?" asked John, who like Craig, worked in the IT department.

It had been the question Craig had been mulling. "We can ask a lawyer, but think who we're dealing with."

"Did they offer you a package?" asked John, who kept folding up his memo.

"Nope. You?"

John shook his head. "They're going to pay us out for tops eight weeks and that's it. After all the years we've been here."

Craig wished he hadn't had two cups of coffee. The antacids weren't working and the bitter coffee brew made him want to belch. "I'll make some calls to HR, okay."

John shoved his hands into his pockets. "Sure. Whatever. I'm making a few calls to look for work. You're lucky, Craig.

You know since Debbie left me, I've been basically living pay check to pay check. You at least, old man, have a nest egg."

Craig was definitely going to throw up or quite literally shit his pants. He didn't have a nest egg of any sort. In fact, thanks to Saturday night's poker game, he owed another ten grand. He'd already missed two mortgage payments on the house and had three overdue notices for utilities. His plan had been to double his take on Saturday night and pay those bills. Since that plan had been screwed up thanks to lousy cards, he'd at least relied on his regular pay to help him out of his latest financial crisis. The piece of paper he kept staring at had royally screwed him.

"Whatever I find out from HR, I'll share. Did Sherry and Tina get notices?"

John stopped by the door. "You don't even know, do you?"

Craig shook his head.

"Sherry got promoted to executive assistant to the CEO and Tina is moving to HR."

Craig pondered the information. He was happy Sherry and Tina still had jobs, but he hadn't seen the shakeup coming. Sherry was okay at her job, but executive assistant material a level he couldn't say he thought her capable of. He had worked with her for over a decade and her silence about her potential promotion felt like a blow. It was increasingly clear to Craig, he didn't understand the women in his life.

John raked a hand through his thinning hair. "Man, I'm cleaning out my desk and leaving. I'm surprised they didn't have security up here to escort us out. They certainly made it impossible to log onto our computers."

"Standard operating procedure. You know the drill."

"I might know it, Craig, but I don't like it. I had four years until I retired with a full pension and it's not fair. Loyalty doesn't count for anything these days."

"You're preaching to the choir, John."

Craig waited until John left and the elevator dinged. Only then did he bolt for the bathroom and lock the door.

Chapter 11

Harold

The kitchen stool dug into his butt and wobbled. The thing had needed to be fixed for years. Harold looked at the clock. He had forty-five minutes until he had to leave for work and the house, unusually quiet, grated on his nerves. Finishing his toast and jam, he rinsed the dishes, something he never did. He eyed the dishwasher, remembering it had broken at the start of the year. Harold went to the basement and got his tools. Five minutes later, the stool sat straight and thirty minutes later, the dishwasher worked like new. He should have fixed those two things months ago. With renewed determination, he went upstairs. The fixed bathroom faucet would definitely earn him brownie points with his wife. Harold eyed the moulding he'd bought at least five years ago. The edges of it peeked out from the side of their bed. The wood came from a fire sale, but he'd never had the time to install it. Well, he'd change things this week. He'd surprise Rose and finally get the moulding installed. He began to mentally make a list while Rose and the girls were away. The quiet of the house he found unnerving. First on his list tomorrow morning, set the alarm later so he could avoid working before leaving for his job.

Six more days until his Rose sailed back into their house and it couldn't come fast enough. Not like he would ever let on to Rose. No way. He encouraged her to have some quality time with Fern and said he understood their need for one-on-one. A bold lie. Harold liked having his wife and the kids around. The house was too quiet without her and this time the girls were staying the week with Fern's kids, which annoyed him. Rose hadn't even bothered to ask him. She simply told him how the weekend would unfold. If she had asked, he'd have said no. She'd of course come back with how it would make things easier for him, but it didn't matter. Rose hadn't asked him. In fact, Rose had barely spoken to him about her plans. She hadn't even thanked him for the flowers, which she'd proudly displayed on the kitchen table. Harold had to admit the flowers were exotic but the bill, one hundred and eighty-six dollars, made him feel slightly nauseous.

"You around this weekend?" asked Toby, when Harold walked into the shop.

His only obligation was to pick up Rose on Sunday afternoon. "Maybe."

"Could use some help for a couple hours, man," said Toby, adding tools to his box.

"For what?" Harold kept an eye out for Bob. These days his supervisor hovered around him like a nasty cough.

"Gotta finish the roof on the cabin. I've got two other guys coming and had been hoping you might join us. Won't take long with the three of us."

And it begins. "Well, let me get back to you, but I can probably swing a couple hours Saturday afternoon."

Toby patted him on the back. "Great. Appreciate it, man."

Harold nodded. He hated being called man or anyone patting him on the back, and having this coming from a twenty-something co-worker irked him.

He loaded up his supply bag and took a van to The Corner. The toilet he'd installed last week had already been yanked from the apartment. At one time, Harold wondered what happened to their stuff, but nothing no longer fazed him. He didn't question it. He simply did as instructed. Harold looked in the van, noting the slightly used toilet, which had a chip on the top left and down at the base. His task this morning, a straight-up installation. Harold highly suspected all the new missing toilets, sinks, faucets, and light fixtures the city installed in the public housing units were exiting for the black market. A number of years ago, he had even come up with a suggestion for a way to track and tag their supplies, but management hadn't wanted to know or do anything.

Jim opened the passenger side of the van and hauled his big frame inside. "How long do you think this job will take?"

"Why?" asked Harold.

"We've got a union meeting at 1 p.m."

Inside a part of Harold died another death. The last thing he wanted to do was sit through a union meeting. Showing up to the meeting was a mandatory part of remaining gainfully employed. "Pretty certain we'll be done by then. It's only a toilet."

Jim hauled out a list on graph paper. "Bob handed this to me as I tried to avoid him. Guess he knew we were paired up today."

Harold took the paper and quickly scanned it. Three new toilets had to be installed, two leaky faucets and a report of leaking water coming from the ceiling.

"By the looks of this list we'll be lucky if we make it out by 4 p.m."

Jim unwrapped a piece of gum. "Yeah, and they're all marked priority. You know what it means if we don't finish on time."

Harold certainly did know what it meant. Both of them would get a report written up, which would go to management. This was what he had to avoid and exactly what Bob wanted.

Monday had turned into a terribly busy day. For a moment, Harold wondered what his wife was up to. Knowing her, bottling pickles or making fudge. Picturing his wife baking always made Harold smile. Rose, a lovely woman on her own, radiated when she threw her heart, which she always did, into cooking or baking. She made Martha Stewart pale by comparison. Her eyes sparkled, her cheeks got all rosy, and the back of her neck where her hair rested would get damp and curl up. Harold could count on two hands the times he had snuck up behind his wife who was so focused on a recipe to kiss her neck and have her playfully squeal. If he timed things right, in the early days of their marriage one kiss would be enough for a quickie in the kitchen before the boys would come home from school and half the time Rose would still have pastry flour on her hands. Harold couldn't remember the last time they'd had a quickie.

"What's so funny?" asked Jim.

"Nothing," said Harold, starting to dream of what his wife would bring back on Sunday when he picked her up. Monday might be difficult but he'd tough it out for the treats he'd get at the end of the weekend. If all went to plan, he'd even score with Rose. A night with Rose hadn't happened with the flowers. Well into week three without sex, surely his wife missed his touch. Harold put the van in drive to start his day.

"Nothing, my ass. I know your wife is away because you were complaining about it last week. And I also know you've got some sweet lovin' coming your way on the weekend."

Harold looked over at Jim. "Can it, Jim. Not like you got anything to complain about. According to the boys, you and Shelly go at it like cats in heat all the time."

Jim laughed, and Harold threw his mind back in the game of work. This is what the boys did. They ribbed each other about their wives or girlfriends in a good-natured way but they had each other's backs. Yeah, there were days when his job sucked, but overall, he couldn't complain.

"Jim, did you fart?" Harold fought with the handle to roll

down the window and escape the pungent odour of donairs filling up the space between them like walking death.

"Sorry, man. Shelley and I went out last night and you know how she likes them donairs."

"She wouldn't like them now. Man, you can't eat that stuff. Something is dead in your stomach. No more farting."

"A man's gotta do what a man's gotta do." Jim didn't even try to look ashamed or embarrassed.

"If you ask me you've got to do number two."

"Well then, we best get the toilet fixed lickety split."

Harold nodded and made sure to keep the window down for the rest of the drive. For a second, he thought of all the times Rose got mad at him for farting in his sleep. For the first time, it dawned on Harold maybe she felt grossed out by him. Mentally he made a note to complete everything on his list, including installing the moulding, and shower before he picked up his wife on Sunday.

Chapter 12

Sean

Sean's heart beat rapidly and his hands felt clammy. He wasn't rushing into a battle scene, but his heart told him otherwise. He eyed the old wharf jutting out from the small island where Fern's family cottage sat and took a long breath. For a moment he thought he should motor on past, but his heart and deep need to see Fern anchored him to the spot. He edged his motorboat to the wharf and gently tied it up to the half splintered wooden post. Armed with the bucket of fish, he patted down his sweater and jeans and ran a hand through his hair. Sean marshalled his thoughts and walked toward the cute white painted cottage with the green trim, all the while praying his heart rate would go back to normal. For a man used to holstering a gun and walking into danger daily, he felt nervous.

He didn't spot Fern, so he walked up the path with the

overgrown rose bushes until the house came into view. The one-story house was a picturesque vision from the past with its dark green shutters, well used screen door and root cellar. The windows were old-fashioned and the frames started at your waist, providing ample view both inside and outside of the place. Not a grand place, it showed its century of age with peeled shingles and overgrown bushes, much like an old man with wrinkles etching his face who'd stopped shaving. It still had country charm. A large rock chimney with a working fireplace made it unique. Inside it had been upgraded a bit with a fridge, but they still used the old kitchen wood stove for cooking. Lights had been wired into the place about twenty years ago, but they were powered by a generator. He knew from last year the girls only used the generator to keep the fridge running. When they left, everything got shut down and turned off.

Sean knocked on the door. No answer. He put the bucket of fish down and wandered to the back where a small shed took up the rear of the property, thinking he'd spot Fern around the corner. No luck. He returned to the front door and remembered last year when Fern showed him around her favourite place. Sean turned to the left of the cabin and cut through more rose bushes. He had scratches on his arms and hands, but the sight of Fern was worth every scrape. She'd fallen asleep in the hammock with a book lying on the ground. The novel must have fallen from her grasp because it had cracked open to lay half bent on the grass. Fern would have been horrified. She prized books and had always taken care of her stash.

Not wanting to startle her, Sean cleared his throat. Instantly Fern bolted up.

"Hi Fern," he said, feeling slightly foolish as his cheeks heated with embarrassment.

Fern tipped her small frame out of the hammock. "Oh my. It's you, Sean?" She sounded incredulous.

"Yeah. Sorry to scare you. I ran into Rose out fishing and she asked me to bring back her bucket of supper for you."

Fern came closer. A foot away, he realized she'd obviously been crying before falling asleep. About to ask her if all was okay, she took another small step and then her arms wrapped around his middle for a hug. Sean hugged her tightly back, thinking this the best day he'd had in a year.

For a long time, neither spoke. Sean didn't want to jinx things. He thoroughly enjoyed the feel of Fern in his arms. She smelled like cinnamon and pine, a heady mixture, turning him on instantly. Her head rested below his heart. A place she'd always occupied. He felt more than saw Fern recover and easily let her escape the intimate embrace.

"It's really good to see you, Sean." A smile played on her pretty lips. "Why don't we go back to the cottage for some tea?"

He adjusted his cap. "I should clean the fish first."

"Oh, that would be great. You can clean them by the wharf and I'll get the water boiling. I made some biscotti this morning with Rose's help and they're delicious."

"Anything you gals make is and will always be delicious," said Sean, grinning.

"Flattery will get you everywhere."

She teased him as she looped her arm around his waist so they could make their way back to the cottage. Did she feel the connection between the two of them but didn't know how to ask or acknowledge it? Fern, still the woman he'd fallen in love with back in high school, was a married woman and off limits. Still, Sean didn't pull away.

They reluctantly released each other when they got to the front of the house. Sean took the fish to clean by the water's edge. Fern went inside to put the kettle on. He returned with four cleaned fish and of course smelly hands.

Washing up at the kitchen sink, Sean felt Fern come up from behind. She once again wrapped her arms around his middle to hug him closely. He towelled off his hands and eased around so he could face her. He wanted to ask her what was wrong, but the moment she tilted her head up and looked at him with those pretty hazel eyes, he did the only thing he could think of and kissed her.

Chapter 13

Fern

Fern had found heaven. Her heart roared to life and every part of her felt excited and alive. The feelings she'd thought long dead. She ignored the warning bells going off in her mind saying good wives didn't do this. For once in her life, she went with her gut instinct.

The feel of Sean's lips on hers made her feel like a teenager again. He was the last person she expected to see and the one person she'd hoped for; like a dream come true. And here he stood in her kitchen, resurrecting the feel of pleasure as it yawned awake within her heart and body. He kissed the life back into her, saving her from drowning in her own internal misery. Making her feel like a desired, beautiful woman.

Fern snaked her arms around his neck, letting her hands glide into his hair. He smelled like the fresh air and clean aftershave. Sean's hands went lower to cup her bottom and haul her even tighter to him. His erection pushed into her belly and she smiled around his lips. This felt like old times. The heady feeling of having a man get excited within a minute of kissing set her pulse racing even more. Boldly she slid her hands to his front and let them slide up and under his shirt. Sean's lips moved to her neck. She angled her neck even more, granting him the right to touch, taste and devour. Her fingers glided over his peaked nipples and she quickly unbuttoned him. He hauled her shirt over her head and there she stood in her everyday beige-coloured bra in the kitchen, wishing for once she'd worn something sexy. But Fern didn't have something like *that* in her wardrobe. Sexy, after twenty-five years of marriage, wasn't something she did or owned. Practical beige-coloured bras labelled Fern, who didn't want to wear a thong. Thongs were a piece of dental floss and supported nothing. Plus, Craig constantly told her not to bother with buying lingerie. So, ten years into their marriage, Fern had said goodbye to expensive sexy outfits and Craig hadn't even noticed.

Now though, Fern held her breath. She wanted to be a sexy woman. At forty-seven, twenty-five pounds overweight and having had five kids, her body showed its ravaged landscape. Without the support of the bra, her boobs sagged south and even with the fifty sit-ups she'd been doing every morning religiously, she didn't own an ab. For well over a year, Fern had been avoiding getting naked by a mirror. She had dimples the size of craters in her thighs and wrinkles a car could drive over on her ass. Now she stood shirtless in the kitchen with her old high school flame.

Sean, who was breathing as hard as her, gazed at her and she let him.

"What are you thinking?" They were a long way from the teenage lovers they had been.

"You are so beautiful."

He always had been a man to say the right thing and the anxious part of her she'd been holding in flew out the window.

He lowered his head and looked at her. Those blue eyes of his were dark with desire.

"You sure about this, Fern?"

Now, this was a good man. Only a man with integrity could ask that question when his erection stood at attention and he still panted from their marathon kissing session.

Fern didn't say a thing. Instead, she took his hand and led him to her bedroom and prayed her sister would take a long time fishing.

Chapter 14

Rose

Sean helped himself to a second piece of fried fish, which Fern had cooked to perfection. "I can't believe all the fish you caught."

"I could have caught more. I had the perfect day for fishing. Thanks for cooking Fern. I'm feeling beat now."

Exhaustion bore down on Rose. She'd rowed to the old logging path and had practically jogged up the road in her rubber boots. A blister the size of Mount Everest had claimed her right foot by the bunion, which forced her to hide her toes even in the heat of summer. She longed to tell Fern what she'd seen. Two new outbuildings were being built and the main road looked to be wider, but the old house hadn't been touched. The rumour in the community had been Willow and her new boy-toy planned to create a number of cottages and sell the place as a year-round hunting and fishing getaway-vacation spot. Well,

Rose knew one thing they didn't. There were no fish in the old, almost dried-up lake nestled close to the old house and deer were even scarcer.

What had been done to the family homestead made her want to throw up. This wasn't supposed to have happened. Their father would be rolling in his grave. The mere thought of strangers walking through the old apple orchard would have set off their father, who had viewed the homestead as his private hideaway. He'd cherished the roots of the place, replacing the carved cross marking the burial mound of a great-great uncle, chopping and cutting back the brush, which always tried to reclaim the pasture. It had been a private place meant only for family.

Rose wondered if Willow even knew they'd buried some of their father's ashes on the property. Probably not. She feared the small memorial they'd created for Lily had been plowed over. When their father had died suddenly, they had made the decision to remove some of the valuable furniture from the old homestead before thieves broke in. Thieves like her own sister, Willow, who liked to call it YOLO (You Only Live Once) weekends and sneak around the back roads of Nova Scotia and New Brunswick to break into people's supposedly derelict camps and remove valuable items. Rose and Fern had been aghast to discover this. Rose felt Willow would never have done stuff like that if Lily had been around because Lily didn't put up with the stupid stuff Willow did.

Willow thought it was her right to take from others, claiming the buildings had been falling down anyway. Rose knew she had lied. After all, she'd seen the holier-than-thou Gospel painting Willow smugly placed on display in her living room which depicted the Last Supper. At one time Rose had worked in an art restoration office and knew the picture would have been in much worse shape if it had been in one of those falling down camps.

"Would you like more wine?" Fern asked Sean.

Rose watched the interaction between Sean and Fern and wondered what had happened while she'd been away doing her so-called fishing. Fern looked relaxed and she certainly seemed a lot happier. Sean had been even more charming. Rose felt like the third wheel.

She excused herself thanks to her fishing exhaustion and let the two of them clean up. Fern handed her a piece of lemon meringue pie. Sean insisted on doing the dishes for the two of them and Fern let him. *Yup, something was up.* Fern had always been picky about how the dishes were washed, which is why she insisted on doing them her way. Rose wasn't going to pry. It might kill her, but she'd wait for her sister to dish the dirt.

After dessert, Rose expected Sean to leave, but he surprised her by saying he'd like to watch the movie. Well, thought Rose, she'd give it to him.

Rose went into her bedroom and returned waving the Magic Mike DVD like a crazed teenager. After all, she had warned him. Fern tried to insist on her favourite movie, but no way could Rose sit through it again.

Rose poured herself more wine and noticed both Fern and Sean had a craft beer in their hands. Rose hated beer. Getting drunk on homebrew at fourteen ensured a lifetime of staying away from the stuff. Rose let Fern and Sean take the old sofa while she wrapped herself in the blanket on the squishy chair. A night chill once again settled in the frame of the cottage. About to get up to light the fire, Rose eagerly accepted Sean's offer of help. Fern quickly got up, only to return with a big quilt. When they finally were all settled Rose thought it slightly odd both Fern and Sean were the ones cuddled up on the sofa. Then Magic Mike came on stage and Rose lost herself to movie magic, showcasing sexy men grooving it on stage like they knew what they were doing.

Rose dozed off and on during the movie. She quietly excused herself when it was over and said good night to Sean. Her sister, like her had been dozing and Rose asked Sean to make sure the fire was out before he left. He nodded and said good night. She got up, loving the woodsy scent in the house and with aching limbs and a sore foot, limped like an octogenarian to her bedroom. Her body would pay dearly for her excursion tomorrow.

Chapter 15

Sean

"I thought she'd never leave," said Fern.

Sean pulled her in tight to his chest "I thought you were asleep."

They were like teenagers under the covers and for the life of Sean he couldn't remember what they'd been watching. All through the movie he'd had his hands all over Fern, under the covers of course, but it had been crazy, bold and hot. Fern had been brazen. At one point she'd unzipped him and had boldly stroked him. It had taken every ounce of control to not groan in pleasure. This was the Fern he remembered. All through his high school years, it had been Fern who had instigated their lovemaking. No one would ever look at Fern and think wild woman, but one day between biology and math class, she'd found an empty storage room and had shown him the time of his life. That memory had been etched in his brain forever. Tonight's was a close second.

"Fern," he said, needing to kiss her.

She knew the tone of his voice and scooted up so he could score. The night eased into midnight. He should get going, but didn't want to leave. Leaving meant saying goodbye to this. He wasn't sure if she wanted to talk about what they'd done and he certainly didn't have the guts to start *that* conversation.

So instead, Sean used his mouth and hands to imprint on Fern how much he had missed her. He prayed she heard his silent voice which said how well suited they were for each other and hoped her body listened to his. They kissed liked drunks OD'd on love with their teeth clashing and their hands constantly reclaiming each other's bodies. At one point, he got on his knees giving her pleasure while she stuffed a pillow over her face to keep quiet. He knew the sight of her like that would always make him hard. They didn't use a condom. Fern didn't have one and the thought things would progress this far hadn't even been on Sean's radar. Fern assured him she couldn't get pregnant and had her tubes tied after the twins and he had assured her he didn't sleep around. Sliding in bare, with the feel of Fern wet and hot around him, wasn't something his teenage self ever had the pleasure of experiencing. Sean had been glad Rose had taken her time fishing. Their first romp hadn't lasted long. Both of them had been molten hot and already on the precipice of pleasure, but Sean made up for it in round two. Now, on the sofa, they were into round three. Fern, a magnificent woman, straddled his lap as she took hold of him in her hand to guide him inside of her. He gritted his teeth, but kept his eyes open. Etching this memory into his brain a crucial must. Even now, he had to fight with his body to slow down, and not climax before she did. He wasn't a teen anymore, but a man who planned to make sure he'd wrung every ounce of pleasure from the woman he'd let walk out of his life years ago.

Fern, like him, had changed. Who didn't after close to thirty years? She'd had five kids and yes, she was rounder around the middle, but he honestly didn't care. He certainly wasn't a prize, but like him, she'd tried to keep age at bay. To Sean, the warmth of Fern wrapped around him a true miracle. Yes, he'd fantasized about her since their encounter last summer but for once in his life, reality not only outshone the fantasy, it anchored him in place. And he needed it.

He hadn't been kidding about not sleeping around. As a RCMP officer in a small community, he'd been given the "off the record" talk. Sure, there had been plenty of women who liked a man in a uniform, but Sean had avoided playing the field. Three years ago, after his nasty divorce and when he'd been on a course in Ontario, he'd been lonely. He'd gone to a bar for a drink and allowed common sense to flee. He'd taken a woman back to his hotel, but while it had been fun in the bed, morning had been an awkward and embarrassing affair. Afterwards, Sean had made do. Now though, this felt right. Not perfect because they were both avoiding mentioning the ugly truth of the situation – she was a married woman. But the feel of Fern in his arms, listening to her talk, felt like he'd finally come home.

A part of him hoped the week wouldn't be the end, but he'd been born a realist. They hadn't talked about her marriage on purpose. It would rear its ugly head later. For now, he savoured the feel of her tongue down his throat and her frantic hands on his chest as she pinched his nipples.

At five o'clock in the morning, he tucked Fern back into her bed, kissed her forehead and resisted the aching urge to crawl into the small single bed with her.

"I'm going to leave now, Fern."

She nodded. She, like him, felt exhausted.

"Do you want me to pop by another day?" he asked with his heart in his throat.

Her eyes were half-mast. "Give me a day to…"

She couldn't say it and he didn't want to hear it. "I'll drop by later in the week."

She gave a sad smile. He knew reality pushed to intrude into her thoughts and he didn't want her to start beating herself up.

He knelt so his knees dug into the wooden floorboards. "Fern. You've got to know I've never stopped loving you."

Her eyes opened. Tears glistened as she tried to hold them at bay.

"I know. I feel the same way, but it's…"

"Complicated," he said, echoing her thoughts. "I get it. Don't regret what we did." The thought of her beating herself up over what they'd done ate at him. He knew her, though, and the minute he left, she'd start to second guess everything. Wanting to minimize the damage, Sean pulled her closer. Who had he been kidding? He didn't want to leave her but it had to be done.

She slowly pulled away. "You wore me out." A smile lit up her face.

He kissed her forehead. "I'm gonna go now, Fern. I'll be back in a few days. Is that okay?"

"Yes."

"I'd like to come tomorrow and the next and crawl right into bed with you, but I think space might be good for you right now."

Her hand played with his hair. "Why do you always say the right things?"

Sean laughed. "Trust me, I don't."

He got up and retucked the blankets around her. The difficult choice to walk out of her room was made. He vowed to give her space in the hope they could talk when he returned. Sean most certainly planned on visiting again. What they'd started, he wasn't walking away from. He might have walked away from his wife, but honestly, his marriage had been over years before the divorce had been finalized.

Closing the door to the cottage silently and getting in his boat to return home when his heart felt like it needed to be there in that old, small cottage lying next to the woman he'd always loved, had to be one of the most difficult things he had ever done.

Chapter 16

Fern

Fern sat cuddled in the old blanket on the front porch. Her body still tingled and she felt giddy thinking about Sean.

"You're looking mighty pleased with yourself."

Fern almost screamed. There before her stood Lily, her sister who hadn't come to the cottage in almost a decade.

Fern tucked her feet under her, urging Lily to join her on the old bench. Lily sat but turned her face to look out at the water.

"This place is still magical," said Fern, hoping Lily would forget her question.

Her sister turned to face her and those piercing blue eyes of Lily made Fern fidget.

"Magic is all around you and you know it. Are you happy, Fern?"

"Wow, big topic for way to early in the morning," said Fern, wishing she'd thought to make herself a cup of tea. Her hands felt like they needed something to hold onto so she burrowed them under the blanket, digging them into the old boards.

"I am happy," admitted Fern.

Lily gave her a penetrating look.

"You think what I did was wrong?" said Fern.

Lily ignored her and turned her back to the lake and who could blame her as a sharp-shinned hawk dove straight down to capture a fish for breakfast.

"Judging isn't something I do."

Fern pursed her lips. "No, solely my department."

"Forgiveness is hard."

A cramp had started in Fern's foot but she didn't dare move. Visits from Lily so close together were unheard of.

"Are you saying I should forgive myself?" asked Fern.

"It's not always about you," said Lily cryptically.

"Why are you really here, Lily?"

Lily remained silent.

"You think I shouldn't have done what I did. Fine. Maybe you're right. I'm not happy. My marriage is a farce and I'm unhappy. What's wrong with capturing some happiness with Sean?" asked Fern, chipping away a piece of old paint from the bench.

"I love you, Fern," said Lily.

Lily's words stunned Fern. Never in all the years had she said those words or heard those words from Lily. Tears clogged

Fern's eyes and her throat constricted. She placed a hand over her mouth to stop from blubbering.

"Oh, Lily. I love you too," said Fern, feeling the tears slide like a river of sorrow down her cheeks.

The kitchen door creaked open.

"What's got you so worked up about?" asked Rose, taking in the scene.

Fern wiped her silent tears away. She stretched out her legs to reclaim the entire bench. Lily as usual had departed. "Rose, I need to tell you something."

"Oh, I do hope it's all the details from last night."

Fern needed to blow her nose. Instead, she tucked the blanket around her body and walked to the railing on the porch where Rose stood.

"No. It's not about that. It's about something else."

"Okay," said Rose, urging her on.

"It's about Lily."

Rose turned and faced her, the whites of her eyes shining back at Fern.

"She visits me sometimes," said Fern, thinking how odd those words sounded to her own ears.

Rose pulled Fern back to the bench. "Tell me everything," said her sister.

Fern swallowed. Starting was always the hardest, but a few minutes later with both of them crying, she realized while she couldn't see Lily anymore, she most certainly felt her presence.

. . .

After the early morning of truth telling, Fern, exhausted, had gone back to bed at Rose's urging. When next Fern opened her eyes, clouds had gathered and it was now a grey, gloomy overcast day with steady rain pelting the old roof and a constant pinging sound echoed through the cottage as the water hit the windows. The smell of baking bread and muffins permeated the cottage. Fern's stomach growled in appreciation. She rolled over. Her breasts were tender and for the first time in about twenty years, she was sore down there. A smug smile flirted across her face only to quickly vanish. Fern immediately got up. She didn't want to travel the bumpy road of guilt. First a bath. Her body needed to soak. Her brain needed to halt the question of why and her stomach most certainly needed food.

"I know you're up. Tea is made."

Rose's loud cheery voice eased her out of bed. Inwardly, she groaned. Putting on her robe, she opened the door to face the Rose inquisition.

"Tea sounds great." Fern bustled around the kitchen to add milk to her mug before pouring the hot, blessed brew.

Rose poured ingredients into a large bowl.

"Bread's hot, if you want some."

"Want some? You're crazy. I could eat an entire loaf. You should have woken me up hours ago. It's past noon. I can't believe I slept so long."

Rose grinned like the Cheshire cat, waiting for her dinner. Immediately Fern knew it had been the wrong thing to say.

"I'm guessing when I left you, you didn't get any sleep," said Rose, winking at her.

Fern ducked her head, took a sip of her tea and lathered butter on a piece of hot bread.

"Fine. I get the hint. I won't pry. Plus, I still can't get-over what you told me this morning. I'm still trying to wrap my head around it. Lily has been visiting you and you didn't tell me. I don't know if I'm envious or not, but I'm here for you, Fern."

Immediately Fern felt tears pool in her eyes. *Rose always says the perfect thing.*

"Some days it's a blessing, but most often I'm left feeling broken. Grandma said it was a gift and a curse what I've got and she's right," admitted Fern, sniffling.

Rose dropped the wooden spoon she'd been holding and hauled Fern for a sisterly hug.

"I miss her so much."

"Me too. We haven't been the same since she left us," said Rose. "I often feel like part of our family dissolved without me being totally aware it was happening and now it's too late."

"Is it?" asked Fern.

Rose nodded. "Enough. We came here to have fun and I know you're avoiding dishing the dirt."

Fern gave a small chuckle. "I'm such a horrible person. I still can't believe I did what I did."

Rose's hands ran up and down Fern's back, offering comfort, sisterly understanding and acceptance.

"Shh, Fern. It's okay. You're only human and I'm actually glad you did what you did."

Fern forced herself out of her sister's embrace. "What?"

"Fern, get real. You've been unhappy for a long time. Don't get me wrong, I'm not saying what you did—and here's where I'd like the details—is okay, but it's clear to anyone with half a brain things between you and Craig aren't so rosy."

"Really?" Fern was shocked. She'd been trying so hard for the past year to put her morning smile on her face, which said all good and right in the world, hearing her sister say she saw through the façade jarred her. If Rose wondered, why didn't Craig? It continued to be the crux of things in her marriage. She had become the invisible wife. If she died, he'd hire a cook and possibly a nanny (and with her luck probably end up having an affair with the nanny) and voilà – Fern, easily replaced.

"Want me to run the bath?" asked Rose.

Fern felt more tears fall and could only nod a yes.

Rose poured two cups of flour into the bowl. "Is Sean coming back today?"

"I don't think so. I told him I need some time." Fern followed her sister to the bathroom with her mug of hot tea in hand.

Rose turned on the water. "Have a good soak. I'll bring you some toasted bread with our blackberry jam and then I want the details. And don't give me that look. I deserve it. If I can't have any fun, at least I can live a bit of my life through you. It's what sisters are for."

"You are the best."

"And you, Fern, are a woman who deserves to be treasured.

I'm glad you had fun. I saw you with Sean and it's the sis I knew years ago. You smiled for the first time in years like you meant it."

"Well, he certainly did make me feel like I was twenty years younger and I totally confess there are parts of me aching and I'm loving it."

Rose laughed. And who could resist Rose's laughter? Certainly not guilt-soaking Fern.

"Sean and you were always great together. I never understood why things ended."

"I ended it," said Fern.

Rose poured some bath bubbles into the water. "I thought as much, but why?"

"At the time I wanted more. I wanted to travel the world, go away to university and leave this place." Fern took a sip of her tea. "Sean wanted to stay."

"So, like the good guy he is, he let you go."

"Yeah. He did. He said he understood and I'd always have his heart."

"Well, that much at least hasn't changed."

"But I've changed. I went away, but missed home so much I jumped to come back home."

"You did?" Rose put the top of the toilet seat down so she could sit on it.

"Yeah. I never told anyone, but I pushed for Craig to move back east when his Mom got sick."

"I'm glad you did. Without you it wasn't the same."

"It's still not the same," said Fern.

"Nice try at diversion, but details, gal. Plus we're not talking about her."

Fern stuck a finger in the quickly filling bath. "We don't need to. She's here with us, but we avoid her like she's a ghost."

"You're already dealing with Lily. Do you really want to tackle what happened with Willow? I take that question back. Fern, I can't go there. And honestly, how can you? What she did to you. What she did to our mother? Thinking about it boils my blood."

"Maybe she had been going through something on her own and didn't have the guts to tell us." Fern voiced what she'd been wondering about for the past two years.

"And it makes it okay for her to choke you?"

"Okay, what she did was wrong." Recalling that day gave Fern goosebumps. Her guard had always been up when she'd travelled and lived in big cities. In all that time, she'd avoided even a slap in her face. All that changed when Willow had tried choking the life out of her.

Fern stripped out of her PJs.

"Don't ask me to forgive and I certainly won't forget. And enough. Get your butt in the tub and I'll return with toast and then I want details on how you got a hickey on your belly." Rose winked at her and then laughed.

Fern blushed beet red and dipped her much-loved, achy body into the hot bath.

Rose shut the door, still chuckling. Fern dunked her head, needing clarity. She lathered her body with the vanilla-scented soap she'd brought, vividly recalling the feel of Sean's slightly calloused hands on her skin. The feel of his hands, more than his heart-wrenching kisses, had set Sean apart from Craig. Craig's hands were always soft. He worked a desk job. Sean had always tinkered with carpentry and he'd told her he spent most of his off time working on a new built-in cabinet for his place. Craig didn't know a hammer from a screwdriver and hadn't cared to learn. Sean had always been a self-taught man. At sixteen, he'd learned as much as he could about cars, which had enabled him to keep the old Pontiac he'd bought running thanks to salvage parts.

Okay. She had to stop comparing the two of them. Craig was a good husband.

Why then do I feel so lonely? Maybe I'm having a midlife crisis. Her finger circled the hickey on her belly. Sean had been a thorough lover and he'd shown her with his tongue, hands and much more how much of a man he'd become over the years. The pleasure she'd experienced had shattered her. He knew it. He kissed her tears away at one time, telling her over and over again how much he loved her, how he'd always loved her but he wouldn't push. Sean never pushed. Looking back, Fern wondered if he had pushed when she'd broken things off in their senior year if things for both of them would have been different. Well, what ifs wouldn't make a life, she reasoned.

Rose opened the door with toast on a tray.

"Eat, darlin'. I'm going to get the cucumbers ready for pickling. I'll be in the kitchen when you're ready to share."

"What time did you get up?" Fern realized for the first time her sister must have been up well before the crack of dawn.

"About the same time, I saw Sean closing the front door," said Rose, taking a sip of what Fern knew to be black coffee. "And I do believe my cell said it had been close to 5 a.m., you naughty woman. I sat in bed re-reading a 1970's National Geographic magazine. They really don't make magazines like that anymore."

Fern smiled and bit into the crunchy warm bread and moaned in pleasure. "This is good," she said with a mouthful of food, hoping no crumbs got in the bath.

"Of course, it's good. I made it. I've got to get back to the kitchen and add more wood to the stove. We're going to be roasting by the end of the day."

Fern bit off another large chunk of the toast. "Give me ten minutes and I'll be ready to help."

"Be ready in fifteen. I'm heating up the jars now."

Fern nodded as Rose left. In short order, she finished off the two pieces of toast and her tea. She'd need at least five more cups of tea to get through the rest of the day. Her mind was a jumble, and pickling always had flustered her. Last year she'd forgotten to add garlic to the dill pickles. Thankfully the only person who knew they were meant to be garlic dill pickles had been Rose. Everyone else heaped praise on her crunchy dill pickles.

What mattered to Fern? She didn't dare examine the question closely. First, she had to get dressed and deal with the pickling task, which would take the rest of the afternoon, or else Rose would nag at her for the rest of the year, or worse, ruin the recipe. Rose was great when it came to baking, but she thought pickling a chore. Fern agreed. But the rewards months later were worth it.

Fern remembered what Sean had said. He'd been waiting months for her to visit the cottage. Maybe she was the gift, much like a jar of pickles, to be savoured months later. Or worse, maybe she now was old and vinegary. With morbid thoughts swirling in her mind, she pulled the plug on the bath and stepped out to face the rainy day. The duty of her life had to be jarred up and put away in storage, much like her memories of Sean if she was going to make it through the day.

"Fern, you are not going to believe what I found," said Rose, running into the bathroom.

Fern quickly got out of the tub and dried off while noticing a scribbler in Rose's hand. "What is it?"

Rose followed Fern into her bedroom. Fern hauled on clothes; her beige bra, which made her smile, gym pants and a shirt.

"It's Lily's journal, I think. I didn't know what it was and there were a bunch of sketches in the front of it so I didn't think anything of it but when you flip it over and start at the back, it's a journal. There's no name, but it's got to be Lily's. She was always scribbling down her thoughts in things like this. I found it while pulling out cookbooks Gram had stashed in her linen chest."

"Wow. I didn't know she kept a journal."

"How would we know? You and I were married and having babies when the twins were in high school. It's what happens to families when a decade separates siblings. Which, if I think about it, is exactly what's happening to my own family," said Rose, following Fern into her room.

Fern quickly dressed while Rose sat on her bed. "And mine. Funny how things turn out. You didn't read it, did you?" asked Fern, eyeing the scribbler.

"Ah, yeah."

"Rose, it's private. You shouldn't have."

Rose laughed and rolled her eyes at her. "Next time you see Lily, you can ask for permission or forgiveness. I don't think she'd mind."

Fern held her tongue and walked back into the kitchen to pour herself another cup of tea. The hot soak of the tub and the guilt of giving into her desires last night were once again threatening to overtake her. Maybe Lily's journal had been meant to be found. After all, the diversion would keep her mind off of Sean.

"I only read the first page. I think we should read this together," said Rose, pouring herself another cup of coffee while checking on the muffins she'd placed in the oven.

The kitchen had become muggy and hot. Fern opened a window a crack, which screeched in protest. They settled on the sofa.

"You ready?" asked Rose, tucking her feet under a light blanket as she got prepared to read a page.

Fern nodded. *Am I ready?* Lately, she jumped into things without thinking of the consequences. It wasn't like her, but people change, or so she liked to believe.

Thursday...April 1, 1999

This day sucks. So much for April Fool's Day. The joke's on me. Dad got mad at me again. Said I didn't do my chores. I've got tons of homework. He doesn't understand and I can't stand English class, plus Willow was supposed to do my chores. I did her chores for two frigging weeks and she said she'd do mine for the next two. Last time I do her a favour. She's been acting weird all week. I think she likes someone. I think it's that Donny guy. I think he smells weird, but she laughs when I say stuff she thinks is stupid.

I know exactly what the smell is – weed. Only an idiot wouldn't know it but it reminds me of a wet skunk, so no thank you. Plus, Donny has spots.

Wayne asked if I was going to the rink after school. I almost died. I thought he and Sherri were an item but Tammie told me they're not going steady anymore. Wayne is to die for. He's in grade 11, on the hockey team and has this cute little moustache he's growing. I couldn't go to the rink today because of this stupid English assignment but I'm going tomorrow no matter what.

Willow's yelling my name. I'm so mad at her for getting grounded for two weeks, I should ignore her. Ugh, if she doesn't shut up, Dad will get mad again.

. . .

Tuesday, April 5, 1999

Willow and I made up. She's going to do my chores and she did my English assignment. Having a twin sometimes is great. I'm glad we're not identical. We're not, but most people are idiots and say we look alike. We always tell them to get glasses. My hair is brown and short and hers is dark and short. I wear glasses and she doesn't. Mind you, she bought a fake pair of glasses in grade 8 and we've been switching classes ever since. I'm good at math and she's good at English. A girl's got to do what a girl's got to do.

"Wait a sec. Did she say they switched classes?" asked Fern, sitting up.

"Yup. How cool," said Rose.

"Ah, it's not cool. I hope my girls don't do it."

"Oh, come on, you're telling me if you had a twin you wouldn't at least try it once to see if you could get away with it?"

Fern shook her head. "No. It's weird. Maybe it's a twin thing. I'm going to talk to my girls about this."

"You might want to hold off on saying anything. They're still young and the last thing you want to do is plant an idea in their heads," said Rose.

"Yeah, you're right. Seriously, this feels way too intimate. I had no idea Willow and Lily did stuff like that."

"Let's see what else they did. You ready for me to continue?" asked Rose.

Once again, Fern nodded and Rose's voice filled the cottage. Fern closed her eyes. Rose's voice didn't sound like Lily's. To Fern it had always sounded gravelly, like Willow's. Lily's voice had always been light and she tended to make all her sentences sound like a question.

I went to the rink after school and Wayne waved at me. I almost died. Then after practice he came up and ordered me a Coke. I honestly can't remember what we talked about. I kept getting distracted by his lips and his hands. He's got huge hands but lean fingers and his lips are totally kissable. He asked if I'd like to go to the school dance next month and of course I told him I'd love to go. I walked him to the rink door and then he gave me a quick kiss on the lips. Heaven. I went to find Tammie, but she was busy necking with Jordan on the side of the rink so I had to wait about twenty minutes before she wanted to leave but I didn't care. That one kiss from Wayne I replayed in my head over and over again.

I found Willow in the fish house, smoking. I couldn't say anything to her, because she's covering for my chores this week, but she knew I wasn't happy. She begged me not to say anything to Mom or Dad, as if. Mom is in her own world and the last thing I'm interested in is speaking with Dad. Plus, I'm not doing anything to jeopardize seeing Wayne or going to the dance. Tammie gave me some condoms she stole from the drugstore. She laughed when I said it's too soon and told me to grow up.

Monday, May 10, 1999

I've been feeling really sick. So sick my Mom let me stay home today. I've got a high fever and my throat is killing me. Even drinking water hurts. Willow thinks I've got strep throat, which is highly contagious. I think I've got a cold. I don't mind missing school. I made Willow take my note to give to Wayne. She promised she'd give it to him. I told him I'd call him tonight. I'm so tired, I'm going back to bed.

Willow says she forgot to give my note to Wayne. What's wrong with her? Something's up. She's avoiding me. She's saying she doesn't want to get sick, but I know my sister and something is not right.

Saturday, May 15, 1999

Mom is worried. I still have my fever and my throat is killing me. I've got a doctor appointment later today. I'm actually sick of being in bed and living in my PJs but I love listening to Prince's song 1999 all day. I've got to get better because the dance is in two weeks.

The doctor thinks I need my tonsils removed. Sounds horrible. It must be serious because I have to go to the hospital tomorrow to see a specialist. I managed to speak with Wayne for like ten minutes last night. He sounded off. Maybe I'm reading too much into things. I called Tammie and left her a message to call me tomorrow after school. I'm so sick of being stuck in the house but I'm also exhausted. At this stage, maybe getting my tonsils out will be a good thing.

Tuesday, May 18, 1999

I'm afraid. Today I'm getting my stupid tonsils out. I wasn't allowed to eat anything after midnight last night and Willow's being weird. She keeps saying she doesn't want to catch what I have and even though I've explained tonsillitis isn't contagious, she's avoiding me. Tammie said she wanted to talk to me but would wait until after my surgery. I can't believe this has happened to me. I better be okay before my exams and the dance.

Friday, May 21, 1999

I'm finally home. The surgery was more complicated. They took out my tonsils and something they called adenoids and then I started to bleed which was terrifying. They decided to keep me in the hospital for a while because of the bleeding but finally I'm being released today. Actually, being in the hospital hasn't been bad. I've read a ton of books and I like talking with the nurses. I even met a nurse from Australia.

She told me all about the place. I'm dying to visit. She told me how people in Australia take a year off after high school to travel or work. What a great idea. When I'm done high school, I'm going to take a year off. She called it a gap year. I'm going to save all my money up and travel there. Willow came with Mom once to visit. She acted like nothing was wrong, which makes me think something's up. I took great pleasure in pointing out the cute doctor who kept checking on me. He said he wasn't a doctor, a resident or something, whatever, he was super cute. Even Willow noticed him. Anyway, now I have a diet of yogourt and soup until my throat heals. Tammie dropped off all my homework so tomorrow I'm going to stay home until Monday and have to tackle some of this stupid work.

Monday, May 23, 1999

I'm so mad I could cry. After school, Tammie told me what she thought had been going on with Willow and Wayne. Wayne wasn't in school today because he's involved with a model parliament so once I got home, I confronted Willow. At first, she gave me a smug smile and tried to brush me off. When I told her, Tammie saw her and Wayne together, she finally confessed. Turns out the day I told her to give my note to Wayne had been the day she pretended to be me. I actually punched her. I'm not sure how we ended up on the floor but both of us got bloody noses and scratches. I told her I would never speak to her again. She told me if Wayne really liked me, he would have known the difference. I hate her.

. . .

"Wow. Did you know about this, Rose?" asked Fern.

Rose shook her head. "Nope. It's low but honestly, knowing Willow like we do now, I'm not surprised."

"You know, I can barely remember the tonsil incident. I remember Mom mentioning it, but hadn't it been around the same time Dad smashed his truck and got a ticket for drunk driving?" said Rose.

"Oh my gosh, you're right. Mom had to get a neighbour to drive her into the hospital. I couldn't help because I was on bedrest with my second. I totally forgot this."

"Well, I'm glad I wasn't living at home during those years. Those two fought like cats and dogs when they were young and it had been enough for me. I'm surprised they didn't get in trouble for fighting."

"Wait a second. While this had been happening to Lily, wasn't it only a few months later Willow got pregnant. You don't think?"

Rose gaped at her sister. "I wish. Sadly, Sam is the spittin' image of his father. I'm guessing she got tired of playing at being Lily and then hooked up with Michael."

"It's unreal how different their lives quickly became," said Fern, finishing her tea.

"I find it sad," said Rose. "I've got to get the muffins out. Let's read more tonight."

"Sounds good. By the way how long is it?"

"Well, I did peek ahead. Lily skips a lot of years. The next entry is when she comes home from Europe because she talks about the big party Willow threw for her as a homecoming."

"She was about twenty-seven. I remember being envious about her travels across Europe."

"Me too, but I have to say, I wouldn't have had the guts to travel on my own. She was so brave."

Fern didn't say anything. Lily, being twenty-seven, had been a lot different from her at the same age. She'd been caught up with babies, Craig and resettling in Halifax. Fern tried to recall how often she talked to Lily back then. She suspected it might have been once a month. After Lily came home from Europe, she'd taken a job at a hair salon and started saving for her next big trip, Italy. That defined Lily. The urge to cry overcame Fern.

"Are you crying, Fern?"

"It feels so personal. I miss her, but I also feel in many ways I didn't know her."

"Yeah, I get it. We don't have to read more if you don't want to," said Rose, putting the scribbler down so she could get the muffins out of the oven.

Fern finally found the energy to get up from the sofa. "Let's see how we feel tonight."

"Sounds like a plan. I know it's sad, but there's this part of me enjoying learning about Lily. I think the age thing made it hard for us to get to know her, even though we were sisters."

"I wonder what Willow would think of this journal?" asked Rose.

"Don't care. She walked out on us."

"I know, but I often think maybe we didn't do enough."

Rose laughed, but not in a funny way. "Do enough? Stealing Mom's land, attacking you? Yeah, I think she did enough."

"Look, I'm not saying I forget or forgive, but you and I both went on with our lives after Lily died. Willow started to change and struggle. Sometimes, I wonder if I had been too caught up with my own family. I was a mess and she was my sister, but can you imagine losing your twin?"

Rose placed the muffins on a drying rack and then leaned on the counter. "I'm sure it was horrible for her. It devastated us all, but you forget, we did try to reach out. We went to visit her countless times but she shut the door on us."

"Maybe she needed time to process. We all grieve differently."

"Come on, Fern. I think you're trying to wear rose-coloured glasses when it comes to Willow. I'm not saying she wasn't grieving but she didn't want our help and honestly, she never did. Enough. We've got a big day ahead of us and pickling, my darlin' waits for no one," said Rose, with a chuckle as she placed more prewashed bottles in the oven to sterilize.

Fern got up from the sofa. "You're right. It's bread and butter pickles today and green tomato chow. Such a fun day."

"At least you got to have a fun night with Sean last night," said Rose, smiling.

Fern grinned but wisely kept quiet as she went to her room

to get ready for the day. She thought she'd be spending the day with guilt a heavy blanket resting on her heart when it came to what she'd willingly initiated with Sean. Instead, her heart felt a newfound sorrow for her two younger sisters for entirely different reasons.

Chapter 17

Harold

The text from his daughter made his day. Ava, his eight-year-old, missed her hamster, Hammy. She wanted to come home. Hallelujah. It was Wednesday and piss-pouring rain. Rose had left on Saturday morning and he'd been steadily going out of his mind. The moulding he'd tackled Monday evening. He even rearranged the laundry room. It wasn't like he had much to do. Rose's boys, Toby and Taylor, fended for themselves, but this had been the first time the girls had wanted to stay with their cousins and he didn't like it. He liked coming home at the end of the day to the sight of them. They even had a ritual where the girls took turns nightly to pick a movie to watch on Netflix and he'd make popcorn and sit in the middle spooned by their warm bodies.

He texted her back saying he'd swing by after work to pick her up and asked if Paige wanted to come home.

"Nope," texted Ava.

She'd obviously got her hands on someone's phone at school because she didn't have one.

Harold wasn't surprised. Paige loved to be with Fern's twins. They were closer in age and liked to try on make-up and stuff, whereas Ava couldn't care or less. Ava lived for sports. Give her a soccer ball and you made her day.

The day sped by and at six, Harold pulled up in front of Fern's house. He knocked on the door and Craig let him in.

"Saved you a couple pieces of pizza, Harold. Come on in," said Craig.

Harold laughed. "You been doing take-out every night?"

"Almost. Don't tell Fern. It's the one time of the year when the kids get to pick what they'd like each night. If she knew, she'd have a bird."

"I hear you. Between you and me, I'm glad Ava wants to come home. Place has been oddly quiet."

"Sorry, mate. I don't know the meaning of quiet. I should warn you, Ava's pretty wiped. The girls had a giggling fit last night close to midnight even though this morning they swore they had been asleep." Craig handed him a plate, indicating he should help himself to the pizza.

Harold bit into the meat lover's piece. Craig puttered around in the kitchen, which Harold found a little strange. Then again if Fern had been present, she wouldn't let Craig into the kitchen.

"Listen, I'm going to work on the job for the guy you told me about tomorrow."

Tomorrow as in Thursday. Why would Craig work for someone on a Thursday?

"Sure. You touch base with him?"

"Yeah, went over yesterday. It's a bigger project than he anticipated, but I'll be fair."

Harold finished his pizza and helped himself to a glass of water. "Great. He seemed like a decent enough guy."

"Yeah, I'm wondering if you know of anyone else who might need some work done?" Craig looked a little sheepish.

"None come to mind but I'll keep an ear out. Thought you'd be pressed with time with work and all."

"Well, as of this Monday, I've got time on my hands. The company made the decision to hire out their IT department. Can't believe I'm almost fifty and now forced to look for work."

Harold put down his water. "Craig, that's horrible."

"Yeah, and Fern doesn't even know. I'm not going to ruin her week with Rose. They need this."

"Man, what are you goin' to do?"

"Not sure, yet. Guess, I'll take some time to figure things out."

"At least you've got investments and savings. Rose and I live check to check and half the time we're lucky if we've got a hundred bucks left over."

Craig turned his back to Harold and began to wash up the dishes.

"You do have savings, right?" Harold felt for the first time a bit of worry for Fern's husband. Harold had often felt like Craig looked down on him, but Rose assured him it wasn't the case. He liked to think they were friends, but wasn't certain.

"Oh yeah, we're all good," said Craig, but Harold didn't buy it.

Ava raced into the room. She wrapped her little arms around him for a big hug. She looked pale and he wondered when she last bathed. If Rose saw her now, she'd have a fit.

"You pack everything?"

"All set," said Ava, backpack in hand. The bag, obviously heavy, had to be almost the same size as his four-foot-two daughter.

"Go get your sister. Tell her I need a hug or she's coming home with me."

Ava yelled, causing both Harold and Craig to wince. For a little girl, she had a mighty strong voice.

Paige came solemnly into the kitchen. "I'm not going home."

"Okay, you can stay but give your old man a hug. Is make-up on your face?"

Craig started putting dishes away. "Trust me, they don't leave this house with make-up on."

"Paige likes for the girls to do up her face," said Ava.

"Stop being a brat. I'm glad you're going," said her sister, who was two years older.

"Girls, cut it out. Paige, be nice to your sister and give me a hug."

With obvious reluctance, Paige gave Harold a hug and then left, but not before sticking out her tongue at her little sister.

Ava put her shoes on while Craig finished off a piece of Hawaiian pizza.

"Thanks for the food, Craig. Let me know if I can do anything."

"Keep your ears open. I'd appreciate it. Listen, don't say anything to Fern if you see her first, okay?"

"You got it." Harold picked up Ava's backpack and small suitcase.

"They'll be home on Sunday and then life returns to normal."

"I hope so," said Craig, putting the kettle on. "Thanks for staying with us, Ava."

Ava didn't even need to be prompted. She said a thank you and gave her uncle Craig a big hug. For a moment Harold wondered if Paige would be so kind to Craig. He hoped so. Any guy losing his job staring down fifty deserved all the hugs in the world.

He said goodbye and loaded Ava into the van. The second they were out of the driveway, Ava dished the dirt on her sister and what the twins were doing. Harold nodded, smiled and encouraged his little girl to tell it all.

Should I call Craig later and tell him the shenanigans going on at night – like the girls sneaking into the rec room to watch scary movies? Harold thought better of it. What good would telling do? He had Ava now and they'd go home and cuddle up on the couch to probably watch the Lizzie McGuire show, which Ava loved. Paige had made fun of her for liking the show, which had been a hit over a decade ago, but Harold liked the funny, good-natured feel of the series. While he wouldn't squeal on Paige or the twins to Craig, he certainly planned to tell Rose. Next year the girls were staying home with him and Rose would have no ammunition to say Fern's place was better for the girls. He'd even tell her about the take-out food, knowing it would tip the scales in his favour. Both Rose and Fern hated fast food, which meant he had a golden ticket to have his girls all to himself next year. He might be a bit frazzled, supper would be more makeshift and often late, but they were his girls and they belonged with him, not at their cousins' house because his wife needed her vacation away from the family. Sure, Rose would come home to a messy house, but the girls got to school, did their homework and he even managed to take them to their extra-curricular events.

Ava stopped talking and stared at him. "How's Hammy?"

"Missing you, and he's going to be excited to see you." *Just like me.* Although, he hadn't cleaned the hamster's cage as promised. Oh well, at least it still lived. That said a lot because the hamster last year had died when Rose had been away and he never wanted a repeat of that drama.

Chapter 18

Craig

Craig was royally screwed. The girls had finally settled. David seemed to be angry at him for something he had no idea about. Duncan still hung with his friends most nights and he hadn't heard from Dale in a while. He thought of texting his eldest, but thought better of it. Dale liked his independence and Craig understood. Now, he sat at the dining room table staring at the spreadsheet he'd created which outlined all the bills due, past due and their finances. As a last resort, he started to look at real estate in the area to gauge what he might be able to get for the house if they had to sell. An hour later, he felt worse. He'd heard the housing market had become flat, but had no idea the true state of things. There were currently forty-five houses for sale in a five-kilometre radius and half were going for less than the assessed value. Craig realized he'd have to go into the bank tomorrow and have a talk with them.

It had felt good telling Harold. Almost cathartic. Speaking the words 'out of work' shocked his ears. Who would hire him now? Sure, he had lots of IT skills, but what nineteen-year-old didn't?

Craig got up and helped himself to a cold beer. Funny, he'd thought getting fired would have encouraged him to drink, but after coming home mid-morning on Monday he hadn't felt the desire. Thankfully no one had been home. Not like it mattered. His kids seemed oblivious to him not heading out the door to work. After only three days home, he felt restless. He'd even put a wash on. If Fern could have seen him, she'd be aghast. Fern liked to separate darks and lights. Craig didn't. He'd done his own laundry all through university and his clothing had been fine. Separating clothing seemed unnecessary.

Tomorrow he'd go for a run, he decided, wondering where in the house his old sneakers could be. Craig looked in the hall closet, the bedroom closet and finally made his way to the mudroom and there they were. He banged them together to dust them off and put them by the front door for inspiration. It had to be at least fifteen years since he'd gone for a jog. At one time, sports had been a routine part of his life, but long hours at work and the demanding schedule of the children had put a stop to his own pleasures. Well, the kids were older and he certainly had time on his hands now.

. . .

He got up early. His morning schedule of 6 a.m. for the past fifteen years had set his internal alarm, and his prostate, which had him visiting the bathroom at least twice a night, had a mind of its own. He packed the kids their lunch and ushered them out the door for school after a quick breakfast. As usual, Duncan barely spoke but he also didn't complain about taking Paige to her school. Then again, he did get the car and Craig suspected Fern paid him for playing nice with his cousins. David, somewhat less grumpy, informed him he had football after school. Once the coast cleared, he rummaged around in his dresser until he found a pair of faded grey gym pants and a usable shirt. He crammed his feet into his sneakers and did a few lazy stretches inside the kitchen before gaining the courage to go outside. With one glance at his watch, he ventured outside and started a slow jog. After about twenty minutes, he realized how out of shape he'd become. Mentally, he vowed to complete a forty-five-minute run. Even if it killed him. After getting a leg cramp and feeling more winded than he anticipated, Craig wondered if he'd be a statistic. Every year he read in the paper about some forty-something man who had dropped dead of a heart attack while running. He had laughed inwardly when reading those news stories, but now he knew how those men felt. Were they running to try to get back on track with their lives? Or were they running to escape the bleak future ahead of them?

Craig wasn't sure why he ran, but he most certainly knew he had to get his finances straight and his head in the game if he planned to keep his family and his own sanity intact. A sense of ownership for what had happened finally hit him and with it, the realization he'd have to tell his wife the true state of affairs. Fern would of course be upset, probably cry and have a fit, but he could count on her to lend him support. After all, Fern never said no and she always liked to have a cause to help. If there was one case needing her attention, it had to be helping her husband find a job pronto.

Craig finished his jog and knelt over to catch his breath. He'd walk home to stretch his achy muscles and then do up a list of potential employers and contacts who might be able to help.

When he got closer to his house, he noticed a police car parked in his driveway.

Still gasping, he knocked on the officer's window. The officer rolled down his window.

"Can I help you?" asked Craig.

The officer gave him a good once over and Craig wondered how bad he looked. Probably dismal considering the officer took his time before answering.

"Are you Craig O'Leary?"

Panting, Craig nodded.

The officer rolled up the patrol car window and stepped out of the car. "Sir, let's go inside."

For the first time since seeing the patrol car in his driveway, Craig felt a sliver of fear skate through him. Had something happened to Fern?

"Sure." Craig led the way to the house and entered the passcode to unlock the door. "Hope it's not bad news?" he said, waiting for a response. When none came, Craig looked at the officer, who seemed as cold as ice. Then again maybe he's been taught to school his expressions. The man certainly was imposing and the amount of gear he wore only enforced the image.

Craig ushered the officer inside and immediately took off his sneakers, placing them outside on the front porch because they stunk. His feet ached. He made a note to buy new sneakers later in the week. "You want some coffee?" he asked, recalling his manners.

"You might want to have a seat, sir," said the officer.

Craig froze. Something bad had happened. Doing as instructed, he sat and with his heart beating like he might have a heart attack he waited for the bad news to be delivered. All the while he started to pray over and over again, to a God he'd neglected, everything be okay with his wife. Craig had come to realize in the short amount of time he'd been home he could not do what she did, day in and day out for their family. He'd once watched a documentary about the importance of keystones and how structurally one small stone could bear the weight of an entire building. That was his wife. She was what made their family function and without her, Craig wasn't sure he could weather the storm already reaching out to tear his family apart.

Chapter 19

Sean

Sean couldn't concentrate. He'd dreamt of Fern last night and after tossing around, finally got up at six in the morning. Even though his house was the same, he felt different. It had been a complete day since his reunion with Fern, but he itched to see her again. He had vowed to give her some time so he planned on visiting her tomorrow. Surely, it would be enough time. He missed her. Yes, their intimacy has been magical, but talking to Fern made him realize her true value. She'd always been his best friend in high school. Opening up to her about the pressures at work, his past relationship with his ex and his worry for his teenage daughters, made him realize how much he treasured being with Fern.

He'd been touched by Fern and she had wrapped her arms around him in ways he wanted to examine all day. However, work called and now he had to get into the office. His plan to visit Fern tomorrow couldn't come soon enough. He'd hoped to have the day off to put the finishing touches to the bookshelf he planned for her. It had been an idea he'd thought of last summer when she'd started listing all the books she loved and since there wasn't a bookshelf at the cottage, he thought she'd appreciate one.

Now, thanks to Nick calling in sick, he had to go to work. He hoped Nick was okay. Lately, he had started to call in sick and it wasn't like him. Nick had been solid. He'd served in the military fresh out of high school, then because he was ambitious and smart, he'd enrolled in the RCMP and hadn't looked back. Sean made a mental note to check in with his co-worker. He knew he and his wife were having some issues trying to have a baby and he hoped it was simply a matter of the flu and nothing more. Either way, in the last month, Nick had called in three times; not a good sign.

Sean straightened his back once the twenty-five pounds of gear firmly covered his body. He downed a coffee and ate a stale blueberry muffin and walked into his dining room, wondering what Fern would think. After his father's death, Sean had reclaimed the old family home. Old defined the place. The house, like many built on the Eastern Shore, had roots dating back to the early 20th century. The stone cellar, lined with seaweed and eelgrass to help insulate it, was a dead giveaway to its age.

Some called historic homes charming. Sean thought those

people were rich and idealistic. Try living in a house over a hundred years old where the cold draft of winter forced you to go to bed in your sweats and hoodies. Over the last decade, he'd poured what little money he had left after paying alimony into the house. First on the list had been adding insulation, new wiring, a new roof and windows. He didn't bother fixing the basement. The root cellar worked fine and when he wanted to tinker, he spent time in the old barn. He'd done the kitchen himself and had enjoyed making the homemade cabinets. What he loved the most were the built-in bookcases he made when he put in the new wall to divide the large kitchen from the living room. He'd built the bookshelves and had wondered even then what Fern would have thought. She had always loved to read and after last summer's surprise re-acquaintance, he had purchased a few classics she'd listed as her favourites. Sean glanced at the bookcase, noting two Jane Austen novels he'd read and somewhat enjoyed, a Daphne du Maurier novel Fern had loved in high school called Jamaica Inn and her new favourite, Life and Death in Shanghai by Nien Cheng. Sean made a mental note to tell Fern about the books he'd read on her recommendation as he laced up his boots. He ached for Fern to see his transformed home. She'd been in the original house when they had dated in school. What would she think of it now? More importantly, getting her into his king-sized bed would feel like heaven compared to the single bed at the cottage.

Thirty minutes later, he pulled up at the small RCMP office in Musquodoboit Harbour. There were four officers on duty daily and each did a two-day, two-night twelve-hour rotation and then had four days off. In all the years Sean had worked for the force, he'd always put in more than the regular twelve-hour rotation because the paperwork required to file for any infraction had become a bloody nightmare. In the last five years, the force had embraced technology like the next best thing. Sean had been brought up old school. He still kept a notebook where he made hourly notes when working to keep himself on track and on task. Now he also had to type something into a computer hourly which bothered him.

The receptionist wasn't in yet so he went to his desk to see what had happened in the last day by linking to the police database site. Normally, Sean didn't pay too much attention to this list, but he noted Truro RCMP asking for assistance with two victims from a car accident from last night.

Sean typed in the incident report and pulled up the two driver's licences. Male victim, Dale O'Leary and female, Scarlett Barron. What were the odds Dale O'Leary had nothing to do with his Fern? Five minutes later with his heart racing and a feeling he shouldn't have had the stale muffin, Sean bent over and tried not to hyperventilate. Next of kin listed for Dale O'Leary were Craig and Fern O'Leary of 33 Radcliffe Drive, Halifax. The accident had happened yesterday night around 3 a.m., which was the witching hour when most tragic accidents happened. Dale and the female occupant had both been airlifted to the Queen Elizabeth Hospital and were listed as critical. Sean immediately called the hospital. Thankfully, when he identified himself as an RCMP officer looking for an update on the two teens brought in last night, they'd patched him straight through to the duty doctor.

Sean scribbled notes as he listened to the doctor's prognosis. When the doctor asked if the family had been notified, it finally hit Sean what he had to do. He reassured the doctor the family was in the process of being notified, thanked him and hung up. For the first time in his long career, Sean understood why sometimes people threw up when they delivered the bad news. He'd done this countless times over his career, but he'd always removed himself from the equation. Sweat glided down his back. Taking a few minutes to get his bearings, Sean touched base with the Truro office and as luck would have it the officer who had arrived at the scene was still writing up his report. He made more notes and informed the officer he'd deal with touching base with the mother, who he admitted to knowing personally. The officer wished him luck. *Luck doesn't like me.* Sean called in to the dispatcher on duty and explained what had come up and what he had to do and let them know his soon-to-be location. The dispatcher thankfully didn't wish him luck.

Not one officer liked this part of the job and some weren't equipped to deal with it. Bearing bad news certainly took a toll on a person, but Fern needed to know what had happened.

Today his task at hand would destroy the woman he loved with all his heart. While it might kill him, he didn't want her to hear the news from anyone else.

He got into the squad car and drove to the end of Upper Lakeville. He didn't bother stopping into the small store and certainly didn't want to run into anyone. Going on automatic, he got into his own boat and started the motor. He wished with a heavy heart he could undo what he knew would destroy any chance of happiness for him and Fern. The thing with duty, it never took a day off.

Chapter 20

Rose

Rose ached to sneak away in the rowboat again and look at the land. She hated keeping secrets from Fern and it gnawed at her, making her fidgety. When she'd first found Lily's journal, she'd thought of keeping it all to herself, but within a minute knew it wouldn't be right. Now, after yesterday's trip down memory lane, she felt sad and angry again. Fern hankered toward forgiveness. Rose wished it was in her, but seeing the land two days ago made her seethe.

She'd barely gotten through yesterday, but thankfully Fern had been in la-la land all day recalling being the naughty wife for a change and they'd had a busy day with pickling. Thinking of Fern being the bad one seemed wrong. Her sister was an adult and she didn't dare judge. When Rose found out her ex wasn't faithful, she had gotten even the old-fashioned way with a few one-night stands.

They had sucked. It had been Fern who had played mother, telling Rose she deserved better. Harold didn't feel like better, but she'd made her bed and had to sleep somewhere. Having a night with Blair would be something. She stepped outside to enjoy the crisp morning, hating how much she wished for a cigarette.

Thankfully the rain had stopped last night and it looked like a lovely day would grace them. Rose, wrapped in a blanket, sat in the old rocking chair she'd moved to the porch yesterday when the heat of the kitchen had become stifling as they'd canned their pickles.

"Why can't you sleep in?"

Rose screamed. She hadn't seen Fern, wrapped in her own blanket almost hidden in an old chair by the corner of the wrap-around deck.

"Fern, you almost gave me a heart attack. How long have you been out here?"

"A while."

"Why? Once again warring with your conscience?"

Fern tilted her head lower and pulled the blanket tighter around her middle. "A little. I'm feeling off."

Feeling off was a code word Rose recognized and the hairs on the back of her neck stood up.

"Well, it's going to be a nice day. What's on the agenda?" Diverting Fern from any of those "off" thoughts a must. When Fern felt off, usually bad things came to pass and Rose didn't want anything to mar their week away.

"Not sure. We've done all the jamming, pickling and

biscotti baking I can handle," said Fern. "I couldn't sleep. I had a weird dream last night."

"Guilty conscience?"

Fern cracked a lopsided smile. "Maybe. Except it wasn't about Sean. It was about Dale."

"You're missing him. No news is good news."

"Yeah, you're probably right. I didn't say goodbye. Not like I'm sure he'd notice."

"Teen years suck." Rose tucked a piece of hair behind her ear.

They both turned to look at the lake as a loon landed effortlessly on the water.

"We never did get a chance to read more of Lily's journal. How about I grab it and we read for a while?" asked Rose.

"Yeah, good idea and if you go by the tea pot could you please top me up?" Fern handed Rose her large mug with a smile on her face. Fern smiling, a good sign.

Five minutes later, Rose returned with the scribbler in hand and tea for Fern. She flipped through a few pages and then settled.

"Okay, let's start when she comes back from Australia."

"Sounds great. You know I never did understand. Why Australia? I mean, it's on the other side of the bloody world!" said Fern, sipping her tea.

Rose eyed her sister like she was nuts. "I'd love to go to Australia. Don't you remember when she was about twelve, I think, she did this school project on kangaroos and she talked about it for years how someday she would go to Australia to see the real thing. Now, we also know the notion got reinforced when she met the nurse who was from Australia when she was getting her tonsils removed."

"You're right. Once Lily set her mind to something, she made it real. She had such drive. They really were, as twins, completely different," said Fern.

"Okay, ready?" asked Rose.

Fern tucked her feet back under her blanket and nodded.

September 15, 2002

I'm finally here. The plane ride took forever but I didn't care. My first time on a plane and it's more than twenty-six hours to get to my destination. I'm not sure how I managed to sleep, but I did. I landed in Sydney and let me tell you it's not anything like Sydney, Nova Scotia. I've settled into the hostel and I even have my own private bedroom. I did a lot of research and I'm going to keep my backpack with me. It's got all my essentials in it and I don't want to lose anything. I called Willow to let her know I arrived safely and while she thinks I'm nuts for this adventure, she finally wished me luck. I wish we were closer, but it's like I've taken one path and she's taken the complete opposite. She's now married with two kids. I still have a hard time getting my head around her choices. Certainly not choices I'd have made and her husband is a douche bag.

Tomorrow, I'm going to go on a few of the free ferries and get a good view of Sydney. Now, off for a drink. This place is so cool. They actually have a café/bar attached to the hostel and people get to hang out in hammocks. Wicked.

September 22, 2002
I've made some great friends here and tomorrow I'm travelling to Cairns with a group of four people. Kerry and Alice are a couple from Ireland who are experienced with travelling. Last year they hiked all through India. Sanja is their friend who they hooked up with in India and Peter is a guy we all met at the hostel. Peter's a few years older and from Texas, but he's nice and certainly easy to look at. We pooled our money together and bought this old clunker of a van which holds six, but with all our bags we'll make do with five. I still can't believe I'm in Australia. The temperature is freaking hot and humid at weird times of the day for me. I'm still adjusting. I can't wait to see Cairns. Sydney is beautiful but it's not as tropical as I expected. Oh, I almost forgot. I found out you have to turn your sneakers upside down and stuff them with socks and to check in the morning for spiders. Turns out almost all the insects are deadly here. Alice had a bird this morning when she found a spider in her shoe. Kerry of course killed the thing which then made Sanja pissed. He doesn't like to kill anything and is vegan. He thought it was gross when Peter went on about eating kangaroo steaks and yes, they do sell them in the grocery store – ugh. No way am I eating a kangaroo. Disgusting!

. . .

The Heart of Family

October 14, 2002

Peter is becoming annoying and he stinks. Then again, after basically three weeks in a crowded van, we all smell. Alice says Peter likes me and I'm all for a bit of fun, but I'm thinking of ditching them tomorrow. We're finally in Cairns and I want to discover this place on my own. I sort of mentioned it to Alice and she totally digs it. I've discovered I love mangoes. They have a number of different ones here and they're delicious. I've got to watch my cash now, but Alice said you can always pick up work in Australia. When I mentioned to her I cut hair, didn't I end up giving her, Kerry and Sanja a free cut. Peter says he's trying to grow his out so thankfully I didn't have to do his. I didn't even have a proper pair of scissors. Kerry bought a pair from a store and I'm surprised they're still speaking to me. I'm missing you, Willow. I called you last night but it went to the machine.

October 25, 2002

I've got a job. How wicked! I sort of fell into it. I walked into a hair salon to look around and I got talking to the lady at the counter and when she found out I came from Canada, she almost died. Turns out she's from Antigonish. We chatted for a good hour and when I mentioned I needed work, she hired me on the spot. I start Monday. It's three days a week, which is perfect as it will give me time to explore more and tonight, I'm staying with Christie, that's the salon owner's name. She said she came out like me to explore Australia in her early twenties and met a fella and the rest is history. How totally weird. She's got a guest shed which is wickedly cool and she said if I like the place, which is like of course, I could stay there for $600 a month. It's not big. There's a small room with a toilet and sink, and a tiny kitchen area with a kettle and hot plate. But there's a BBQ outside and honestly, it's what everyone uses, and there's only an outside shower but it's private. The sofa pulls out into a bed, suits me fine. I'm going to tell Christie yes for staying with her and the plus side is it's only four blocks to the salon. Christie recommended I get a bike. Her house is three blocks from the beach. This place is heaven. When I told her, she laughed. She said it's why she never went back home to NS. I'm not sure I could do that, but for now, it's nice to feel sort of settled while I get to explore the area.

"What a sweet deal. She had been lucky. I do remember her sending me a postcard from Cairns and telling me about meeting a gal from the province," said Rose.

Fern shooed a spider out of her way. "Maybe I should have travelled more."

"You still can. At least you two can afford it. The farthest we can make it would probably be Antigonish."

Fern wrinkled her nose. "Don't get me wrong, I like Antigonish, but to be truthful, I'd rather save up for a big vacation. We should plan for one. You and I. We should save up and get away."

Rose laughed. "Ah, yeah, Fern, we are away. This is it."

"No, silly. I mean like get on a plane and go away," said Fern.

Rose recognized the look in Fern's eyes. She had started to get excited and already started to plot and plan. Rose yawned. She'd let her sister scheme away, but in her sad reality, being financially solvent to escape wasn't in the cards.

"Let's plan it for in two years," said Fern.

Rose nodded. Maybe she could squirrel a bit of money away each month.

"You know it doesn't have to be far. We could hit New York."

Okay, why did her sister have to name her favourite all-time city to visit? Because Fern knew her inside and out. Rose closed the scribbler. "We'll see. Okay, enough reading for now. I'm getting out of this place for the day. The weather's going to be great. I say, let's go fishing," said Rose, smiling. Fishing made her happy. Fishing would keep her thoughts off the land and most certainly away from dreaming of going to New York. Fishing would also divert Fern from beating herself up. The perfect plan for the day.

"You know, maybe you're right. As much as I love all the baking and pickling, I think a day outside will do me good," said Fern, getting up from the bench to stretch.

"I'll get the gear ready. You can pack the lunch. We'll eat the muffins in the boat."

Rose had a mission. She was a gal with a plan. Fern laughed. "Sounds great."

Rose got up from the rocking chair still wrapped in the warmth of the blanket and ambled over to where Fern stood. Without warning, she engulfed Fern in a sisterly hug. Fern returned the hug and Rose savoured the feel of her sister's strength.

Twenty minutes later, they were geared up and seated in the row boat. Rose had made Fern row. They were heading to the Falls. Rose planned to do fly fishing, which is why she wore hip waders and Fern was going to plunk her line over the rowboat, and not catch a thing. Fern hated catching fish. She liked fish, but hated watching them gasp to their death, which is why Rose always took care of them quickly.

"I forgot how much rowing sucks," said Fern.

Her sister swatted at a horsefly. "Exercise. It's good for you."

"I do exercise. I go to the gym three times a week, but it does no good. I could fast and I'd gain weight," said Fern, causing Rose to laugh.

"Drama queen. And I have to say I'm pretty certain Sean liked what he saw."

Fern gave Rose a look her sister found hard to decipher.

"Well, he didn't complain," said Fern, trying hard not to smile. "I still can't believe I did what I did."

Ah, now her sister planned to open up. "And why do you think you did what you did?" asked Rose, gently. Her sister did have control of the rowboat.

"Honestly, Rose, I feel like a well-worn rug."

Rose got it but needed her sister to spell it out. "Like how?"

"Craig has no understanding of what I do. I'm sure he thinks I stay in my PJs all day until I have to get the kids. He doesn't need me anymore. And what do I have for all the years I've stayed home with them – nothing. Not even a pension. You know I used to be a feminist in my university days. What happened to me?"

Fern looked like she might cry. Rose couldn't handle her sister being emotional while kicking herself for having some fun. "Fern, you did what was right."

"Right! I've got nothing. No skills. Rose, when I had to get a laptop, I had to take Dale with me because I had no idea what to get. Duncan set it up and I still can't seem to get my pictures off the freaking cloud so I can get them printed. When did this happen? When did I become a cliché? I'm going to tell you something. I hate being home. I hate when I wake up and the first thing I think of is what will I make for supper. Who does that?"

"Women do it. Men don't. Fern, it's the same for me."

"But you work," said Fern.

"I'd love to have been able to stay home."

"No, you wouldn't. It has slowly killed me."

Rose pulled her ballcap lower and tucked her hair behind her ears. Mentally, she made a note to get a haircut when she got back. "Then get out and get a job."

"Who would hire me?"

Rose gave her sister a pointed look. "Fern, you have skills. You do tons of freaking fundraising for your community. I have no idea how you manage to raise thousands of dollars, plus you're great with people."

"But Rose, it's not who I thought I'd be."

"And who was that?"

"Wendy Mesley," said Fern.

"Who is she?"

Fern rolled her eyes.

"I'm guessing she's an author," said Rose.

"Nope. She's a CBC reporter. I met her once in Toronto when she gave a talk and she stunk like cigarettes. Still though, she's the reason I first wanted to become a reporter."

"Then why did you go into finance?"

"Because I also like numbers and knew I could secure a job in that field. I used to watch The National with Dad and I can still remember the first time I saw her anchor it. Dad turned to me and said, 'That could be you, Fern.' It had been like a light bulb went off. From that moment on I wished I could be like her."

"Wait a second. Isn't she the one who married that old guy on The National?"

"Peter Mansbridge. Yeah, they got married and then divorced and then she had breast cancer, but she still does the news."

"Does she have kids?"

"Not sure," said Fern.

"Fern, you told me you hated your job in Ontario. And can you imagine going through life without kids?" asked Rose.

"Okay, I might have hated my job. And no, I can't imagine

life without the kids. But it would be nice to be with adults and make my own money. I feel like I'm insignificant and have nothing to show for it. And don't get me wrong, Craig's been a good husband, but we've been off for a number of years now. Maybe we've grown apart. I honestly don't ever think, 'oh I should go tell Craig.' Instead, I think of ways to avoid doing my monthly 'duty'."

Rose chuckled while swatting at the flies. "Please do not say 'duty' again. It's something our mother would have said. And, I'm fairly certain it hadn't been a chore with Sean."

Fern grinned and pursed her lips. "No, that had been loving like it's supposed to be. For the first time in years, I felt alive and more importantly, present."

"Fern, it sounds to me like you've got some serious thinking to do about things. I can't give you advice, but you have five wonderful children and a husband who I'm sure still loves you."

"I think Craig likes to say he loves me, but the words are meaningless. He's hardly home and when he is, he's simply watching sports on TV. We used to be close, but it's been at least five years now since we've actually planned anything together. If I want us to go out to a restaurant, I'm the one who has to plan it. You know last month when he hinted we might hook up later in the evening, I pleaded a headache and he didn't bat an eye. I never thought I'd become the woman who views having sex with her husband as a chore, but being with Sean made me realize something."

"What?" asked Rose.

"I want more out of this life," said Fern, smiling with a mischievous look in her eye, making Rose grin.

"Don't we all. Fern, I try to avoid having sex with Harold."

"What?"

"Oh, come on. Do you think you're the only woman with problems? I've been with Harold for eleven years. You've been with Craig for twenty-five years. We're at the age when things break down. Marriage being the number one thing. I honestly don't think marriage is normal."

"How do you think Mom and Dad did it?"

"Ah, yeah you did grow up in the same house as me, right? Fern, they barely spoke to each other and then they got separate rooms. It's how they survived. Plus, you and I both know Mom would never have left Dad. She's incapable of making a decision."

Fern stuck an oar in the oar lock and rubbed her palm. "Tell me about it. I never knew that about Mom until Dad died. Rose, it's your turn to row. My arms are killing me."

"Stop being a baby. We're almost there. Are you going to tell Craig about Sean?" Rose had to ask; the question killed her.

"Yes, I am."

"Well, I'd think long and hard about it."

"Rose, I can't not tell him. It's not fair to him."

"Life isn't fair, but I'm going to tell you something. He's not going to take it well. You sure you're ready to handle the consequences?"

Fern looked over her shoulder. Rose suspected she probably wondered where the Falls were.

"You lied about the Falls being close."

"Obviously, your memory sucks. Angry at me a little?" teased Rose.

"I see what you're trying to do."

"What I'm trying to do, sis, is get you to row faster. You keep rowing at this rate, and it'll be lunch time before we make it there. Trust me, my intentions are not malicious."

"No, you're trying to show me how remaining silent would make things easier for me."

Rose tied a fly to her line. "As usual, you're making me seem deep and I'm *so* not. I think staying quiet until you sort things out makes sense."

"Do you think he'll be mad?"

"He is a guy after all. Wouldn't you be mad?"

"Seriously, Rose, for the past year I've been sort of hoping he'd have an affair."

Rose winced. "Oh, that's pretty bad. You might say it, but you don't mean it."

"I'm not so sure."

"Fern, honey, you should have said something about how you've been feeling sooner. Why did you wait for this weekend?"

"It's not like I didn't want to tell you. I didn't know what to say. Hey, Rose, I'm feeling lost as a person, as a mother and a wife. I've been faking fine for a long time, but with Sean I felt something..."

"I'm sure you did." Rose laughed.

Fern giggled. "Not what I meant. I felt alive. I also realized something. You're right. I need a job. When I get home, I'm going to find something to get me out of the house."

"I think it's a good idea and promise me something," said Rose.

"What?"

"Wait for a few days before telling Craig. Perspective can be a good thing." Rose wondered where her depth of knowledge came from.

Fern nodded.

Smiling, Rose pointed to her right. "Around the bend and we're there."

Fern stopped rowing to push a piece of hair off her face. "I don't know if I should look. It's probably five more freaking miles and my arm muscles already hate me."

"I'm not kidding."

Fern smiled and tried to sound like their mother. "You had better be telling the truth, Rose Anne-Marie Faith Siteman."

Rose chuckled. "You will never master it. Only Mom can say my full name and make it sound chilling. You, sis, make it sound like a weird religious thing."

"Because it's a weird name."

"And Fern Constance Reverence Siteman, isn't?" teased Rose.

"All our names suck. Willow Thyme Jane Siteman and Lily Blue Pepper Siteman. I used to think Mom had been on drugs when we were all born," said Fern.

"Actually, according to today's magazines, we're in style. Mom and Dad were ahead of the times. Today celebs name their kids things like Orange, Apple, Sky, Dream, South, North...basically anything."

"And it's why I picked simple ordinary names for my kids."

"I agree with you. I didn't even want to give my kids middle names, but both of the men in my life at the time forced me to," said Rose.

Fern picked up her rowing pace. Rose was pleased they had ventured into more neutral territory of which celeb had named their child the weirdest name. She couldn't wait to get to the Falls and knew exactly how Fern's arms felt. Hers still ached from her recent journey down the lake.

An hour later, they were both eating the packed lunch and Rose felt mighty proud of herself for reeling in two large fresh water perch from her lucky flies. They hadn't been lucky until they caught the fish, but the pretty fuchsia flies were now placed strategically next to her other two lucky ones.

Rose finished her sandwich and wrapped up the cookies she'd save for later. "Want to go see the land?"

Fern almost choked on the bite of tuna sandwich loaded with mayonnaise and crunchy dill pickles. "What? You mean now?"

"It's around the bend."

Fern crinkled her forehead like she might contemplate the idea.

Rose pushed ahead. The need to share her secret had been cancerous. Fern had to see what she knew. The land was being raped. Changed. Their land was being built and made into something else. Something their father would have hated.

"I'll row. It's a good hour, but I row fast and it's only a thirty-minute hike in." Rose knew she pressed her point.

Fern rewrapped her sandwich. "You've been there."

Rose nodded once and waited for her sister to rant at her. Instead, Fern started packing their stuff back into the basket. "Fine. Show it to me."

Rose tried not to smile but wanted to. Fern hadn't been near the land for over four years. So much had changed in their family in such little time. First their father's unexpected death, then their mother's stroke and dementia diagnosis, but worst of all had been the treachery of having Willow steal land right out from under their mother for personal gain. Her parents hadn't been wealthy by any stretch of the imagination, but the family land on their father's side had been passed down for over three generations.

Rose pushed the boat out into deeper waters and then quickly got into place to start the hard row around the bend. Who needed to do bicep curls at a gym when you could row for a good hour and get the intended effect?

While rowing she told Fern about her first time visiting the land. Unburdening felt like a climax. Fern didn't say a whole lot, which worried Rose. They reached their destination, a small beach which had a logging path cut into the forest. The path ran inland to their family's property. Rose stripped out of her hip waders to more manageable rubber boots. Fern placed her hand on her shoulder.

"It's only land, Rose."

"Wait till you see it," said Rose, pursing her lips. She didn't understand why Fern wasn't as excited to share in the discovery.

Fern zipped up her jacket. "We shouldn't be here."

"Don't lie to me. You're dying to see it, but you won't say it."

"Do you remember the time we snuck up here together to escape our toddlers and discovered Lily making out with…"

"Mitch MacDonald. How could I forget. What a sight. I'm happy to say I've never seen something like it again," said Rose.

"How old had Lily been then?"

Rose marched ahead. Fern followed. Her steps were slower as she manoeuvred around the boulders and muck. Since Rose had already been there a few days ago, she led the way, showing her sister where to walk to avoid getting her boots sucked into the devious mud trying to claim shoes as souvenirs. "She would have been seventeen. Not like we hadn't done the same at her age, but coming face to face with your sister getting it on had certainly been unnerving and embarrassingly funny."

"Poor kid. Lily, got mad at us and said what are you doing here while Mitch took off out of the house before we could stop laughing."

"Oh my gosh, I had forgotten. Lily had been so upset at us. She didn't find it funny, but it had been. Strange, how she didn't write about it in her journal."

Fern slipped on a rock but quickly found her footing again. "Maybe she did. I think she might have had a number of scribblers with her journal entries. You know I'm enjoying us reading the journal. It's been years since I've thought about her adventures and I feel like enough time has passed without me blubbering all the time at the mere mention of her name."

"I totally agree. I worried when we started it might be too much, but the more we read, the closer I feel to her."

Fern nodded as she started to closely watch her footing. They proceeded with little talk as they eased up the big hill.

"I'm totally out of shape," moaned Fern, placing her hands on her hips to catch her breath halfway up the hill. "Why do I feel like I'm trespassing on land our family has owned for over one hundred and sixty years. This feels so weird."

When they crested the last hill, Rose heard Fern gasp. She knew exactly what she felt. She'd felt the punch to her gut a few days ago when she'd dared to give into curiosity.

Rose pointed things out to Fern she probably didn't see. There were four small cottages being constructed near where the stone wall had been. Dozens of trees had been felled to make way for a proper lane to the lake and they were building what looked to be a large barn. The beautiful meadow which their father had religiously mowed now lay as a mess with large tractor tracks. It looked like a wounded battlefield and she had to gulp not to give into the wave of emotions tearing through her.

"Do you think she got rid of the memorial we made for Lily? And what about Dad's grave?" asked Fern.

"I honestly don't know. Knowing Willow, she probably bulldozed the area," said Rose.

Fern collapsed to her knees, not caring they'd get wet and

mud-stained. Rose knelt beside her sister and draped an arm around her shoulders. "This wasn't supposed to happen."

"I can't believe she'd get rid of the memorial for her twin sister. Do you think she knew about Dad's grave?" asked Fern, her breath huffy as she fought for composure.

"We can take a look around. I'm not sure if she knew or cared about what Mom wanted done with Dad's ashes. She wanted this land and stole it to get it."

"I can't believe she'd intentionally ruin his grave. He was her father."

"But you're forgetting Fern, Dad loved her more and wanted her to have this," said Rose, waving her arm around the area dramatically. "Don't you remember those words she threw in our face like a two-year old child and not a grown woman? This had nothing to do with Dad. Getting this was what she wanted. I think they've been planning this for years. It makes me sick."

"Where is everyone?"

"I think the crews come up on the weekend. They're probably all his friends and he's probably paying them with trade or something."

Rose stood up and helped her sister to her feet. When Fern started to make her way down to the main house, Rose marched quietly behind her. Fern peeked through the kitchen window.

Fern used the sleeve of her jacket to wipe grime from the old window to peer more closely inside the house. "I miss this place."

Rose looked inside. The kitchen table with the peeling black paint they'd grown up with sat like it waited for them. The old farm stove which looked a lot like the one at the cottage called to Rose. Fern knelt down and lifted the large flat stone which had always been there and voilà, she found the key.

Rose gasped. "Are you going in?"

Fern fitted the key into the lock. "This is what you wanted, wasn't it?"

Okay, Rose gave her sister one big point for hitting the mark. She craved to see inside. Fern did the dirty work and a minute later they stepped inside. The place smelled exactly like how Rose remembered. A touch of mothballs combined with musk and a hint of old cedar wood – heaven. They moved from the kitchen to the pantry, each of them reaching out to touch a few precious objects they recalled from their childhood. The old sofa and saggy chair still resided in the living room and when they went upstairs, the old beds were still in place.

"Not much changed," said Fern.

"Well, not yet. Lots has changed on the outside. I suspect they're waiting until the outside is done before demolishing this place."

Fern stopped on the last step of the stairs. "Do you honestly think she'll demolish it?"

"Yes," snapped Rose. "It feels weird being here."

"You're right. Did you ever think this would happen to our family?"

"I'm not sure. She always acted entitled. She demanded

things from Mom and Dad, neither of us, including Lily, would ask or accept, but no. I never thought it would come to this."

"I hate I can't even call her to get help with Mom. I had been desperate enough once to beg Mom to call her and get her to take her to an appointment. You know what she did? She dropped off Mom. Dropped her off. It's like she doesn't realize or care Mom has dementia. You know the receptionist called me because my number's an emergency contact, saying my mother was distraught."

"You never told me, Fern. I've been telling you for over a year she doesn't care about Mom. She got what she wanted. They don't help at all. We're the ones who took care of Mom when she lost her driver's licence. We're the ones who moved her into the city. We're the ones who organized four dumpsters and spent countless hours cleaning out her place. We even had to wear masks because of all the mould. She wouldn't lift a finger unless to help herself to something she wanted – like this land. If we hadn't hired a lawyer to ensure Mom's other assets couldn't be taken from her, she'd have it all and then what would have happened to Mom?"

Rose hated having to go into all the sordid details, but Fern had a soft heart and sometimes needed a reminder about all the work they'd done for their mother, and continued to do for her. "Let's get out of here. I wanted to show you so you'd know, but now I feel sad."

"I simply want some help with Mom. I feel like I can't do it all. Every week I have an appointment with her doctor, a specialist or the foot doctor, and that's not including grocery shopping for her or simply trying to find time for a walk. If not her, then it's one of my kids. How can I manage all of it and get a job on top of it?" said Fern.

I've been selfish. Rose placed a hand on Fern's shoulder and made her sister look at her. "I try when I can to help with Mom, but I'll try harder. You need a life. Get a job and get out of the house."

"Thanks, Rose. I'd be lost without you, but you, like me, juggle your own children and you also work. Never in my wildest dreams did I anticipate dealing with my seventy-three-year-old mother like another child I had to take care of. Last week I realized she'd been wearing the same shirt for the past two weeks. I called the caretaker who comes in to clean her place and wash her clothes and asked her to keep a list of what she finds in the laundry hamper. When I looked at it, she had worn one pair of socks and one underwear for two weeks of clothing."

"Fern, you should have said something to me." Rose urged Fern out the front door.

Rose locked up the house and tucked the key back where Fern had found it.

"I planned to tell you later this week after our weekend."

"She needs more help," said Rose.

"And are you going to join me for the battle?" asked Fern, moving slowly back up the hill.

"Yes, of course, I will." Instantly, Rose anticipated their mother getting angry and then crying. It had become their routine.

"Well, before that I'm going to a drop-in meeting taking place at the hospital next week for family and caregivers who look after loved ones with dementia."

"When is it?" asked Rose.

"Tuesday night at six."

"I work until six, but I'll come once I'm done."

Fern hugged her sister. Rose saw the tears in her eyes. "We'll get through this together."

"I know, but I'd like Willow to share in this burden and it's that which makes me angry. Not the land. Not what she's doing to this place, even though I'm upset it looks like she didn't keep his grave," said Fern. "I can see the memorial for Lily. A few tree branches are covering it up, but it's still at the beginning of the pathway to the lake."

Fern pointed to the left and Rose followed her line of view. "Oh, good. I had worried she'd cleared it all out. I'm actually surprised she kept it. I wonder if she ever thinks of her?"

"I'm sure she does, but she'll never admit it. Plus, it's not like we're on speaking terms at the moment," said Fern. "You know , it's not fair. She gets to live her life and all is rosy for her and we're the ones dealing with Mom. Let's get back. I need a drink," said Fern.

Rose smiled at her sister. "Thank you for coming with me."

"No more secrets. You should have told me."

"It killed me not to. I'll make supper tonight and you can finish the scarf you're trying to knit."

"Trying is the key word. I have no idea how my girls can whip these things out in a day or so."

"It's because they love to knit. You don't. Do you remember the time Gram tried to teach you to knit?"

"I tried once a year." Fern walked back down the muddy trail to the boat.

"That had been the point. You hate knitting but you're good at other things."

"Lately, I feel like I'm not good at anything."

"Okay, you don't get to have a pity party. I'm the one rowing back and it's because I'm the nice sister."

"Rose, I feel like you're my only sister."

The truth of her sister's words echoed around them like a gust of wind almost knocking Rose off course. Rose felt a deep ache behind her eyes, but those tears had dried-up years ago when she realized pretending Willow had died was better for her sanity and those she loved.

Chapter 21

Fern

Fern was glad they'd gone to the land. In a weird way, seeing the family homestead had been therapeutic. She'd loved the property as much, if not more, than Rose and Willow. She remembered losing her virginity to Sean in the lumpy old double bed upstairs. She had memories etched in the walls of the place and letting go was difficult, but she had to. The memory of Lily and Mitch felt fresh in her mind. It had been one of the few times Lily remained mad at her for weeks. Eventually, she'd forgiven them and they had both shared a laugh at the awkwardness of it all.

Lily forgave. She got mad like a firecracker but within a few days, her sweet nature returned and she'd erased it from her memory. The same could not be said for Willow, who kept a running tally of all the injustices she felt they'd done to her over the years without a thought to absolution. Lately, Fern wondered if she too walked down that narrow path of absolute conviction. *Wouldn't it be easier to forgive and forget so they could work on rebuilding their relationship?* Rose would say no way, but Fern wasn't so sure.

Anyway, most days she didn't have time to dwell on the land. Dealing with her mother's demands overrode her days. Fern worried about her mother and deep down felt her mother's disease might kill her. She had to let it go.

It had been a silent affair as Rose rowed back to the cottage. Rose, immersed in her own thoughts of her time at the land, didn't notice the silence or remark on the emptiness with chatter. Fern had felt off all morning and it gnawed at her. The dreams lingered like flickers in her mind.

First, she'd dreamt of the time Dale had been probably six and he'd picked a huge bouquet of daisies for her. It had been the first time he'd been stung by a bee. He'd cried, but handed her the flowers saying he'd picked a bunch for her because he loved her bunches. Fern had iced his bite and thankfully the swelling had gone down after a few hours. The second dream had been even stranger. It had been the time when a yellow finch had flown into the living room window. Before she could run out of the house, Dale had. He'd returned with the small creature in his hands. Fern had put the bird in a shoebox and prayed for it to wake up, explaining to Dale sometimes they got stunned and if left alone they'd regain consciousness. It had been a sunny day so they placed the box on the deck. By midafternoon, Fern realized the bird had died. Explaining death to Dale had been difficult. Fern recalled him asking, "If we bury the bird in the ground, won't it get reborn?" They had been going to a nearby Anglican church for about six months at the time. Fern assumed they'd been discussing resurrection in the Sunday school program. She'd asked Dale if that's what they were teaching in church and he said no. When pressed, her eldest had looked at her and simply said. "I believe the bird can do some good if we bury him in the ground." Fern got it so they quietly, while the younger children had been napping, dug a small grave in the backyard for the finch. In the summer, a batch of beautiful daisies had sprung up over the grave. Dale had made a point of reminding her it was the good from the finch. Speechless had best described Fern. She'd nodded and said yes, marvelling at the simplicity of life from a child's point of view.

Two dreams in one night, each featuring her eldest, Dale, made Fern fidgety. Her head ached and her stomach felt off. Maybe she shouldn't have had the tuna sandwich with all the mayo.

Rose cleaned the fish by the beach and then went to chop some kindling for the stove. Fern peeled a few potatoes for their supper while sipping her white wine. She surveyed the shiny mason jars of pickles with pride. They'd start packing things up probably tomorrow, but for now all their gifts were on display for them to look at with pride and awe. Beside the mustard pickles and crunchy dills, they had made hot yellow bean pickles with garlic, bread and butter pickles, chow, pickled beets, biscotti and enough fudge to sink George's boat.

Fern shoved more wood into the stove and didn't see who

stepped through the door of the cottage. She assumed Rose had returned. "I peeled the potatoes for supper."

"Fern."

Sean's voice slammed through her. She turned and for a moment felt caught by surprise. He stood in his RCMP uniform, looking mighty good. Fern dumped the rest of the wood she'd been cradling in her arms and rushed him for a hug. The stiff starchy uniform brushed against her cheek. Sean held her, but then he slowly eased her out of his arms. Instantly, *that off feeling* reclaimed Fern.

"What is it?" Her voice pitched an octave higher than normal. She worried something had happened to her mother.

"You need to sit down." Sean ushered her over to the sofa.

Rose came in. Sean gave her a look and Rose moved to sit beside her sister.

"Fern, last night there was an accident and Dale was injured."

It took a second for Sean's words to register. *Dale injured. How? What had happened?*

"What do you mean?" Fern tried with all her might to make sense of what he implied. Her fingers laced themselves together through the woolly quilt lying on the sofa.

"He was driving and it looks like he might have fallen asleep at the wheel. He and his passenger were air-lifted from Truro to the QEII. Fern, they're both listed in critical condition."

"I don't understand. Dale doesn't have a car. How could he be driving?" Fern clenched her teeth and sharp pain travelled up her neck. She could barely speak. Her heart ached and it felt like someone was sitting on her chest. "It's study week for him, so he's home working on university stuff."

"Who had been the other passenger?" asked Rose.

"A girl. Her name is Scarlett Barron," said Sean.

Fern cried out. The sound like a wounded animal filled the house.

"What? What is going on? Why would he be with her? I don't understand this," said Fern, now crying steadily and on the verge of losing it.

Sean directed his question to Rose, who gripped her sister's hand. "I take it you both know who Scarlett Barron is?"

Rose cried. "She's Willow's daughter."

Sean gave a deep sigh, and ran a hand through his hair as he rose from the sofa. "Fern, you need to go to the hospital now."

"This can't be happening," said Fern, over and over again. She rocked herself back and forth on the sofa. "Dale's okay. I know he's okay. This isn't happening."

"I'll get her jacket and purse. Fern honey, Sean's going to take you to the hospital. I'll be there ASAP. Sean, when you get back, ask Kelly to call Harold for me. Kelly has his number. You need to go now, Fern. Dale needs you."

Fern stopped moving and then looked at Sean. "How bad is it?"

Sean pulled Fern's listless body into his and held her hard. "It's bad. He's in a coma. They did surgery last night to stop the internal bleeding, but they think he might have a small bleed on his brain."

Fern cried hard. She didn't have the strength to move. How

could this be happening to her? Rose muffled her cries with her hand, but she became a busy bee. Rose grabbed Fern's purse, helped her get to her feet and into her sneakers. She placed her arms in her jacket all the while with Sean's help. Fern heard Sean's voice offering love and comfort and saw the tears he tried hard to keep at bay. She couldn't have him breaking down. She knew it.

The world went into slow motion for Fern. *I'm having an out-of-body experience.* Rose's mouth moved, but Fern didn't understand the words. Sean was talking. *Is this how a stroke felt?* She couldn't decipher what was happening. Someone pushed her arms into a lifejacket, but her body felt numb.

Time disappeared. She didn't remember the boat ride from the cottage to the dock. *How could that be?* Fern saw Kelly pacing on the dock. More words which didn't make sense passed between Sean and Kelly and then Sean slid her into the passenger side of the RCMP cruiser. The next thing she knew, the sound of the siren filled the silent screams in her head as they sped down the country road to the highway. Once they were on the highway, Sean turned off the siren.

"I'm here for you, Fern," said Sean, whose hand she gripped. Funny, she didn't remember reaching for his hand. Had he driven like a madman one-handed the entire time they'd raced down the windy country road?

The drive to the hospital felt both too short and too long. Fern prayed the entire time. She prayed to the God she'd discarded like a worn sock. She prayed to the faith she'd forgotten, but her mind still knew verbatim the psalms she silently said in her head over and over again like nursery rhymes. At the back of her mind was the rancid thought that this is what befell bad women. This, her sin. A price had to be paid for giving into the temptation of pleasure. Even though it was the twenty-first century and that septic cliché of a whisper sounded ridiculous, she couldn't shake it.

An hour later, Sean pulled alongside the emergency department entrance. He parked and walked her inside. He spoke to someone at the front desk and then she silently followed him to the elevator and together they stepped out onto the seventh floor. They hadn't spoken the entire drive. Fern couldn't utter words. Sean took charge.

"He's in room 709A," said Sean, leading the way.

Fern followed, robot-like. Her mind had become mush and it took all her energy to keep breathing. She noticed weird things. The halls, painted light beige, needed another coat of paint to cover the chips and dented walls. The smell, antiseptic with a hint of cleaning fluid, failed to get rid of the overriding scent of urine and decay. As they walked through the halls, nurses rushed silently by wearing sneakers like they knew when they started their shift it would be a marathon.

The door to 709A had been closed. Sean quietly opened it and there lying on the bed was Dale, her nineteen-year-old baby.

"Thank you," said a man Fern recognized as Craig, her husband who had his arms around her before she could fully register the room, Dale or even him. Fern still couldn't speak. Craig cried as he gripped her tight. Sean shut the door. All she could look at was Dale hooked up to a ventilator and a ton of machines. Some were beeping and some weren't. Craig sobbed like an angry child. Stoic, Fern knew she had succumbed to shock.

She forced herself to take a step fully into the room. "What happened?"

Craig pulled himself together. "I don't have the full picture yet. Duncan said…"

"Is Duncan okay?" Fern couldn't deal with living if one more of her kids had been hurt.

"Yes, he's fine. He said Dale told him he and Scarlett were going to a concert. Dale and her were sharing the driving."

"I didn't even know they spoke?" said Fern, feeling like a fool.

"Me either. Anyway, they think he fell asleep. It's not good, Fern."

Fern looked at her son and thought what an understatement that was. Not good was having a bad day. Not good was knowing your mother was incapable of changing her clothing. Not good was a frigging flat tire. This situation was beyond words. Her head felt fuzzy. Craig, sensing something, helped to usher her to a hard-plastic chair.

A doctor knocked gently on the door and entered. "Have you made your decision?"

"What?" asked Fern, looking from the thirty-something doctor in his pristine white lab coat to Craig. "What's he talking about?"

"Sorry, I didn't realize you two hadn't discussed the situation. I'm Doctor Singh. Your son came in early this morning.

They managed to stop the internal bleeding, but he's brain dead."

Fern looked at her son. The doctor talked, but the words were meaningless. She reached out and picked up Dale's hand. His hand felt ice cold. She noticed the scar above his chin. He'd gotten it when he had been five, when Duncan and he thought they were Superman and could fly between their bunk beds. She noticed the stupid ring tattoo he got last year on his pinkie finger. She'd always hated his tattoo. How odd it had become the only looking alive thing on her son.

"The passenger with him is still in critical condition and needs a liver."

"Sorry, I'm not following you. When will my son wake up?"

The doctor gave Craig a look. Fern stood up, the plastic chair with the steel legs scraped the floor. "When will he wake up?" She didn't recognize her own hysterical pitch. That sound she'd heard only from other women.

"I am sorry, but he won't. The ventilator is keeping him alive. We noticed he didn't sign his donor card and your husband mentioned the passenger was his cousin. Without a liver, she'll die. We tested them and his liver is a match. We don't normally do this and I've advised the MOTP about the situation and they're going to send someone in to speak with both of you."

Fern looked at Craig. He shook his head. He didn't know what the doctor said either. "The what?"

"Sorry. Bad habit with the jargon. MOTP stands for the

Multi-Organ Transplant program. They'll give you the run down on how things progress."

Fern looked at the doctor. He might as well have been an alien. Did they train doctors to talk like they were listing a to do list for groceries when dealing with soon-to-be hysterical parents whose child was dying in front of their eyes? He must have understood her look, which said she wanted to kill him because the doctor said he'd give them time to talk and return later. *Later?* There would never be a time she could contemplate what he asked of her.

Fern felt herself slipping away. The world had gone dark and she had fallen into an abyss. This had been the *off* she'd felt all day. Her child, her baby, the boy she'd spent fifteen gruelling hours to give birth to without any drugs so he'd have the best start in life was leaving her. That knowledge burned her core and she felt utterly helpless. The feeling – she couldn't do anything to make this right hurt so much she couldn't breathe. All the air in her lungs had evaporated. She wanted to die. She'd gladly die if she could save Dale. Dale, her strong sensitive one who sat with her to watch Game of Thrones and Vikings. Dale, her first-born who cried in her arms when he got dumped by his girlfriend in grade six. Dale, who she had taught in one day to ride a bike. Dale, who had a sixth sense when it came to the times she made brownies or chocolate chip cookies so he could claim the batter in the bowl. How could her Dale be brain dead? How could her Dale keep this secret from her?

Fern sat back down. Craig took her hand. She looked at their joined hands, not recognizing the sight. When had been the last time they'd held hands? An odd thought, but she couldn't shake it.

"I can't believe this has happened. He needs to wake up."

"Fern, he's not going to," said Craig.

Fern tried to take her hand out of his hold, but he wouldn't let her. "Look at him, Fern. Did you hear what the doctor said?"

"Yes, Craig, I heard it but I'm not taking his word. I want a second opinion. He could be wrong."

"Don't you think I want him to be wrong? Fern, I can't believe this has happened. I didn't even know he kept in touch with her."

"Me neither."

"What should we do?"

Craig spoke in a soft voice, shocking Fern. He sounded resigned. It petrified her. She relied on Craig to be strong because she was falling apart. Didn't he see she could barely breathe?

"I'm going to ask for a second opinion. I'll be right back."

Craig let go of her hand and took Dale's. He bent over the bed and his shoulders shook with tears. She couldn't cry. If she cried, the floodgates would open and for once in her life, Fern wasn't sure she would find the strength to stop.

Stepping out of the room, she went to the front desk area where some nurses were. "I'm Fern O'Leary. I want a second opinion on my son Dale."

The nurse gave her a look she had come to recognize. Pity. "I will call Doctor Singh for you."

"Wait. Is he the doctor who spoke with me earlier?"

"I'm not sure. He had been on rounds so he probably did stop by."

"I don't want him. I want a second opinion. Please get me another neurologist, another specialist."

"It might take a while. I will give Dr. Sangster a call for you."

"Thank you. I'm not going anywhere," said Fern, trying to force a smile but failing.

The nurse placed two pens in her front pocket. She wore a smock with pink bunnies on it. Maybe it made patients smile. The effect, lost on Fern.

"There's hot water for tea and coffee in the kitchen and the lounge is at the end of the hall and there's a minister on call."

Minister on call? Fern shivered. Religion had been a foundation of her youth and the early days of her marriage with the children. An image of Dale playing Joseph in one of the Christmas plays flashed through her mind. Did she want a minister? What could it hurt?

"Are you okay?" asked the nurse.

"No, no I'm not. Will you please call the minister for me?" said Fern. Her chin wavered. The tears were gaining. She bit the inside of her cheek, forcing herself to stop.

The nurse got up and came around the desk. She took Fern's hand in hers and led her to the small kitchen. Fern watched her put on the kettle. Nurses didn't normally do this. "Do you want coffee or tea?"

"Tea," said Fern, starting to shiver.

With years of experience probably dealing with hysterical parents, the nurse placed a tea bag in a white Styrofoam cup and darted out of the room to open a door across the hall, returning a minute later with a hot blanket which she draped around Fern.

"It's shock. You've had a shock to the system. I'm going to take you back to your room and I'll bring you the tea and call the minister. You need to sit. You need to be strong," said the nurse.

By this point, Fern couldn't even read the nurse's nametag. Her eyes were too blurry with tears. She sniffled loudly.

"Everyone cries here. It's okay," said the nurse, engulfing her in a hug.

This woman didn't know Fern, but she knew her pain. Fern cried. The nurse rubbed her back. The kettle clicked off, but neither one of them moved. Only when Fern felt like she had a grip on herself did the nurse let her go.

"There's a washroom around the corner," she said, like she knew Fern needed to reclaim her space. Fern thanked her and like a zombie walked to the bathroom.

When she came out, Sean stood in the hall. Once again, the sight of him in his work uniform was a shocking sight. He smoothed his hands down his pants. It was a nervous tick he'd had since those elementary days. His eyes crinkled when he noticed her look.

"Bad habit I can't shake. Are you going to be okay?" he asked. "Stupid question. I'm so sorry, Fern."

Fern shook her head and bit her lip. Exhaustion stirred like a heavy body of water to envelope her. "Probably not. Thanks for coming to tell me and for driving me here."

He looked up and down the hall and she followed his gaze. They were alone. He pulled her to him and the feel of his arms around her felt wonderful. Something she didn't deserve.

"I've got to go, but I'll come back tonight," he whispered, giving the top of her head a kiss.

Fern eased out of his hold and took a step back. "Don't. I've got to deal with this. You go back to work. I'll call when I can." She tried hard not to gauge his reaction.

Sean took a step toward her, like he wanted to embrace her again.

Fern put her hand up, halting him. He gazed at her and nodded. Fern tried getting a hold of her emotions, but her chin quivered again. She couldn't and didn't dare take solace in Sean's embrace.

He stopped and looked at her. "I'll go. You call me, okay? I'm here for you."

Fern nodded and watched him walk away. She couldn't go back to Dale's room. She first needed to see Scarlett. Back at the front desk, she asked about her and got directions to the other end of the hall. Scarlett was in room 721D.

Fern walked to the room. She knocked on the door. Willow, the sister she hadn't seen in two years, opened the door. Fern felt a kick to her solar plexus. Willow looked exactly the same. Barely reaching five feet, her black hair rested in her usual fashionable bob, but she looked terrible. Her face was a splotchy mess. She'd been crying and Fern knew her face conveyed the same message.

"Did you know about this?" asked Fern.

"If you mean did I know they were going to the concert, yes, I knew," said Willow.

Of course, Willow would know. It hurt Fern more than she cared to admit.

"Come on in. She's not doing good. They said she needs a liver," said Willow, blunt as ever, citing what she wanted without a care for others.

Fern stepped to the foot of Scarlett's bed. She'd always liked Scarlett. Lithe, tall, funny with a quick wit, she had always seemed brave. Now, battered and bruised, she resembled a bloated doll lying still on the bed.

"She had surgery this morning. She's got a broken collarbone; two broken ribs and a piece of the vehicle must have pierced her liver." Willow plunked herself back down in the same dark blue plastic chair sitting in Fern's room. Willow turned and looked at her.

"I'm sorry about Dale."

Fern couldn't speak. She didn't know what to say. This wasn't how she had ever envisioned facing her sister after what had happened between them. She couldn't even bring up their mother's issues. Nothing compared to what they were both dealing with at the moment.

"Have they done this before?" Fern thirsted for knowledge.

Willow nodded, giving Fern a hard look. Fern choose to ignore the tears in her sister's eyes. Instead, Fern didn't say anything else. She backed out of the room and shut the door. Betrayal. It's what she felt from Dale and it hurt like a deep rusty knife being plunged into her heart. Much like how she'd felt when Willow had wrapped her hands around her throat to choke her. Shock. Betrayal and a deep sadness the relationship she'd had with her sister and what she'd thought she'd had with her son had evaporated within thirty seconds.

Returning to Dale's room, Craig lay bent over their son.

Fern wanted to shout at Dale and ask him a dozen questions. Why had he kept his relationship with his cousin from them? Did he do it to protect her? Had she been so selfish? Fern wasn't sure she could have faced them having a relationship and maybe Dale knew it. She'd like to believe he lied to her with a purpose, but Willow had known. Willow knew they'd done this more than once and Fern felt crushed. She was Dale's mother. He should have told her. Now she'd never hear his voice again or his side of the story. Instead of sorrow, a rush of anger flooded to the surface scaring Fern.

"Why did he do this? Why didn't he talk to us about his plans?" she asked, reclaiming the hard-plastic chair.

Craig, who hadn't heard her come in, lifted his head off Dale's body and looked at her.

"Fern, what does it matter? It's done. It was an accident. We need to deal with it."

A knock on their door forced Fern to swallow what she wanted to say.

"May I come in?" said a twenty-something woman.

"I'm Janice Malone, the minister."

Craig got up and shook her hand and urged her inside. Fern remained sitting but she held out her hand. She wasn't sure she'd done the right thing to request a minister. A few minutes later, Janice asked them to form a circle around Dale and bow their heads in prayer. It surprised Fern how comforting the action felt.

"Do you have anything you'd like to say to Dale?" she asked them both.

"I love you, son. I've been so proud of you. I..." Craig stumbled. Fern reached out and gave his hand a squeeze. "I don't know what to do. I don't want you to leave us. I'm not sure we can let you go."

Fern looked at her husband. Those were the words she'd have said. They weren't so dissimilar after all.

"And you, Fern. What would you like to say?"

Fern wet her lips. "I can't let you go. A part of me will die. I don't care if I'm selfish. Stay with us. Please, I'm begging you."

"That was good. Tell him how you feel. Do you think your other children would like to speak to him," she asked.

The thought of the children seeing Dale like this robbed Fern of any hope and breath. Craig openly cried. Fern realized she'd never seen him cry before and she found it oddly unsettling.

"I don't know if we should put them through this," he said, and bless him, he was right. Did she want them to remember their big brother like this? The thought hurt so much she couldn't speak.

Janice took their hands in hers. "It is your decision. I am

here to help in any way I can. You might change your minds, but again it's up to you both. Would you like me to stay here and read to him from the Bible?"

Craig nodded. Fern went over to the side table and took a sip of the now tepid tea the nurse had obviously brought to her room while she'd been with Scarlett. She sat back down and listened to the drone of Janice's voice as she read a passage from Corinthians.

Over the sound of the machines keeping Dale alive and with her mind trying to make sense of the words, the minister read of love, faith and hope, Fern recalled the two dreams she'd had last night. Her gut told her: Dale had been trying to speak to her. The knowledge for the first time since she'd heard the news gave her a sense of peace. Or maybe she had become so exhausted from the shock her body and mind were forcing her to finally take a much-needed breath and absorb what happened. Dale, her baby, her first-born was dying. She brought him into the world and it was only fitting she'd be with him at the end. It wasn't the natural order of the universe, but the thought of Dale dying on his own, in the car, would have killed Fern.

Chapter 22

Harold

Harold surprised himself by how much he liked Toby's cabin. Small but wholesome, Rose would call it sparse. Basically, it consisted of one large room. Toby had made a sofa area at the back which could easily be used as a bed. They were currently working on creating a kitchen area.

"Thanks again, Harold for helping," said Toby.

Harold nodded. He had a mouth full of nails and was intent on finishing nailing the kitchen cupboard to the wall. Task completed he said, "Sorry I couldn't come when the guys all came down, but I'm glad to help now. We're almost done. I like your place and the land is amazing."

"The boys were helpful, but to be truthful there were too many people who needed more management than I like."

"I'm thinking lots of beer flowed," said Harold, glad he missed the gathering. These days he tried to avoid liquor.

"Oh yeah, which is why they needed lots of management," said Toby, grinning.

Harold placed his hammer on his belt. "Well, with the days getting shorter, I think one more night and this will be complete. I heard you're planning to surprise your wife. That's nice."

Toby sheepishly nodded but didn't make eye contact.

"All good with Karen?"

"She's finding the pregnancy difficult."

Harold laughed. "I have no idea how women do it. Rose's last pregnancy convinced me to get snipped."

Toby winced. "She's been moody lately."

"It's the hormones. Rose cried all the time. Even a tissue commercial made her cry. But in the end, it's all worth it. The baby will become the centre of your world."

Toby picked up a piece of wood he had sanded to make the countertop. "I'm hoping. I had thought with the pregnancy she'd be happier."

"I'm sure once the little one comes into the world she'll be thrilled. Are you planning to be with her for the delivery?"

"That's the goal."

"Well, let me tell you, I'm glad I showed up for the big event. It's a real eye-opener to what women have to do. I'm not the squeamish type, but I'm telling you it's intense."

"Yeah, I heard. I'm not sure how much help I'll be, but I would like to be there," said Toby.

"Holding her hand will be helpful. Now, I've got one more cupboard and then I'm going to have to call it a night."

"Again, Harold, I appreciate you taking the time out of your busy schedule to help."

"Well, the only busy part right now is waiting for Rose to come home. She's up with her sister for their annual getaway week at their grandmother's cottage."

"George told me. He said he hoped to time their return to the mainland for some goodies."

Harold added a few more nails to his hand while chuckling. "Yeah, George would be right. Those two come back with boxes full of bottled pickles, jams and enough sweets to fill our freezer until Christmas."

"Are you complaining?"

"No way. I love it, but…"

"You miss her," said Toby, finishing Harold's line of thought.

"Yeah, man, I do. I would never discourage Rose from going away with her sister, Fern but I'm always counting days until she returns. The house is too quiet without her."

"You're lucky, you know," said Toby, measuring the last part of the wood he wanted for the counter.

Harold gave Toby a quick look. He didn't want to pry, but he got the impression not all was grand between him and Karen and it made him sad. He hoped the baby would bring them together, but he wasn't stupid. Adding a kid into the mix in many cases often became the wedge driving couples apart.

"Yeah, I do know that, but marriage is work. It's not like you follow a set of instructions and all goes well. Rose and I have our ups and downs, but honestly, I can't imagine my life without her."

Toby nodded and then they quietly turned their minds to the tasks at hand.

Harold gave a last wave at Toby. "See you tomorrow," he yelled.

"I'll be in late. Karen's got a doctor appointment and I promised I'd go with her."

"Make sure you let Bob know."

"I will. Thanks again," said Toby, as he got in his car.

An hour later, Harold opened the door to his house and within a minute, his youngest wrapped herself around his leg.

"I've been waiting all night for you to get home," said Ava.

"Perfect timing. We just got home from our long walk and she begged me to watch her favourite show with her," said Kate Oakley, who had been babysitting the girls for years.

"Thanks, Kate," said Harold, handing her two twenty-dollar bills.

"No problem. Glad to help and perfect timing. I'm not a fan of the Lizzie show. See you later, Ava," said Kate, leaving.

Harold walked into the kitchen, thrilled to see Kate had, as usual, cleaned up the mess. She'd been babysitting the girls for the past four years. "Ava, give me five minutes to shower and then I'm all yours."

"Okay, I'll get Lizzie McGuire all ready for us," said Ava, in her sing-song voice, which filled Harold's heart with warmth.

Harold smiled and then raced up the stairs to shower.

Tomorrow after work, he'd fix the leaky faucet in the upstairs washroom and he couldn't wait to show Rose his surprise. He'd worked all weekend on adding a new stand-up shower to their downstairs bathroom. He finished fixing the drywall last night and while his body ached from working all day at work and then at home, he couldn't wait to see the look of total surprise on his wife's face. It was what fuelled him these days. Pleasing Rose, he realized, made him feel great.

Harold wished his old Dodge van could go faster as he sped down the highway and weaved his way down the small country road to the end of the late. The call from Kelly had knocked him on his ass. Dale and Scarlett both critically injured in a car accident on their way back from a concert in Ontario. It didn't make sense. He couldn't get his head around it and couldn't even begin to imagine how Fern and Craig felt. Kelly had offered for George to drive Rose into town but Harold didn't accept their offer. He had to be with his wife. He'd called the school and Ava would be picked up at the bus stop by their neighbour, who said she could spend the night and told Harold not to worry. Rose would be proud of him for taking care of things.

He pulled into the canteen parking lot at the end of the lake. Kelly stood waiting for him. "George will take you out to the cottage," she said.

"Would it be okay if I went to get her on my own?" he asked.

"Sure. Not a problem. I can't believe this happened. Do you have any more news on how they're doing?" Kelly wrung her hands and had tears in her eyes.

"No. Last I heard Fern was with Craig at the hospital."

"Well, we're praying for them."

Harold thanked her and then got in the small boat. A few minutes later, he docked at the old wharf by the cottage. He sprinted up the stone slabs and opened the door. Rose practically threw things into boxes. The minute she saw him, she rushed into his arms. He'd been hoping she'd reach for him.

"I've got you," he said to the top of her head.

She sobbed into his chest. Harold fought not to cry. He didn't want to ruin the moment. He enjoyed holding Rose in her time of need? A trickle of guilt edged into his consciousness. Given the circumstances of what had happened to Dale and Scarlett, finding a sense of relief in holding his wife might be viewed as wrong. Harold quickly told his subconscious to shut up.

"I can't believe this," said Rose, once she'd gained composure.

"I know. It's surreal."

"So much has happened to our family in the past few years and now this…"

"Rose, we'll get through this. The family will get through it."

"How? Fern will die if something happens to Dale."

"No. She'll want to die, but she's like you – a strong woman. She'll get through this. She and Craig will get through it."

Rose looked up at him. Harold leaned down. He had an overwhelming urge to kiss her tear-stained tears away.

"I'm not strong, Harold."

Harold made a coughing sound – half choke and half laugh. "Rose, you are the strongest woman I know. You raised those boys of yours with love and dedication and not once have I ever heard you complain about your ex. You work two jobs to ensure our kids can do the things they love. You make me feel inadequate, and sometimes you scare the crap out of me, but most often you amaze me."

"I amaze you? I feel like you don't even see me."

"See you? Rose, I know you take care of our family and if I haven't said how much I love you, I'm an ass. I try to do things I think you'll like. I sent those flowers –"

"You sent the flowers?" she said, giving him an incredulous look.

"Yeah, who did you think sent the flowers?"

Rose looked away and the feeling in Harold's gut that he hadn't been paying enough close attention to his wife made him go still. "Rose. What's going on?"

She wrapped her arms around his middle and hugged him tight. "Harold, I'm the sorry one. Lots has been going on."

"What do you mean?"

"Well, it's not me, if you're wondering, even though lately things have been off between us."

Harold's arms circled his wife's small frame. She smelled like cinnamon and cookies. "That's life, Rose. We lead busy lives. It doesn't mean my love for you has died or I think any less of you. I've missed you, Rose."

Rose looked at him and then she took his hand in hers and led him to her bedroom. Clothes were all over the floor which made him smile. Rose had always been a clutter bug. She'd go for days leaving her droppings all over their bedroom and then without warning, go on a cleaning frenzy and even iron his work pants.

"How inappropriate would it be if I wanted you to hold me?" she asked.

Harold didn't say anything. Instead, he cupped his wife's face in his hands and kissed his love into her, hoping she'd realize she meant the world to him.

Chapter 23

Rose

Rose reached over and let her fingers trail along her husband's chest hairs. He smiled at her with love shining in his eyes. Maybe it was the cottage or the circumstances, but their lovemaking had been tender and she'd cried out with pleasure. Rose hadn't realized how much she needed his love until he'd kissed her tears away and with skill proved he knew his way around her body.

"We should get going, Rose, but I don't want reality to come crashing into our lives. This has been perfect. I'm glad you picked the big bed," said Harold, propping himself up on the pillow as he pulled Rose to his chest.

"Thank you for coming for me."

"You're the love of my life. What's happened is a family tragedy. Of course, I'd come for you," said Harold and he meant it. His love keep their marriage afloat. Rose's love met Harold's halfway, but it had to be enough. After years of giving all her love to her first husband and then being betrayed, she had become damaged goods. She couldn't give all of herself to another person and wished it wasn't so.

"Why did you put a password on your phone?" she asked.

"What?"

"Your phone. I noticed last week you added a password."

Harold laughed. "Yeah, I did. There are a few guys around the shop I don't trust. Want to know my password?"

"No. It's okay," said Rose, wrinkling her nose.

Harold bent his head and kissed Rose's lips. "It's Rose."

"What?"

"My password, it's you. You own me. You are my password to a happy life. Without you I'd be nothing."

Rose felt relief while also feeling guilty. She shouldn't have asked, but those old fears from her first marriage were scars she carried deep. Harold said he understood. Harold loved her. Harold with his pot belly and all his faults, which he had a list of, would do anything for her. Would he do the one thing she wanted most?

"Harold, when things settle down, I want you to go to AA."

She waited for Harold to chastise her. Instead, he settled back down into the bed and pulled her even closer.

"For you I will. Couldn't hurt and the last thing I want to do is hurt you. I'm so sorry about the other night."

"I was so mad at you."

"I know. I was mad at myself. I should have known better. Guess I don't. I'll do it with your support."

Rose smiled. A hopeful sign and today of all days she'd grab it and hold tight.

An hour later, things were packed up tight for the year. Harold hauled the generator back into the shed and finished stacking the rest of the chopped wood under the tarp. Together they loaded up George's boat with boxes of goodies. They didn't speak as Harold drove back to the campsite.

Kelly paced the dock waiting for them. She looked like she'd been crying. Rose hoped she didn't start crying again because she barely kept it together.

"Any more news?" asked Rose, rubbing her stomach. Nausea made her want to throw-up.

"Sean called to tell me Fern's with Craig and from what I could gather, it doesn't look good for Dale, but they're getting a second opinion."

"We're going straight to the hospital. I'll give you a call once I hear more. Tell George thanks for the boat. We appreciated it," said Harold, hauling the boxes out of the boat and loading up the van.

Rose grabbed a box she'd made for Kelly. "This is for you. Let us know what we owe you for the things."

"Forget it. This will more than make up for it. I can't believe this has happened. Call me when you hear more. Keep me informed and let me know what we can do," said Kelly, grabbing Rose for one of her big momma-bear hugs.

Rose hugged her back. Kelly had been a long-time friend

and they had remained close throughout the years. Rose promised to keep her updated. With a final hug, Harold urged her into the van to hit the road.

Once they were on the highway, Harold reached over to hold her hand.

"We'll get through this," he said.

She held to his power of conviction. They'd get through this. Fern would get through it but it would change her forever. It's what tragedy did. Rose knew first-hand. When her ex betrayed her, something in her died. It was still dead, but she had lived. She'd sheltered the boys as much as she could and survived the loss. But the death of a child was an unimaginable horror all mothers dreaded. A part of Rose also felt guilty and relieved it hadn't happened to her children, which caused her to shiver. She said silent prayers the entire drive to the hospital and vowed to go to church next week. Would God listen to her plea for help? If there was one thing her family needed now, it was faith. She fought the hysteria to laugh, realizing they were royally screwed.

Chapter 24

Craig

Craig was falling apart. Pieces of him must be flaking off. Would the doctor prescribe something for his anxiety? He didn't have the guts to ask. The doctor attempted to make sense of the chart and lines from the machines keeping his son breathing. *Best not to distract him.* Craig hated the machines. He hated the sound they made—incessant beeping—but he couldn't keep his eyes off them. He kept praying for a miracle but it wasn't going to happen. That only happened in the movies and while the spectacle of his life played out like one at the moment, he was the only one completely in tune to his downfall. Worse, Craig couldn't tell Fern. She couldn't handle another blow and learning he'd lost his job might be one thing but discovering they were financially screwed on top of this...he didn't have the heart to add to her misery.

Fern murmured something to Dale while holding his hand. Craig had done that for hours. Sad he couldn't recall the last time he'd held his son's hand. Had years gone by without him touching his son? He wiped more tears from his eyes. He'd cried more in the last few hours than in his entire life. He hadn't cried this much when his parents died. Then again, nothing equated the loss of a child.

"I'm going to get some ice," he said to Fern.

She didn't respond. Should he ask if she'd like more tea? Over the years, Craig had come to realize tea held magical qualities for his wife. When they'd fought, he'd bring her a cup of tea and she'd sip it, sigh and calm down. Every morning, for decades now, he'd brought a cup of morning tea to her in bed. It had become their ritual. She liked it so much she'd even told Rose and her friends about it, which had impressed Craig enough for him to keep doing the small act of kindness.

Craig opened the door and stepped into the hall. The lights were dim. He checked his watch, 10:30 p.m. Where had the time gone? Craig asked a nurse where the lounge was and made his way down the softly lit corridor. Inside the lounge he found the small space where the ice machine and cups were kept and helped himself to a glass of ice water.

"Craig?"

Lost in his own thoughts, it took Craig a second to realize the voice didn't belong to his wife, but rather her sister. He'd always thought Willow crazy but seeing her now, looking exhausted and crushed, he realized how much the sisters resembled each other. Fern had mousy reddish-brown hair, Rose had straight shoulder-length light brown hair, Willow had black hair cut into her usual bob and Lily, who looked the spitting image of Willow, wore her hair always in a ponytail. Willow's eyes were puffy from crying. Craig realized he probably looked a sight. He didn't care.

"Willow," said Craig, turning back to fill up a second Styrofoam cup full of ice for Fern.

"Will you talk to her?" asked Willow.

Craig waited until the machine stopped. He'd always thought Willow to be a pathological liar and a real nutcase. After assaulting his wife for no good reason, he simply couldn't stand her. In fact, the day when his wife came home hysterical with her neck bruised and told him what had happened, he'd urged Fern to press charges. Fern of course couldn't do it to her sister. And Willow had known.

"I'm not sure what you're asking, Willow. Did Fern speak with you?"

"Sort of. She came in to see Scarlett. She'd not doing good."

Craig sucked on an ice cube. Not doing good? His son was brain dead while her daughter had a chance at life.

"Fern knows Scarlett needs a liver. The doctor said ..."

"I'm not sure what the doctor said to you, but we've got our own problems."

Willow reached out and touched his arm. Craig, not a violent man, barely resisted punching her. This woman had been the reason his wife had cried herself to sleep for months, and spent six weeks in physiotherapy twice a week. Willow had tried to choke the life out of his wife.

Craig narrowed his eyes. Willow removed her arm. A wise choice.

"The doctor said the chances were better if Scarlett had a liver from a relative."

Craig straightened and rolled his shoulders. What she asked unnerved him. "I'm going to stop you right there, Willow. Not going to happen."

"But the doctor told me Dale is brain dead."

Okay, maybe he'd punch the doctor instead. "We're getting a second opinion."

"When?" asked Willow. Her tears flowed freely.

Craig didn't buy the crocodile tears act. He'd come face-to-face with the crazy Willow enough over the years to know she was the supreme actress.

"None of your business."

"Craig?" said a voice he knew well. Rose coming to the rescue.

"Bye Willow. Don't bother us again." Craig brushed past her to move into the lounge.

"Unbelievable, I've been waiting for hours to get in. They made me and Harold wait. We're freaking family, but they said there were too many people on the ward. I told Harold to go home and deal with the kids. I'm so sorry. Where is Fern?" asked Rose, obviously not seeing Willow.

"Hi Rose," said Willow, moving into the open.

Rose gave both of them a sweeping look. "What's going on?"

"I'm going back to the room. We're in 709, down the hall

second door to the last on the left," said Craig, exiting before WWIII started.

"I'll be there in a minute," answered Rose.

Craig wasn't interested in their sisterly drama. He had enough with keeping it together. The doctor would be back in Dale's room in twenty minutes. Craig needed to have a private talk with him. He wasn't sure he bought all of what Willow had said. He needed more information. He hoped for knowledge that would make breathing easier.

Chapter 25

Sean

The drive back to Musquodoboit Harbour was laboriously slow. It had been on purpose. Sean took the old number seven highway, weaving through Preston, Lake Echo, Porter's Lake, and Chezzetcook. His thoughts were in a jumble. He hated leaving Fern, but seeing her with her husband, a man he hadn't met before, unsettled him. He'd heard about Craig, but seeing the man in the flesh another matter. Over six feet with a head full of hair, under normal circumstances his Irish charm would probably have won over Sean. Today he'd looked like a man broken in half and who could blame him.

Sean backed the cruiser into a spot when he got back to the station. He flexed his fingers and took a fortifying breath. Every part of him ached deeply and he couldn't let on. His eyes strayed to his watch. Four more hours and his shift ended.

Tonight, he'd be home alone again. Funny, how his plans had evaporated so fast.

Before leaving the cruiser, Sean texted a message to his youngest daughter. "Missing you."

An hour later, with his head buried in paperwork, his cell vibrated.

"Miss you 2," typed Clarissa.

Sean found himself grinning. He quickly texted back. "Want to come for a visit?"

"When?" she texted.

Sean looked at his schedule pinned to the side of his computer and checked his watch. Two o'clock which meant 7 p.m. in Calgary. He dialled her number, needing to hear his daughter's voice.

"Hi Clare." He'd never called her Clarissa. It had been the name his wife had insisted on. He'd hated it on day one and had always called her Clare.

"Dad? Is it really you?"

When had he last talked to her? Sean felt like a deadbeat father. It must have been a good month. He sucked at being a parent. "Yeah, it's me. Thought you might want to come for a visit?"

"I'd love to," she said with no hesitation.

"Great. Check with your mom and text me the dates which work for you. Do you think your sister will come?"

"Nay, she's got flag football and is swamped with courses. But you know me, I'm more flexible. I'll check with Mom first and get back to you, but it'd be great just the two of us. How's the place shaping up?"

"A lot better than the last time you saw it."

"Couldn't get much worse," she responded, which made him laugh.

The last time Clare had been to Nova Scotia, the homestead had a leaky roof and the plumbing didn't work. She'd be amazed at the transformation.

Sean let Clare go. He looked forward to seeing his daughter again. With it came the harsh realization of the sorrow tearing through Fern. He eased back into his chair, feeling the weight and trauma of the past few days catch up to him. As removed as his daughters were from his life, the thought of losing one of them made him feel sick.

He hoped Fern would call him, but vowed not to bother her. He'd check in with the duty nurse to get updates, but in his heart, he knew it wasn't good. Dale, her son, had looked dead and the nurse had said he'd had a bleed on the brain. Sean prayed for a miracle for Fern, but he'd seen enough tragedy in his line of work to know he was a realist at heart.

Chapter 26

Rose

Rose thought if she ever saw her sister again, she'd punch her in the face. Well, it hadn't happened yet.

"Guess you know what happened," stated Willow, moving to the ice machine to fill up a cup with water.

"Why?"

"Why what?" asked Willow.

Rose felt her cheeks heat and her stomach churned uneasily. Willow had that effect on her. "Why had Scarlett been with Dale?" asked Rose, as an old surge of anger toward her sister started to ignite.

Willow had always acted superior to Rose. She got what she wanted or felt she deserved and consequences went out the window. All her life, she took from their parents with a smile on her face and it always made Rose angry. All of Rose's life she'd worked hard to step out of her parents' shadow and look where it got her – nowhere. Yet, somehow Willow who hadn't worked a day in her life, managed to con their mother into handing over the one hundred and twenty-five acres to her.

"You know, Rose, I'm not sure why Scarlett and Dale stayed in touch. Maybe it's because they, as family, like each other."

There was that annoying tone in Willow's voice Rose hated.

"Family. You're so full of it. Don't play like you're above what you did. You stole Mom's land and attacked Fern," said Rose.

"I'm not getting into this with you. Scarlett needs a liver and Fern isn't going to help."

It took a second for Rose to absorb what Willow said. Physically she took a step back. "You honestly expect Fern to help you? You are such a taker. Priceless. After what you did to us, to her specifically, dream on."

"If it was your child, you'd expect it," said Willow, taking a sip of water and trying to appear calm, but Rose noticed her rose-coloured cheeks. Playing it cool and acting indifferent had always been Willow's way with her parents to get what she wanted. Rose didn't buy it.

"But that's the difference. It's your child. Don't ask her for this. Did you even apologize for attacking her?"

Willow didn't say anything. It was how she acted when the truth got thrown in her face and she didn't like it. *Well, screw her.*

"If I were you, I'd get on my knees and beg for her forgiveness and maybe she'll consider your request, but I'm going to tell you something…you could beg all day and I'd never give you what you want," said Rose, mustering the courage to leave the room before she felt the need to get physical with her sister.

Rose's legs trembled and her head pounded. Once she rounded the corner, she spied the washroom. She darted inside and locked the door, needing a moment to collect herself before she came face-to-face with Dale. What Willow said rattled her. Dale, brain dead and Scarlett would die unless she got a liver. Why Dale's liver? Why couldn't Scarlett take any liver? Didn't livers grow back? A zillion questions zoomed a million miles through her head. Times like this, bad times, caused her hand to twitch. She wished for a cigarette. Pathetic, but she couldn't help it. Peeing and then washing her hands, she took a moment to examine the exchange with Willow.

The last time she'd felt this way had been when Fern had called to inform her about Lily. At first, Fern had been crying so hard Rose couldn't understand her, but once she got the gist of it, she'd been stunned. Two days before Lily's death, she'd had lunch with her sister, who had been home for less than six months. She had already started to plan her next adventure, either Iceland or Vietnam. The two destinations were as opposite as day and night. Lily worked that way. She had a sheet listing pros and cons for each place and had animatedly talked about each. Rose thought her sister nuts to want to go to Vietnam, but she didn't dare say anything to Lily. She'd learned over the years obstacles were things Lily liked to tackle. Iceland at least sounded safe. Rose eyed the latest tattoo on Lily's arm. Lily had described it in detail but at the moment, Rose couldn't remember what it meant. A deep sadness for the loss of her sister hit her. Rose splashed some water on her face. So much tragedy in so little time for her family to absorb and now more, she thought, trying to get it together.

Willow would never apologize to Fern, because doing so would admit guilt. Willow was smart in her own way. If she said sorry, she gave herself away. It's what she had been doing with their mother for years. Admitting their mother had dementia meant what she did to their mother had been beyond cruel. It had been a calculated move to ensure Willow got what she wanted, regardless of her own mother's needs.

Thank goodness Fern had power of attorney and the insight to recognize Willow's next steps. Fern had ensured all of their mother's lawyers were updated on their mother's medical condition. If they hadn't done it, their mother would be in the poor house. With a sickening feeling in her stomach, Rose realized not three months after stealing the land, Willow had brazenly, with Scarlett in tow, walked into the bank with their mother and tried to remove Fern from her bank accounts. Then they'd marched their tiny asses straight to their mother's country bumpkin lawyer to get Fern removed as power of attorney. Thankfully, the lawyer recognized she couldn't make any changes to their mother's will due to all the medical files Fern had sent her way, which clearly stated the progress of their mother's dementia.

Now Willow had the audacity to ask and expect Fern to sign over Dale's liver to Scarlett. For a second Rose thought she might throw up. *How did our family come to this point?*

She washed her face with the cold water and used the

scratchy brown eco-friendly paper towel to dry off. She felt like crap. Fern needed her. She'd be the strong one for once. A role reversal for sure. She almost cracked a smile.

Rose peeked her head out the door to ensure Willow wasn't in the hall and only then did she make her way down the corridor to Dale's room.

At Dale's room, she took a deep breath and then slowly opened it. The sight of Dale lying lifeless on the hospital bed hooked up to machines robbed her of breath. Fern got up from her seat and probably sensing how Rose felt, pulled her through the door and ushered her into the plastic chair she'd vacated. Rose couldn't form a word. She knew it would be bad, but knowing and seeing with her own eyes was so much worse than the illusion of what she'd conjured. Looking at Dale's pale body, hooked up to the machines, Rose realized no amount of prayer or belief in magic would change his reality. Her tears fell unchecked. *So much for being the strong one.*

Chapter 27

Fern

Fern had listened to the second doctor give her opinion of Dale and she'd been civil and polite. Too polite. Rose had held her hand in a death grip, but still she'd managed to nod, ask a few questions and pretend the diagnosis the doctor gave made sense or helped. Craig had held Dale's hand. Fern focused on breathing. Breathing meant life. *Wasn't the machine giving life to her son?*

Fern couldn't remember the neurologist's name. When she'd left, Craig had finally let go of Dale's limp hand and excused himself. She suspected he had gone to cry somewhere without Rose seeing him collapse. Appearances. They were both trying to keep up a shield saying they were okay. Fern wanted to scream. She was not okay and never would be whole again. The scratch in her normal life had been solidly cracked open and no repair job would replace what she'd had. The good days were gone. She got it now.

An hour later, Rose left, quietly excusing herself and finally Fern sat alone with her son. She sat on the side of his bed, brushed his soft brown hair off his forehead and willed him to come back to her. His hair looked the same but most of him she couldn't identify. His face had become swollen and covered with bruises. They'd taped his eyes shut. Even his arms and fingers had ballooned up. Somewhere under all the swelling lay the son she'd birthed. She tried to find him but it felt futile. As before, she sensed he had gone. This knowledge, the prickly premonition she'd felt a week ago. The *something* had come and taken her boy. Taken the joy out of her life and changed her family irrevocably. It felt surreal. All the steps that went into a family dealing with decisions like this were now a deck of cards she had to play. But she couldn't shuffle the deck and didn't know the rules of the game. If only she could find the right instructions.

Both doctors had declared Dale brain dead. Both specialists urged her to donate his liver to his cousin because family matches meant Scarlett had a better chance. Could Fern remove her sorrow and anger at their deception? Not today. The wound felt fresh and oozed with a septic poison no medicine could cleanse. Her family owned the title of dysfunction but saying no to Willow's request made Fern feel like a failure. *I am not the guilty one. I am not the bad person.* Thinking it didn't make it feel any less real.

Why hadn't he told her? Why keep the fact he kept in touch

with his cousin a secret? And worse, how did she miss it? Fern wanted all the sordid details. When did they decide to meet, how did they organize it and why did he feel he couldn't tell her? Yes, Dale had been distancing himself from her for the past few years but she'd chalked it up to him asserting his independence while he navigated becoming a young adult. This type of secrecy felt like a brutal betrayal of his love.

Fern leaned over and kissed Dale's bruised cheek. Machines beeped and their constant electrical-motored sounds had become, over the course of hours, a comfort. They were doing their job – keeping her son alive. Maybe somewhere along the way, she'd failed in her job as a mother to keep him safe. Craig would laugh at her reasoning. She had insisted on driving her kids everywhere and usually freaked if they wanted to go out for a walk in their sidewalk-lined neighbourhood after dark. She used to tell them bad people came out in the dark.

The sad reality was bad people existed at any time of the day. Fern had to cling to thinking of Willow as awful because seeing how she had looked as she gazed at her daughter started to tug something free within her she'd thought she'd knotted tight. Right and wrong. What Willow had done to their mother had been wrong. The grey matter that kept coming more into focus when Fern thought about it was Willow hadn't wanted the land to leave the family. It had been Craig who had pointed it out after the family meeting. He'd been the one who had said, what does it matter; let her have the land to keep it in the family. Fern had actually been thinking maybe he'd been right and had arranged to meet with Rose to convince her, but then the bomb quite literally fell. Willow had texted them from the lawyer's office telling them the deal had been done. The land was hers. The cut from that both she and Rose had keenly felt. Often Fern thought she should have explained more to Willow the debt their mother had accumulated. Craig hadn't thought it would have helped, but Fern wasn't so sure. Rose had taken Craig's side but then Rose didn't see in shades of grey. Rose believed in right and wrong and Willow had crossed the line. Lately, though Fern wondered if they hadn't all crossed a line. Sisters were sisters and forgiveness was an integral part of that odd definition of what sisterhood meant. Seeing Willow, looking as torn as Fern felt, had made her want to reach out but taking those steps required more energy than she could spare at the moment.

Craig returned. He looked even more haggard.

"I ran into Rose on the way out. They're going to bring their kids over and they're all staying at the house tonight."

Funny how Fern hadn't thought of her other children all this time. One more thing to deal with and she'd collapse. Thankfully one side of her family had at least stepped up to the plate.

"Do the kids know?" she asked.

"I asked Harold and Rose to say he's in the hospital. I think we should be the ones to tell them, unless you feel we should bring them in."

"No, I don't want them to see him like this. I don't want this to be their last memory of their big brother," said Fern, choking on the tears attempting to break free. Spit gathered in her mouth and she fought not to vomit.

"Let's go home and come back in the morning."

Fern cast a hard look at Craig. "I can't leave him." She couldn't step beyond the walls of the hospital. Doing it meant a goodbye of sorts.

"Okay. I get it. How about I go home and tell the kids? I'll come back in a few hours."

Was she a bad mother in that she wasn't capable of the task? Would hearing the news from her lips make it any better for them? Fern didn't know the correct response. She nodded to let Craig deal with them. Craig gathered up the cups they'd accumulated and placed them in the garbage. He then went over to the hospital bed and whispered something in Dale's ear and kissed his closed eyes. Fern hugged herself and cried. Craig had done the same thing at the wake for his mom. She'd asked him then about it and what he'd said later at night when they were spooned next to each other under the warm covers stuck with her. He'd said it was an Irish thing. He'd told his mother to have fun in the land of the fey and he'd kissed her closed eyes, which is what they did.

Craig hugged Fern's shuddering form, whispering words of love and comfort. She tried to let herself be engulfed in his strength, but felt too numb. He mumbled he'd be back shortly and she urged him to stay until morning. They had until morning to make their final decision unless Scarlett took a turn for the worse. Craig, like her, abhorred the idea of giving anything to Willow's family.

"I don't want him cut into bits," he'd said, looking at her with a pained expression.

She got it. They were a united front. Dale would remain whole. After all, if he'd wanted to, he'd have signed his donor card. In reality, Fern wondered about her son's beliefs. Did she know him? She'd thought yes, but now was no longer certain. He'd kept his relationship with his cousin a secret. She liked to believe he'd done it to spare her pain, but the deceitfulness of it burned her. She'd birthed Dale. She'd raised him to be good person. But in the end, he was his own man. He'd done things his way and he'd done what he'd wanted. If he'd wanted to be a donor, he'd have signed the bloody back of his licence. Fern would not make the decision for him.

About thirty minutes later when Fern knew she'd dozed off, a soft knock at the door woke her.

"Come in," she said, her voice a gravelly husk.

"May I come in?" asked Willow.

Rose didn't get up from her chair. "Fine."

Willow stepped into the room. Did she expect Fern to ask about Scarlett? Fern kept quiet.

Willow went to the foot of Dale's bed and stood there. Fern finally looked up at her sister.

"I shouldn't have asked. I'm so sorry for everything. I did think you knew they were seeing each other. I didn't question it. Maybe I should have," said Willow, her words tumbling out fast while she twisted a ring on her finger.

Fern recognized this side of Willow, anxious and nervous

but truth layered her words. An authenticity she hadn't heard from her sister in a substantially long time.

Okay, this Fern hadn't expected. She blinked and tried to gather her wits, but her mind felt sluggish and exhaustion bore down on her.

"Forget I asked, Fern. I get it. It's too much. I can't believe this has happened," said Willow, speaking quickly but with an honesty Fern wasn't sure she recognized.

It was more from Willow than Fern had heard in over two years.

"He's dead." Fern tasted the bile she'd been trying to keep down since hearing the news. Uttering the words surprised her. They were sharp and succinct and powerful beyond measure.

"Is there any chance?"

Fern bowed her head and looked at the old ceramic floor. "Two neurologists examined him. No brain activity. Their words, not mine."

"Scarlett is going septic. She's on powerful drugs, but it's not looking good."

Fern didn't say anything. She didn't want more information. "Are you at all sorry for attacking me?"

There, Fern had said it. She'd asked the million-dollar question she'd wondered about for years.

"I had a lot on my plate and you have always put me down and..."

Fern stared incredulously at her sister. "Put you down? I haven't-"

"Yes, you have," interrupted Willow.

"Willow, you attacked me. You choked me because I asked a question and you wouldn't answer me."

"I cleaned the bathroom."

"Then why attack me? Why?"

"You make me crazy and with all the stuff happening in my life, I was stressed out."

"Grown-ups don't attack people."

"There you go again, Fern. 'Grown-ups', that's what I am. I snapped."

Fern had suspected as much months later after she had finally been able to sleep through the night without shooting pain ratcheting up from her shoulder blade to her neck.

"It happened," said Willow.

"Like this. It happened. You never admit when you're wrong."

"And you always admit when you're right," said Willow.

Fern wasn't sure what that meant, but she'd had enough. "Get out."

"You do realize we're both probably losing our children by the morning," said Willow, adjusting her sweater to cover her chest.

"I don't wish it and never would. I hope Scarlett gets a liver but ..."

"But it can't come from your son because you hate me so much."

Well, Willow, you got that right.

"Don't kid yourself, Fern. If Rose's children needed something you wouldn't hesitate. You're not so holier-than-thou as you like to believe. Deep down we aren't so dissimilar."

With those remarks, Willow left, sucking all the air out of the room as her words bounced around in Fern's brain like a yo-yo. Was she like Willow? Would she give Dale's liver to save one of Rose's kids? Probably.

Fern laced her fingers together and closed her eyes, hoping for darkness. Why were all the tough decisions a slap in the face?

"Mom," said a voice sounding so much like Dale, Fern jerked awake. Instinctively she wiped the drool from her chin. She'd fallen asleep and obviously with the darkened room a nurse had shut off the light and left her alone. Her heart pounded in her chest and her feet were asleep and tingly. Could she be dreaming?

"Mom. Mom. I need to talk to you."

"What?" she managed to ask, forcing her brain to register it wasn't Dale speaking. Duncan, who could be Dale's twin, knelt at her side. A tear-stained face greeted her, but determination stared at her from his steel-grey eyes. Dale had thrown full-body tantrums and even bashed his head against the ceramic kitchen floor once to get his way. Not Duncan. He had simply stated what he wanted and when told no, he'd walk away and ask again and again for days until he wore you down and eventually you gave in so you could have him move on. Steely determination and the jut of his chin told her something big was on his mind.

Fern grasped Duncan's hand in hers. It felt warm, so different from the cool, clammy touch of Dale's.

"You've been here a while, haven't you?" she asked.

He used the sleeve of his light blue hoodie to wipe his face. "Yeah. A while. I...I didn't know what to expect. He doesn't even look the same."

"I know what you mean. At first, I thought it might not be him," said Fern.

"It's him," said Duncan, wearily.

"Yeah, the stupid ring tattoo he got certainly helped."

Duncan gave a soft chuckle. "You know I tagged along with him when he got it."

"What?"

"Yup. I had been his moral support. He said he'd done ton of research on it, but I think he saw a store downtown and thought why not. Plus, I managed to talk him out of getting this huge octopus he wanted along his arm."

"An octopus?" Fern couldn't help but chuckle. The image of Dale with an octopus on his arm was comedic. What would an octopus symbolize? Aren't tattoos something meaningful people get inked on their skin? Once again Fern found her eyes darting to the black outline of the ring on Dale's swollen finger.

Duncan sat in the chair Craig had occupied. He pulled it closer to Dale.

"He was going through this phase of wanting to be cool and thought a tattoo would instantly do it. Plus, there had been a hot chick working in the store so part of me wondered if that had been his motivation."

"Now that sounds more like your brother. Did she have black hair?"

Duncan simply nodded.

"He certainly had a type. Do you remember his last three girlfriends?"

Duncan wrinkled his nose as he thought about her question. The move made him look younger and emphasized the sprinkle of freckles across his nose and cheeks.

"Oh yeah, they all had shoulder-length black hair. Weird. I wouldn't have made the connection, but I guess he had a type."

Duncan all but choked on the words 'had a type' and it pained Fern.

"So, why didn't you get one?"

Duncan reached out and touched Dale's hand. "I had thought of it but I don't like needles. Plus, as much as he said it didn't hurt when the girl applied the needle, I could tell by how tense his face got, it did. He teased me mercilessly for weeks after, but I'm good with it."

Fern looked from Duncan to Dale. They had looked so much alike over the years she got why people found them hard to identify. Now they looked completely different. One alive, the other dead. Fern quickly composed her thoughts. Falling apart wouldn't help Duncan. "I'm glad you didn't get one. I'm surprised you came."

She grasped Duncan's other hand and gave it a squeeze. "Did Dad explain things to you and the kids?"

Duncan kept looking at his brother. There were fresh tears in his eyes again as he cleared his throat. "I had to see him. I can't believe this has happened. I thought it would be a lot louder."

"You mean the machines." She understood the need for chaos and not the silence of death.

He nodded. "Yeah. I told Dad I needed to see him for myself. He understood it."

"How are the girls and David handling this?"

He looked like he wanted to bite off her head for asking such a ridiculous question. Of course, her kids were basket cases. She was functioning, but barely.

"The girls went hysterical. Auntie Rose settled them down. David and I had a long talk."

Fern tucked her hair behind her ears. "Thank you. Thank you for doing that." Her chin quivered. She had to be strong. Duncan had come for a reason. He needed to muster his courage to speak.

"David's going to take this hard. He's always looked up to Dale."

"We all looked up to him. Why didn't they stop and spend the night somewhere? Dad said they think he fell asleep at the wheel. Thinking about it makes me angry again."

"You came to say goodbye. I get it. I didn't want the girls or David to see him like this." Fern tried to reassure herself she'd made the right decision for her children.

"I know. I get it. Dad explained things. I...I simply had to see him. Dad told us about Scarlett. Mom, I know you and Willow don't get along."

Fern got up from the plastic chair and pulled Duncan in for

a hug. "Shh, it has nothing to do with my relationship to my sister. I don't feel we can make the decision for him."

Duncan pulled out of her embrace. At almost eighteen, at six-foot-three, the tell-tale frame of his O'Leary heritage peeked out from his lanky teenage build.

"Mom. Dale would want you to do this. He'd want Scarlett to live. He'd actually want to save as many people as he could. Did you know he planned to apply to paramedic school in a few months?"

Fern sat back down. More surprises. No, she had not known. Was this unexpected? Yes. Dale, had been a second-year bachelor of science university student. Hadn't they talked about engineering school? Fern raked a hand through her hair. It felt knotted and could use a good brushing, but the effort was beyond her. "He never talked about it with us. He never told us about Scarlett."

"I know. He didn't know how to."

"But you knew," said Fern, instantly wishing she hadn't spoken the words out loud.

Duncan gave her a sheepish look. "Yeah, I knew. I begged him to tell you, but he said you wouldn't understand and you'd get mad. You and Dad can be so intimidating. He planned to tell you about paramedic school after this trip. He knew you wanted him to go to engineering school but it wasn't him. Sometimes it's hard to say no to you and Dad."

Honesty was often the hardest thing to hear, but Fern forced herself to listen. She urged Duncan to reclaim the seat next to her. "Tell me more. I need to understand all of this.

We've always been there for all of you but you're right. Maybe we've been too pushy."

Like I was too stubborn to listen to Willow. The thought slithered through her subconsciousness. If she'd listened to Willow, would their family be so dysfunctional? The bigger question is, would it have saved her son, Dale? That line of thinking instantly made her feel sick. The blame game seemed to be becoming her game of choice. Fern knew she couldn't take the time to fully examine things at the moment.

Instead, she turned her mind to Duncan, which meant forcibly turning her attention from Dale and the quiet hum of the machines. Duncan talked and talked. Telling her things, she'd never suspected of Dale and of him. Where had she been all the years? She hadn't known half the stuff he mentioned about her children. He told her about their plans to go work abroad for a few months and help build a school in Guatemala. He told her how Scarlett had become involved in a lot of international charities. She'd already gone to Cuba to help build a school and when she'd told Dale, he'd jumped at the idea. *Scarlett doing charity work?* This knowledge baffled Fern's mind. Maybe this was how all parents felt when the ugly truth of things got laid out like this – with your child dead on a hospital bed.

"We would have supported his decision," she said.

"Would you? Dad and you are always going on about how important it is to get your education. Dale hated university. He hated doing the International Baccalaureate program in high school, but he did it for you. He tried to talk to you and maybe he should have forced the issue, but he wasn't happy."

Her child hadn't been happy? Surely if she re-examined things in slow motion, she'd find evidence contrary to this. He had seemed happy, hadn't he? In her mind, Fern replayed every car ride with him, all the supper table conversations and it shocked her to realize how little he spoke. She honestly hadn't realized. Ignorance, a painful stab to her heart.

"You want us to give Dale's liver to Scarlett?"

Duncan nodded and squeezed her hand. "He'd want you to do more. He'd want you to donate as many organs as possible."

Fern hiccupped and then lost it. The scrape of the plastic chair on the floor as Duncan moved closer to her echoed in the small room. He gathered her in his arms. A complete role reversal.

"It's okay, Mom. He'd want this."

They were both crying, trying without success to get their emotions in check.

"I don't want it," she said, once she could talk.

"I know. But we have to think of what he'd want." Duncan ran his hands up and down her back, sounding older than his years.

"Are you sure about this?"

"Yes. I know my brother. We talked a lot."

A truism melting her heart. As children, they were thicker than thieves. If she punished one, she'd find the other sneaking into their room to offer comfort. Was this what had happened? Duncan stepping to the plate to voice what Dale couldn't?

"He should have signed his donor card," said Fern, weakly.

"Yeah, he should have. Don't forget he got the card almost five years ago when he had been going through his dick phase."

Fern laughed; the sound was foreign to her ears.

Duncan let go of her. "Sorry, I probably shouldn't have called him that."

"No. It's okay. He wasn't a saint, but to us he had been perfect. Do you remember the time he came home at 3 a.m. trying to sneak into the house?"

"Oh yeah. He got pissed at me. The plan had been for me to leave the front door unlocked. I totally forgot."

They sat for what felt like a long time, talking about Dale's not so finer moments and some of his finest with the beeps of the monitor's part of the soundtrack. This, more than the power of prayer, soothed Fern's soul. When the nurse came in, Fern urged Duncan to head home and help take care of his siblings. She'd have to talk to Craig about all of what Duncan had said, but a sense of relief in making the decision settled in Fern's heart.

When the nurse exited, reminding Fern to help herself to anything in the kitchen, Fern got up and kissed Dale's closed eyes.

"I'll be right back, son," she said to the room.

Fern dug her fingernails into her palms as she strode down the hall. She had a new mission. She could do this. She had to, even as her heart fluttered in disbelief with her decision.

Chapter 28

Craig

Craig longed to drown himself in alcohol, but he couldn't do it to his family. They needed him to be strong when he felt so defeated.

His cell vibrated in his pant pocket. He'd fallen asleep on the sofa after telling the children about Dale. Thankfully, Rose and Harold had been there to help. At first, Craig had thought he'd want to tell his kids on his own but he couldn't do it. It had been Rose who had ushered them all into the downstairs family recroom with the comfy sofas. It had been Harold who said Craig had something important to say and who had assured them at the end Rose and he were there for them. Craig, for the first time in his life, had been grateful to Rose's family. Even Rose's kids went above and beyond. Her boys had cooked supper for his family last night and now Rose, in less than twenty minutes, had scrambled eggs and made pancakes for breakfast.

"Hello," said Craig to his cell.

"Craig. I need to speak with you," said Fern.

Craig sat up straight. Hope flared to life. The specialist had been wrong. Dale would be okay. "What's up?"

"Duncan came in last night and talked with me. I'm going to sign the papers for the doctors."

Craig's breath left him. They'd talked about this. He didn't want Dale cut up. Hadn't he made his views plain as stale bread? So much for a miracle. "We talked about this, Fern. We're not doing it."

"It's not only for Scarlett. He'd be helping about ten people."

"I don't care," said Craig, and he honestly didn't. Did it make him a bad person? Probably, but having his son cut into pieces to save someone made him physically ill.

"Craig. This isn't about us. This is about what Dale would want."

"Fern, we were a united front. How do you know he'd want this?"

"Duncan told me. Did you know they were planning to go to Guatemala to volunteer to build a school?"

"What?"

"Our boys were planning a trip to do some good. Dale planned to drop out of university and take a paramedic course."

Fern talked a mile a minute. She had set course on a mission.

He wanted her to stop talking. From his wife's tone of voice, it wouldn't happen. "I'm coming in. Don't sign anything until I get there." Craig hung up on his wife before she could urge him on.

Craig quickly showered and brushed his teeth. He grabbed two pancakes on the way out the door and promised his kids and Rose he'd call with updates. Did agreeing to give Dale's liver to Scarlett count as an update? He felt pretty certain it could be a yes, but he wasn't about to tell Rose, Fern had changed her mind. Rose would pitch a fit and he didn't blame her.

At the hospital, he couldn't find Fern. He thought for sure she'd be in Dale's room. He wasn't about to walk to Scarlett's room to find her and she wasn't answering her cell. He texted her. Fern hated text messaging. Craig highly suspected she didn't understand how to use the feature on her cell. So, Craig did the only thing he could do. He forced his butt back into the plastic chair beside his son's bed.

Later, a knock on the door, broke his melancholy thoughts.

"Come in," he said, hoping Fern would prance through the door with a change of heart.

"I'm Judy. The social worker. Do you have a minute?"

Time stood still at hospitals. Those in the profession knew it as a weird warped time reversal thing no one talked about. He'd been holding his son's hand for almost two hours, lost in thought. He ushered the pretty thirty-something woman inside. Her blonde hair fell almost to her shoulders and she had pale blue eyes. Tall, dressed in light blue slacks with a white blouse, she looked like a teacher. She promptly claimed the other plastic chair and then launched into her appeal about how pleased the hospital was they had agreed Dale could be a donor. She told him as much information she could about all the people Dale, his son, would be helping. Craig didn't want to listen. He needed to remain angry with his wife. She'd signed the consent forms without waiting for him. Forced to pay attention to the woman, something started to shift inside him. She gave more details about his son's gifts, which had been the word the social worker used. Some PR person made a mint off of transforming body parts into gifts.

"Now the only part your wife said she wouldn't consent to are his eyes."

"His eyes?"

"Yes. She said quite clearly he needed those for his journey."

Craig flexed his toes in his too tight sneakers. Tears welled in his eyes. She'd remembered. "Yes. Yes, he does."

The woman reached out and patted his leg. A tender moment amid the misery.

"If it's any consolation and I know it's small, I had to make this decision about six years ago for my daughter," she said, pulling back her hand to help re-establish a boundary. "Like your son, a car accident claimed her life. I took this job to help other parents. It is the toughest decision any parent can make, but you are doing the right thing. I believe it with all my heart."

Craig didn't know what to say. Did it matter she'd lost a child, like him, in this horrific way? He wasn't certain. "I'm sorry, I've forgotten your name."

She reached into her clip board and pulled out a business

card. "Judy. This is my card. Please feel free to call me anytime. I already spoke with your wife earlier this morning. She asked me to talk with you alone. She said you weren't in favour of the decision. How are you feeling now that you have more information?"

Craig thought about all the people his son would help. He felt man enough to admit he did feel like a weight was being lifted. "A bit better."

"And it's all we can ask for. Trust your heart. This decision is not the end of Dale's life. He will live on. It is the greatest gift anyone can give. I'm going to leave you now. The doctors should be here any minute. Before they take Dale into surgery, you and your wife will have one last time with him to say your goodbyes."

Craig nodded. He felt shaky. His heart hurt. Judy reached out and took his hands in his. "Would you like me to stay with you, Craig?"

"Yes," he said, meaning it. Where was his wife? Why wasn't she here? "Have you seen my wife?"

"She mentioned she had something she had to do. I'm certain she won't be gone long."

Long enough to allow the doctors to cut Dale into pieces like slices of meat. Craig thought about the people his son's body parts would make a difference for and tried to find comfort. He failed miserably.

Chapter 29

Fern

Fern fidgeted in her seat. Her watch said it was seven in the morning. She had been the first patron in the small downtown Dartmouth café located across from the library. Thankfully, it wasn't packed. It smelled like sweetened butter which had been slightly burnt. Fern felt nervous and the smell made her nauseous. Before making the final decision to give Dale's liver to Scarlett, she'd arranged with Willow for a private talk in a public space. She didn't trust her sister enough after her deranged moment of trying to kill her and needed some space from the hospital setting. Ten minutes later, both she and Willow were sipping their brew. Fern couldn't taste the Earl Grey tea. Could Willow's taste buds savour her Café Americano? She hoped not.

"Fern, I'm sorry," said Willow.

"Yeah, we all are. They should have stopped somewhere for the night."

"No, I mean...yes, you're right they should have stopped but I'm sorry for everything that's happened. There's no excuse for what I did to you, but I snapped. I...after the incident, I went to see my doctor and she prescribed some medication for me."

The admission knocked Fern almost off her seat. Willow apologizing felt long overdue. "I should have listened to you about the land. I had been stubborn."

Willow gave a jaded smile; a look so similar to Lily's mischievous grin Fern's heart fluttered. "I think emotions were high all around. I didn't want to let it leave our family."

"But taking Mom to a lawyer behind our backs."

Willow took a long sip of her coffee. "Well, it wasn't like you were going to agree, so you left me no choice."

A knot twisted in Fern's back. "You're right. Both Rose and I wouldn't have agreed. I tried to explain to you Mom needed the money. She still had a mortgage on the house."

"I'm sorry for how I got the land, but not sorry for the land."

Fern pursed her lips. A few more people had come into the café, the beginnings of the morning rush. She felt the tell-tale tingles of a headache brewing. "Well, I've given it a lot of thought. You want Dale's liver and I'm willing to allow it, but you have to give up something."

Willow's eyes narrowed. "The land."

She's one smart cookie. Fern nodded.

"That's not fair."

Fern gave a small hurtful chuckle. "No, you might not think it is, but it's the deal."

"Does Craig know about your deal?"

Craig most certainly did not know, but she wouldn't disclose such to Willow. "Of course."

"Did Rose put you up to this?" asked Willow, leaning back in the chair to tuck her hair behind her ear.

"No, she didn't," said Fern, forcing herself to take a sip of tea. The Earl Grey tea tasted too flowery and it wasn't having the calming effect she'd hoped for. *I actually thought of this all on my own.*

"Have you seen the land recently?"

"As a matter of fact, I have. Seems like you've got lots of things taking place on the land." *Things our father would have hated.*

Willow ran a hand through her hair. "I've invested more than I wanted to. If you take the land, which I'm not saying I agree to, I'm going to have to be compensated."

"How much did you invest?"

Willow gave her a crafty look. "Well, I wouldn't say I invested my cash, but Kane did and I can't sign the land over to you because of that."

Fern wanted to howl with laughter. Her sister basically thought to scam her and it sounded like she'd succeeded with Kane. "If you didn't contribute a dime to the land and it's solely in your name, you can sign the land over to me. It's as simple as that, Willow. If you want Scarlett to have Dale's liver, I'm expecting you to do the right thing."

"Oh, shut up, Fern. If I give you the land, what do I get?"

Flabbergasted best described Fern. The fact she had to say it out loud shocked her. "You, Willow, get your daughter. I get a dead son. I'm the one losing in this bargain no matter how you spin it."

Fern looked around the café. A line had formed at the cash and the smell of fresh cinnamon buns had overtaken the burned butter smell from earlier. "You can think about it."

Willow leaned toward her. "You're going to play hardball with Scarlett's life?"

Fern tilted her head. "I'm not always a pushover, Willow. I might have naively thought we could reconnect as sisters, but I don't think it's going to happen."

Willow scoffed. "Sisters? Really? My only sister had been Lily and she died."

"Wow, that's sad. There might be a decade between us and you might hate it, but we are related by blood. We were all crushed when Lily died."

"No, you weren't."

Okay, maybe we didn't feel the blow like she did, but still Lily's death cut us all. "You're always looking for a fight with me. Did I experience grief with Lily's passing, yes. Was it the same grief you experienced, no. It's never been about one person loving you more in a family. You are still my sister. I do care about you."

"Lily and I were connected. She had been my twin. Something died inside me when she did."

"I believe it. You know, both Rose and I were worried about you after Lily's death. We tried to reach out to you."

"I hated the both of you."

And still do. "Because we had each other," guessed Fern.

"Yeah," said Willow, sounding for the first time fatigued and sad all at once.

"I had wondered about that, but we were both hurting also and as incapable of dealing with Lily's death as you were."

"I felt like I couldn't even mourn. I had to deal with four kids."

"So were Rose and I," cut in Fern, feeling the need to remind her sister they had been in the same boat.

"It wasn't the same, Fern. You had Craig and Rose had Harold. I had no one."

"You had your husband."

"By that point, we weren't speaking. I felt like I was on my own."

"You weren't, but I think you wanted to be."

Willow took another sip of her coffee and nodded. "Maybe. I had a complete breakdown a month after her death. I at least managed to check myself into the hospital. I spent six weeks there. Have I shocked you yet?"

Fern pushed her backpack on the floor out of her way. "No, I had wondered. I'm not surprised. You needed help and I'm glad you went and got it. Both Rose and I had called your house numerous times, but your husband always said you were out. We thought since you wouldn't return our calls you wanted privacy. I'm sorry. We should have pushed more to be with you."

"Honestly, maybe I did want to be on my own. Life for me hasn't been easy."

Fern barely resisted rolling her eyes. Whose life has been easy, she thought. However, she wisely restrained herself and silently urged her sister on. "I'm sure it wasn't."

"Lily and I were completely different but the same. It's weird. I wish I could explain what we had but I can't. She had been the do-gooder who planned her life and once she set her mind to something, she did it. I mean, who saves up for years to plan a trip to Australia? Lily, that's who."

"And then Europe and Italy. She wanted to see the world. Did you know she was planning another trip?"

"Oh yeah. She kept talking about Iceland or Vietnam. I kept talking about which kids TV shows the boys were watching. But, in many ways, I lived for her adventures."

Fern realized something. She and Willow were having a normal conversation. The tension in her back eased. "Why did you stop coming to grandma's cottage with Rose and me?"

"Oh, Fern, it was way too painful. You and Rose were like Lily and me. I'd hear you finish Rose's sentences and see how you interacted in the kitchen and it would make me almost spiral out of control. After the hospital, I learned to avoid situations that would trigger me," said Willow, smiling. "Basically, you and Rose."

"I had suspected as much. How are you coping these days?"

"Same as you," snapped Willow.

The rebuke was a subtle reminder how fast Willow's mood could change. "I'm glad we talked. I think it's time I left, but thanks for meeting with me."

"Have you changed your mind about the land?"

Fern shook her head. "Oh no, the deal stands. I'm glad we could talk like two normal people and I am sorry for what happened to you, but it doesn't change what's on the table."

Willow eyed a young man who walked by. "I'm surprised, this doesn't seem like you."

People change. Fern knew it first-hand. "I guess it shows you how little you know of me." Fern handed a piece of paper with the name of her lawyer and street address to Willow.

"What's this?"

"I'm giving you two hours. If you don't show up by 10 a.m. the deal is off. She's drawn up the papers so you can sign the property over to me."

"You'd let Scarlett die."

Fern got up from the table. "No, that would be on you. Oh, before I go, I've got something for you." She dug inside her backpack and pulled out the scribbler containing Lily's journal. "We found this at the cottage and I think you should have it."

"A scribbler?"

"Start at the back. It's one of Lily's journals. I think you'll find the reading enlightening," said Fern, placing it on the round café table. "Willow, I am sorry for how things played out. You were never alone and more than anything, I feel hurt you felt that way. Both Rose and I would have bent over backward to help you."

Willow nodded but her attention had become transfixed on the scribbler. Fern left the café, wondering as she always did when dealing with Willow what she'd do next. Two hours to decide: let go of the land to save her daughter's life. Any other person wouldn't have to blink to accept the deal but Willow always thought of herself first.

Honestly, as Fern started the car, she wasn't sure if Willow's heart or moral integrity switch would live up to her expectations. They certainly weren't living up to her own, but she'd learned something from Willow: being tough to get what you wanted meant being willing to make difficult decisions.

Chapter 30

Rose

Rose rearranged Fern's baking cabinet. The lack of order drove her nuts. Nothing had a label and the spice rack was a hopeless mess of bags and jars. *How does she find anything?* She had to keep busy. She'd called into work and told Blair what had happened and then called her boss, who had assured her she could take as long as needed. Next, she'd mustered the courage to call her ex. He'd been politely surprised, but far enough removed from their family for so long the shock of it didn't fully register and didn't affect his plans to jet off with his girlfriend to a paradise island. She'd made breakfast and Harold and the boys had cleaned up. They were all at loose ends. Her girls were up with the twins. They weren't handling it well. What did she expect? David's silence made her sad. When Duncan finally came home, she all but pounced on him.

"Is she okay?" *The better question is, are you?* Rose bit her cheek. She didn't want to start mothering Fern's kids. Duncan had been upset in the beginning but he'd quickly stepped into the protective brother role. Last night he'd spent a lot of time with David, who had completely lost it, which of course had set the twins over the edge. At one point, Rose thought they could all use some drugs to get through the night. Instead, they'd all cried and hugged each other and talked about Dale. As weird as it felt, it had helped.

"Yeah. David, want to go for a drive?" asked Duncan, clearly needing time alone with his little brother.

David, who had been sitting on the sofa, staring at the TV without absorbing it, said yes instantly. Within minutes, they were back out the door and hitting the road. Rose felt relieved. She could handle her kids, but Fern's were a different matter.

"I'm going to take the girls to our place for a bit," said Harold, coming down the stairs. He'd obviously showered and changed and had already packed up. Harold never liked to be far from home and today his need for routine she found comforting.

"Sounds good. Can you drop me off at the hospital?"

He plunked his duffel bag down by the front door and then came over to where she stood with one arm on the kitchen counter to haul her in for a much-needed hug.

"Of course. Did you want to shower first?"

"No. I'm good," lied Rose. She knew she looked terrible. Getting in Fern's shower seemed too intimate for her sensibilities.

Harold gave her a sweet kiss and then said, "I'm going to give them the twenty-minute countdown."

Rose revelled the feeling of Harold's arms around her. Something had clicked with the two of them thanks to the magic of the cottage. He kissed the top of her head and let her go. Rose packed up what little clothing she'd amassed at her sister's house and forty minutes later, once again walked into the hospital. This time she knew where to go. A sad reality, which she hated.

She stepped off the seventh floor and its cheery lights disarmed her. Shouldn't the world be in shades of grey? She momentarily paused by Scarlett's door. The urge to peek in and see how she fared gave way. Rose knocked on the door.

A nurse opened it. "Sorry. I was looking for Willow."

"We're getting her ready for surgery," said the nurse, ushering Rose out the door.

"Oh, okay," said Rose, backing out while wondering if that news could be good or bad. She made her way down the other hallway to Dale's room. Inside she could hear Craig and Fern arguing. *What was going on?*

Rose thought twice before opening the door. Did she want to know why they were fighting? Had Fern told him about Sean? Rose hoped not. Not the time or place. There would never be a good time, but surely Fern understood now had to be the worse choice. Not sure what to do, Rose wandered into the lounge. She clicked on the TV and watched CBC Newsworld, a channel she detested. She tried to get the remote to click to another channel but no such luck. They should have home repair or cooking shows playing non-stop in the lounge. Who wanted reality when you were on this floor? Fantasy home renovations where everyone at the end got their dream home and baking shows which made you hunger for decadent desserts were essential sources of entertainment when faced with life and death choices.

Rose had always been more into home renovation or cooking shows. Fern often made fun of her for not following the news. Rose didn't want to see images of children being blown to bits. She'd take fluff any day over reality, which as she sat in the stained worn sofa, felt raw and hard enough.

She got up and went into the adjoining kitchen to make a cup of coffee and sat back down, wondering how long she'd have to wait. About ten minutes later, Fern came into the lounge. Visibly shaken, with her face flushed, she looked worse than yesterday. She still wore the clothes she'd worn at the cottage. Then again, so did Rose. Yesterday felt like a life time ago.

"He…Craig…he…we lost everything," said Fern.

Rose couldn't follow the conversation. She urged her sister to the sofa, grateful no one else had come into the lounge. "Fern, what are you talking about?"

"He lost his job. He told me."

"He'll get another one," said Rose, rubbing her sister's back.

"You don't understand. He gambled away our savings."

This Rose hadn't foreseen. "Gambled away? What do you mean?"

Fern shook her head. "I should have known. He did this to me before. When we lived in Toronto. He told me he stopped. In fact, before moving back home, we'd had this big fight about it. He said he didn't do it anymore. He lied. Worse, we now have nothing."

"Calm down. Maybe you're overreacting."

Fern grabbed Rose's hand. "I'm not. All the money in the kids' savings account for university is gone. He thought he could make things right by making a big wager last week and he lost it all. You know, maybe this is what I deserve."

Rose knew where Fern headed. She'd been down that self-destructive road before. "Fern, no one deserves what's happened to your family. You didn't do anything wrong."

Fern gave a hurtful laugh. "Oh, Rose, there you're wrong. I should have told him."

"No. Now is not the time. You both have enough to deal with. Whatever is going on financially will get sorted out. Craig is resourceful. He'll find another job. Trust me, he's not the type of man to walk away. You know it. He didn't walk away before. He's been successful here. This I'm sure is a hiccup."

"Maybe deep down it's what I want. Maybe I want him to be the one to walk away so I don't have to own up to my mistakes."

"Is that how you view it?"

Fern looked at Rose with weepy eyes. "Yes. No. I'm not sure. It felt wonderful."

Here she started to cry in earnest. Rose drew her sister in for a hug. She understood what the 'wonderful' her sister referenced. She'd avoided talking about Sean on purpose, but he'd called her this morning asking about Fern. He had wanted to call Fern. Rose had told him to give her sister time.

There would be lots of hugs between them over the next few days but this hug had a message; she understood.

"Wonderful is good. You deserve wonderful. We all do. Let's try not to overreact. Are you up to giving him a call?" asked Rose, in her gentle voice.

Fern shook her head. "I can't. I... maybe I shouldn't have done what I did. This is my fault."

"Fern, you are not responsible for what happened to Dale. And, it takes two to tango. Listen, this is not the time to examine what happened. An awful lot has crashed into you in very little time. You are in no condition to make any decisions. I think you should wait a while before talking to Sean. As for Craig, he's admitted his mistake and it's just money."

Rose gave a hurtful laugh. *Just money.* She'd been struggling for years to make ends meet for her family and losing all that money was not a laughing matter. If Harold had depleted their savings, she'd be furious.

"Let's deal with this, with Dale first."

Fern pulled back, trying to regain her composure. "I signed the donor forms."

Rose sat back into the squishy leather sofa. She didn't know what to say. Deep down she'd highly suspected Fern's sense of fairness, goodness and family would force her hand. She'd been right.

"Craig's furious with me. He doesn't want this," said Fern, searching in her purse for a chap stick.

"What made you?"

Fern applied the lotion to her cracked lips. "Duncan. He came in to plead Dale's case. What he told me about my own son shocked me. I really didn't know Dale. After discovering more about him, I couldn't say no." Fern reached back into her purse for a tissue. She blew her nose and stuffed the used tissue back into her handbag. She probably had a mountain of used tissues wedged into the small leather purse.

Fern hiccupped. "How is it I didn't know so much about my own son?"

Rose clasped Fern's hands. "Fern, you are a great mother. The thing is while they are our children, they are also their own persons. I can honestly tell you I'm thankful I don't know everything."

"But Rose, the things Duncan told me were so opposite to the Dale I knew it startled me. It made me realize I need to listen to my kids more. Actually, I need to listen to everyone more. Duncan said Dale wanted to tell me about his plans but he didn't want to disappoint me. How awful my own son felt he couldn't talk to me."

"Fern, I'm sure you didn't tell Mom and Dad everything."

"No, but my relationship with them had been strained," said Fern.

"Difficult defined the state of things between them. The thing is, parents can only try their best and you did."

"But I would have accepted him wanting to become a paramedic and volunteer overseas to build a school. I would have been proud of him," said Fern, pushing her hair behind her ears. "It hurts he felt he couldn't tell me."

"A paramedic, how cool."

Fern nodded. "Yeah, the more I think about it, the more I can see it would have been the right choice for Dale. Now...now it's too late."

"Oh, Fern, I can't begin to imagine how difficult this has been for you. My heart is breaking for you all, but you will get through this."

"You do know Scarlett will get his liver," said Fern.

That's what the nurse meant about Scarlett being prepped for surgery. Rose digested the news and felt relief.

She leaned into her sister's space. "How do you feel about this?"

"Relief," said Fern, attempting a smile.

"Me too. The thought of losing both of them had been killing me. Does it make me selfish?"

"No. It makes you human. The only part I said they couldn't take were his eyes."

Rose nodded, not sure she wanted all the information, but if her sister felt the need to go into those gory details she'd listen.

Fern slouched on the sofa. "I'm glad Craig told me now. I'd rather get all the blows squared away."

Rose understood and realized how exhausted her sister must be. Her conversations were bouncing all over the place. "What are you going to do?"

"The doctors will let us say our final goodbye before his surgery. Then we'll get things arranged for his funeral."

"Let me help," said Rose.

"Do you think you and Duncan can work on his obituary? I don't think I can handle it. I'm starting to feel completely exhausted."

"Yes," said Rose. Something tangible she could do. "Do you want the funeral in the city?"

"Yes. This is his home. His friends are all here. Call a funeral home and make arrangements, please. After surgery, he's going to be cremated. Craig wanted a wake, but I told him I couldn't handle going through all of what it would entail."

"It's in my hands. Don't you worry about it."

"Thank you, Rose. I can't begin to tell you how much this helps. And thanks for listening. You're right. It's only money. I've calmed down now. I think I'll go back and sit with him before the doctors take him away."

"Want me to join you?"

"That would be nice. Thank you."

Together, linked hand in hand, they made their way back down the now familiar hallway marked with scuff marks and walls desperately crying out for new paint to Dale's room.

Craig, perched on the tip of the plastic chair, had his face in his hands. His skin looked grey and his eyes puffy. He reminded her of a deflated balloon. Rose got how he felt.

"I'm so sorry, Fern."

Fern crossed her arms and Rose watched her mouth tighten into a grimace but she finally sighed and then went over to give her husband a sad smile. "I'm glad you told me. Let's get through this and then deal with things. Rose is going to sit with us before they take him away."

"She told you?" asked Craig.

"Yeah, sorry to hear about your job. I'm sure things will work out. I'm going to make the funeral arrangements and Duncan will help with the obituary. You two don't need to worry about anything."

Craig got up from his perch and took hold of Dale's hand. The sight tore into Rose's heart.

He mumbled, "I wish it were me in that bed."

Fern sat and remained silent. Rose didn't know what to say as Craig wiped a tear from his face and told her to have a seat. The silence felt oppressive but breaking it with banal talk seemed sacrilegious. The door swung open to usher in two nurses.

"They're ready for him," said one of the nurses.

Rose wished she'd stayed in the lounge. Instead, she mustered her courage and went over to say goodbye to Dale. She stood next to Craig and Fern followed next.

"See you on the other side, son," mumbled Craig.

"You have my heart with you. I love you," said Fern.

Fern's words were so true it took a minute for Rose to realize they were waiting for her to say something.

She cleared her throat. "I'm so glad you were in our lives and we will all miss you. I will take care of them for you." Fern tucked her arm around Rose's waist, hauling her in for a squeeze. They all had tears streaking unchecked down their cheeks. Then with a nod from Fern, the nurses wheeled Dale and the machines out of the room.

The vacuum emptiness of the room felt raw and Rose realized taking a breath hurt. Fern collapsed into the chair; silent sobs shook her body. Craig tried to hug her but she brushed him off. Rose understood. Fern had to deal with the situation and the blows were piling up on her subconscious. She had to sort things out on her own. A Siteman trait, through and through. Sad, how much Rose understood her need to cocoon herself. No pretty butterfly at the end of the hibernation would emerge. Instead, it would be a woman, bruised and scarred deep with a tragedy no one would see. She would once again be forced to fake a smile to get through the day.

Rose had to leave. She knew her sister had to deal with the loss of her son, privately. "I'm going to head home. Harold took the girls to our house for a while. I'll make supper and we'll bring it over to your place tonight." Rose tried to make it all sound normal, when the day felt like a hurricane had barreled through their family.

"Thank you," said Craig.

Rose looked at Craig and Fern. Would they weather this storm together or would one of them break free? She didn't know what to think. And thinking too far into the future hurt her head. They'd take one day at a time, like her, and get through it.

She quickly gave a last hug to her sister and then only when she had exited the floor did she call Harold, telling him she'd catch the ferry. He'd pick her up on the Dartmouth side. She gave him the update. Dale's liver would save Scarlett. While part of her felt like once again Willow had won, she also knew Fern couldn't have lived with herself knowing Dale could have saved Scarlett and they'd done nothing. It sickened Rose she had those thoughts, but it wasn't in her to forgive and forget. That usually was Fern's way of looking at the world. However, Fern agreeing had surprised even Rose. Maybe Willow had finally apologized to Fern. Rose highly doubted it.

Rose eyed a woman smoking by the parking lot. Screw it. On her way home, she was stopping at the corner store for a pack. Life after all was too short and today, she'd give into her craving.

Chapter 31

Harold

The next day, Harold called his boss and explained what had happened. Thankfully, being in a union allowed him to take time off to deal with the family crisis. It had become a crisis his wife tried her best to stem. It wouldn't work.

Craig had told him he'd lost his job. He hadn't said anything about gambling it all away. Harold couldn't get his head around it. Craig had always seemed uptight and strait-laced. He didn't fit the type of guy who would go to a seedy bar, let alone one of those mysterious poker places which popped up and disappeared faster than the authorities could track.

Forty-eight hours had passed since the first phone call. After supper, he'd taken Fern's girls back to their house. She had wanted them with her tonight. He understood. He laid in bed with Rose by his side. She kept nodding off. He hadn't said a thing when she'd asked him to stop at the corner store. He knew she'd bought cigarettes, but Rose didn't need a lecture. She needed sleep. He too craved sleep but it eluded him. His mind kept rehashing all Rose had told him. Before she'd turned on her side to go to sleep, his wife calmly informed him, while at the cottage, Fern had slept with Sean.

"Who is Sean?"

"He had been her boyfriend from high school. I always thought they'd get married but then they broke up and life happened. He's divorced. I heard he had a nasty divorce. Anyway, he's been back on the Eastern Shore for a number of years. He's an RCMP officer. Still pretty good-looking for a guy his age," said Rose.

"How good looking? Scratch that. But why did Fern sleep with him?"

"Well, I'm not a therapist, but Fern hasn't been happy for a while. Not sure what's going on but it sort of happened, according to Fern."

"Rose, this isn't good. Does Craig know?"

"I don't know but I'm certainly not saying anything. It's not my place. I've got to sleep. Tomorrow I'm going to work with Duncan to write up the obituary for Dale and start making the funeral arrangements."

"I'll stay home and help," said Harold.

"Thank you," Rose said and then promptly rolled over and went to sleep.

When she was sleepy, she crashed. When tired, he got wired.

Would the girls go to school on Monday? Secretly he hoped

they did. Routine helped, but he wasn't sure they were up to it. Rose's boys had been helpful and Harold knew they were crushed with Dale's death, who was four months younger than Rose's eldest.

Rose's family was fraught with difficult and touchy subjects, but Harold did wonder if anyone had told their mother. He suspected in the chaos of the past few days, both Rose and Fern hadn't. He certainly couldn't do it. Half the time when he picked her up, Sylvia didn't know who he was. She jokingly said it, but in his heart, Harold knew it took her a good five minutes before all the cylinders fired and she made the connection. He'd offer to tell her but knew Rose and Fern should be the ones. It wouldn't matter. An hour later she wouldn't recall the conversation. She carried a notebook around with her and wrote down conversations. Harold felt it resourceful. She certainly didn't want to admit to having dementia but knew she wasn't completely up to scratch and note-taking helped her cope. What Harold didn't like were her mood changes. She'd once told Rose off simply because she wouldn't stop at a corner store for Sylvia to buy more lottery tickets.

Wow, Craig a gambler like Sylvia. *How strange and tragically sad.*

He vividly recalled the day he'd had to go into the Porter's Lake pub to find Sylvia. It had been eight months after the sudden death of her husband. Rose had gone in for carpel tunnel surgery the week before and her arm had been in a cast and Fern had been laid up with the flu. Rose had been trying all week to reach her mother and finally on Friday he'd agreed to go down after work to check on her. Harold had surprised himself by volunteering for this task.

His relationship with Sylvia was not the best. She tended to talk down about her girls, a trait he hated and one he was thankful Rose hadn't inherited. First, he drove all the way to the Shore, thinking he'd find her eating supper and watching the news but she hadn't been home. By chance, he spotted a neighbour walking and after introducing himself he inquired if she'd seen Sylvia. The woman had said her husband had driven Sylvia to the pub. Harold had been shocked. He had known from Rose her mother liked to gamble, but he'd always assumed she'd simply bought lottery tickets. How wrong he'd been. He walked into the pub and sure enough, Sylvia sat on a stool playing the slot machine like there was no tomorrow. She hadn't been happy to see him but he managed to eventually pry her away by offering her a ride home. On the drive once again to her house, he'd casually asked how she got to the pub. He knew she'd lost her licence months ago. Sylvia talked about her kind neighbour who would ask to drive her to the pub and then she disclosed she lent him money for the slot machines. She had said it had to be their secret because his wife would get mad. Harold immediately knew he'd have to deal with it. The neighbour had been taking advantage of her.

After making sure Sylvia had supper and had settled back at her house, Harold got in his truck and had called his wife. After explaining what he'd discovered, Rose had been pleased he'd dealt with things but she hadn't been surprised. Rose agreed to talk to Fern and they'd figure out how to deal with Sylvia's out of control gambling problem. Harold had driven to the neighbors' place after Sylvia had pointed it out on the way home. He tried to confront the man on his own but his wife, who obviously knew something had happened, wouldn't give him five minutes. Finally, he came out with it stating he wasn't to ask for money from Sylvia again and the four hundred he'd borrowed this week had better be returned ASAP to her. The wife had been furious with her husband, who hadn't even attempted to deny the claim.

A few weeks later, in one of those rare humid May evenings, the neighbour had walked to his shed, found his shot gun and ended his life. Harold couldn't believe it when he'd heard the news. For a while he feared his confrontation had been the tipping point, but Rose assured him the man had problems for decades. Either way, every time he had passed the house on his way with Rose to Sylvia's place, it made his skin crawl.

Harold rolled over in bed and lightly placed his arm around his wife. In her sleep, she cuddled closer to him and the weight of her nestled to his body felt wonderful. He felt happy with the positive shift in their relationship and tried not to think about how it came to be.

Chapter 32

Rose

Her list got longer by the minute. And every time a task was completed, Rose felt like bursting into tears. She knew Fern and Craig were home and wondered how they were faring. Dale had been cremated and his "gift" of a liver was stashed inside Scarlett. Rose hoped it did its job. Fern had told her many other parts of Dale were helping other patients. When Rose thought about it, she felt ill. Fern had been proud of her decision, but Craig still struggled with it. Rose didn't know what to feel. The sense of relief she sought hadn't hit her yet. Dale had made the ultimate sacrifice. Why did things feel so messed up?

The bell rang. Who could it be? Rose gulped down another large sip of the coffee Harold made. Harold let Duncan in. Duncan, who acted like the big brother, offered to help her write the obituary. Rose wondered if she'd ever stop comparing the two brothers.

"Hi Rose," said Duncan, shaking off his jacket and handing her a piece of folded loose leaf. At one time it had been crumpled and obviously stuffed into his jacket pocket.

Rose gently unfolded the paper. "This is going to make me cry, isn't it?"

Duncan bowed his shoulders and nodded. She pretended not to see the tears. If she gave him an auntie hug, a river would flow.

"I've got to call the minister but for the life of me I can't remember the name of the church your parents went to."

"St. Peter's. It's Minister Young, but I think he's away."

"Away?"

"I heard he's doing a year in Africa, or something."

Of course, he is. "Okay. Would you rather I try a different church?"

"No. We didn't go often, but it had been our church when we were little. I think whoever does it will be okay," said Duncan.

Rose thought him a real trooper. *What must he be going through? He lost his big brother and is automatically forced to step into the "big brother" shoes.*

"Okay. I'll deal with the church. So far, I'm thinking the minister should speak, but I honestly don't think your parents will be able to. I know your mother can't, but I didn't ask your dad. What do you think?"

"He's a wreck. I'd say no. I'm not sure about me..." said Duncan, looking at the floor.

He couldn't face her. He, like her, struggled for composure.

Rose touched his arm. "Duncan, I'm not asking you to speak. You have enough on your plate. Your help is so appreciated but..."

He raised his face and took a step back. His eyes were full of tears but he fought not to cave. He stuffed a hand in his pocket. "I'd like to speak, but honestly I think I'll lose it. Plus, I think the girls will need me."

The out. The girls. The twins. "You're right. They will need you. I think the minister can handle everything. I would like to play some music Dale liked."

"He liked rap."

Rose fought not to flinch. *Rap? Could any rap be appropriate for church?*

"I don't know any rap. Can you help my boys put together a playlist which would be church appropriate?"

Duncan nodded with a wry grin.

"I'll take on the minister and the service in the hall. I promise you won't be disappointed."

Duncan took a deep breath. "Okay."

Rose fidgeted with a string hanging from her sweater. "The boys are in the basement. How about you head down and tell them. I'll bring some of the brownies down in a few minutes. I'm going to start making calls, okay?"

Duncan swivelled his head toward the top of the stairs leading to the basement. "Auntie, we really appreciate you helping with this. I can't stay long. I promised to take the girls shopping for an appropriate outfit."

He's taking the girls shopping. Rose couldn't get her head around it. "Duncan, I'm sure my girls have something in their closet the twins could use. Want me to take a look before you have to march to the mall with them?"

He bunched his hands into his pockets. "Yeah, I'm really not looking forward to taking them to the mall, but Mom can't do it. I'll take any help at this point."

Rose nodded. She suspected Fern lay curled in bed crying her eyes out. Who could blame her.

"Got you, and I don't blame you. Shopping is not something they should be doing at the moment. I promise in thirty minutes you'll be out of here and if I can't find something for the twins, I will do the dirty for you and take them to the mall. You're doing enough," said Rose.

Duncan gave her a real smile and then walked down into the basement they'd converted into a recroom.

Unlike Fern, who had a basement converted into a state-of-the-art recreational room equipped with top-of-the-line games, Rose's basement consisted of two used carpets placed directly over the concrete floor, an old TV and an ancient computer. Rose knew her eldest had hacked into some system and all the games they had loaded were pirated, but she couldn't do anything about it. Harold viewed it as ingenious creativity. Harold had found an old sofa someone had placed at the curb for garbage. It had been in surprisingly good condition. He picked it up once it got dark and voilà, they had a usable rec room.

Rose took the phone and Duncan's letter, along with her reheated coffee upstairs to her bedroom. She didn't want any interruptions as she digested Duncan's scribbled notes.

- Dale had been captain of the high school football team.

- He planned to volunteer to build a school for children in Guatemala. Rose re-read the line. *Really? That's what Fern had meant.*

- He loved to go to concerts.

Rose wasn't sure the minister should mention anything about concerts. Because of *said* concert he died.

- Dale had joined the university's debate team.

Rose had to bring the letter closer. Duncan wrote something after debate team and attempted to scribble it out.

- He thought they were a bunch of idiots.

Rose cracked a smile. Good to know he wasn't perfect and her face muscles still knew how to move upward.

- His favourite book, Spud.

Rose never heard of it and wondered its relevance.

- Favourite beer, Propeller Pale Ale.

Good to know he had inherited Fern's taste for liquor.

- Classified, his favourite rapper.

Even Rose knew the famous rapper from Enfield, Nova Scotia, and she grinned in earnest.

- In his spare time, he volunteered at the food bank.

Fern hadn't mentioned that either. They could certainly use it.

Why did funerals only talk about the good things? The Dale she knew had been sullen, barely spoke to adults and as a teenager had terrible acne. He'd once punched a hole in his bedroom wall because Fern had grounded him. Rose knew this because Fern had cried on the phone the next day disclosing what a jerk her son had been to her in front of their guests, and he had been grounded. Rose had said welcome to the teenage years, which at the time were a living nightmare for her. Even with Fern's kids going through their own teenage tantrums, they had seemed like nothing compared to Rose's kids, who were both caught doing drugs, smoking, drinking, and one had even admitted to breaking into a car. Thank goodness, he hadn't gotten caught.

Now, the secrets and lies surrounding Dale and Scarlett's relationship, their road trips, and the concerts they attended felt like an insurmountable Everest all on their own.

Why can't children talk to their parents? Rose almost laughed with her thoughts. She had certainly avoided her parents most of her life. Her father had been a drunk and she had learned early on to avoid the times when the bottle took precedence. Nothing Rose could do measured up to her mother's expectations. Maybe this cycle of life faced many families. Those crushing expectations ended up crippling children. It certainly had consequences for her.

She'd run away a few times. Fern had come after her the first time when she'd been twelve and had gotten into trouble for something ridiculous. Rose struggled to remember what had happened, but nothing popped into her mind. Fern found her down by the Falls. She had been frantic for her and it had somehow made Rose feel better. Her sister had of course found her scribbled note which had plainly stated, "I've left home for good." Rose remembered thinking Fern would be mad at her but her sister had rushed to hug her and cried, saying, "Please don't leave me alone." Rose had felt undone. She'd promised never to run away again; a bold lie.

The day after Fern went away to university, Rose had left home, intending for it to be for good. She hitched her way from the country to the city and then made her way to Fern's place, where she had rented a bedroom in a woman's house. The woman had been a friend of a friend from their church. When the woman answered the door and she'd asked for Fern, the woman correctly guessed she must be her sister and ushered her in. Rose had found the thought of Fern moving away increasingly agitating and frightful and had finally broken down.

Rose smiled, recalling how the woman offered her a soda and a sandwich. Then patiently, the lady had explained Fern needed time to find her way. The woman gave her ten dollars and a bus ticket, and showed her how to pick up the Zinck bus which would take her back to the country. She encouraged Rose to call Fern later and visit her sister in a couple of weeks. No one had offered Rose comfort of that nature in such a grown up way before. Rose had felt better with the substance and did as the woman instructed. To this day, Fern still didn't know she'd run away to find her and it had to remain a secret. After the first two weeks without Fern home, Rose started to adjust. The twins had been going through their deplorable elementary years and Rose hadn't wanted anything to do with them. She learned to make herself scarce. When home, she either cleaned the house or babysat. Two chores she loathed.

Writing her sister's son's obituary topped all things she abhorred. Rose struggled to turn her thoughts to the present and make headway. Duncan had said he couldn't stay long and she suspected he was helping with David, who of all Fern's children, had the hardest time with Dale's death.

After speaking with the minister, who she agreed to meet tomorrow, Rose went into Paige and Ava's room, kicking clothes littered on the floor out of her way. She dug through Paige's closet and found one black dress, and a black skirt and light sweater which would work for Allie and Ella. None of the shoes from Paige would fit the twins, who had tiny feet, so she'd leave Fern to deal with footwear. Armed with her bundle, she wrapped up some brownies for Duncan to take home.

"I'll give your mom a call later tonight," said Rose, as she ushered Duncan out the door.

"I'll let her know and you can fill her in. Now that I don't have to deal with the mall, I'm going to take David for a drive."

Did Craig or Fern know what took place in their household? Duncan, with his boyish shoulders, was bearing the pain of his siblings. Dare Rose say anything to either of them?

She'd talk with Harold later to get his view. Rose didn't want to step on any toes, especially with everyone being hypersensitive, but Duncan had lost a brother too and needed to process his grief. Knowing her husband, he'd say Duncan stepping forward might be his way of handling Dale's death.

Rose's head hurt. Working on arranging things for the church and the service were tasks she never thought she'd have to contemplate.

"I hope you don't mind I brought home supper," said Harold, walking through the door armed with Chinese take-out.

Rose smiled and brushed the tears from her eyes. "When did you become a mind-reader? You've made my day."

Harold placed the bags on the kitchen counter and then hauled Rose in for a hug. "I knew you were working on church arrangements and thought you might need a boost. I even picked up a bottle of red wine."

Rose reached up and kissed her husband. "This is exactly what I needed."

"I saw Duncan in the driveway. I'm amazed he's still standing."

Rose found the bottle of wine and quickly twisted off the screw top. She poured them each a glass. The boys, who obviously smelled the Chinese food, dashed up from the basement to dig in.

"He's handling way too much," said Rose, grabbing plates and utensils for the boys. "Save some for your sisters."

"They hate Chinese food," said Toby, piling enough food on his plate for three people.

Rose thought to rebuke this claim, but knew the girls would be happy with grilled cheese sandwiches, so she'd let her sons eat their fill.

"Rose, I'm dishing out ours before it all disappears,"

announced Harold, as Rose sat down in the living room to enjoy her wine.

She flicked on the TV and breathed a sigh of relief. Jamie Oliver with his posh accent cooked up a feast in thirty minutes. Rose could watch a marathon of Jamie cooking. Harold liked to tease her she found the British chef sexy. Any man mastering food in the kitchen fulfilled Rose's fantasy.

Harold sat down beside her, handing her a plate of Chinese food. Rose bit into lemon chicken and smiled. She gave her meal a solid five stars and her husband a loving look, for he truly understood her. Balancing her plate and wine while they nestled together on the sofa, Rose thought, it was the best fine dining she'd had in a long while.

Chapter 33

Fern

Fern had become a fraud. She knew it to the marrow of her bones. She sucked at being a mother. Honestly, she shouldn't have had kids. At sixteen, she'd vowed never to have children. She should have stuck with her life plan—escape the fishing village and move to a big city and never look back.

All she did now was re-examine her life, the children's lives and wonder where it all went wrong.

"Mommy, are you getting up?"

Allie nudged closer to the bed. Only Fern could tell the twins' voices apart. Craig always got it wrong. Fern remembered once getting angry at Dale for saying so what if he couldn't tell their voices apart. She rolled over in the bed to face the wall. The memories were going to kill her. The bed dipped as Allie and Ella scrambled next to her. Allie's cold little hand rubbed

Fern's back. Her owl-like eyes, large and expressive, for a minute reminded her of Dale. Then again, everything reminded her of him.

"We love you, Mommy," they said in unison.

A vocal trick they didn't need to master. Fern liked to think they spoke to each other in the womb because the second they had talked it had been as one. Fern had always loved it, not so much Craig or the other kids. It had set them apart. To Fern it had been a good thing.

Allie, a force to be reckoned with, led the way. Ella had always been her shadow and sidekick. Fern had talked about this with Craig. He'd thought she was crazy to worry and said what did it matter. Obviously, nothing mattered. She'd tried to be a good parent and had thought staying home, ensuring they had healthy lunches and homemade suppers, waiting on her children all the time and not having a career, were worthwhile sacrifices. She knew better. It had all meant nothing.

Had her mother tried to convey this to her? She recalled returning home and informing her mother she planned to stay home, and her mother had pleaded with her not to. Had this happened to her? Fern felt a tidal wave of emotions, raw and painful, surge up. She remembered fighting with her parents to apply for university, but then her mother secretly helped her fill out the student loan applications all the while whispering not to tell her father. Her mother typing in her fast, neat secretary way a resume so she could apply for jobs to save money for university. How proud her mother had been when she'd graduated; how sad she'd been when she'd moved away and how the look of fear had entered her eyes when she'd announced she was staying home to raise the children. They had a big row and for two weeks Fern hadn't spoken to her mother. Her mother warned her she'd regret her actions. How apt the truth of her words had been.

An ache for her mother hit her. Fern longed to go talk to her mother about Dale, her life, and her unhappy marriage, but the roles had reversed. Maybe though, seeing her mother would be helpful. She knew Rose and Harold had broken the news to Sylvia and she'd been upset. Maybe in a few days, if Fern could muster the energy to leave her bed, she'd spend some time with her mother. Sometimes, even a simple hug from her mother made her day. The question would be what type of day would she find her mother in. Some days the repetitive nature of talking with her mother left Fern exhausted.

"Did you hear us? We love you, Mommy," said Ella.

Fern almost choked on her words. "Oh, my sweets, yes I did hear you. I love you both so much."

Fern couldn't say more. Talking required effort and today she had no more tears to shed. She felt like a dried husk. Her quota of energy was all used up. She didn't have the stamina to face the world of her children. Deep down, she knew it was wrong. They needed her but she could barely breathe. She felt useless. Dale had been cremated. Lit on fire. Her stomach clenched and she broke out in sweat and tasted blood in her mouth. The urge to be sick, again, made her reel. After saying one final goodbye to Dale in the hospital, she'd barely made it into a washroom before throwing up. Then she'd come home to diarrhea. Her body, breaking down, seemed apt. She deserved it.

Sometime later, the twins left her. Alone. She needed space. Had to blanket the sorrow, which had become a powerful emotion, teasingly anchoring her to the bed. The loss of her first-born. She wasn't going to make it. She heard of people having breakdowns before and now understood. Everything hurt. The bedside clock said eleven o'clock. They'd been home since 7 a.m. Fern didn't think she could make it through the day.

She didn't know where Craig had escaped to in the house, but hoped he coped better. The drapes were drawn and she laid in the dark bedroom. She tried to think of anything but Dale's body being burned in the crematorium and failed. Craig had wanted them to bury Dale in the ground. Fern couldn't do it. She couldn't keep him safe against the decay and the bugs and maggots marching to invade her boy's body. She couldn't stomach the idea of something eating him. Fire had seemed the less invasive force of nature. But now Fern kept remembering the large bag of ashes from her father when he died years ago. She thought ashes would be like fine grains of sand but they weren't. Ashes were not powdery, but ground up bones and teeth and while some might say sand-like, they certainly hadn't felt like the fine powdered white sands of Clam Harbour beach her fingers knew intimately. It had surprised her.

The fight over burial and burning with Craig had sapped what remaining strength she had. The drive home had been stifling with silence, treachery and secrets; as poisonous as a rattlesnake's strike. She should have told him about Sean, but speaking of passion and something she couldn't put into words, seemed disrespectful to their plight. Fern had kept her mouth shut and gone straight to bed.

"I made you some tea."

David? Rose forced her eyes to open. They were so puffy from her tears they felt glued to her skin. She turned over and forced herself to a sitting position.

"You made me tea?" She didn't know David knew how to make tea. She'd never once seen him in the kitchen.

He walked slowly into the dark room, carrying the hot mug nervously. Cautiously he placed the tea on the side table.

"Thank you. Is your Dad up?"

David shook his head. She patted the side of the bed and urged him up. He didn't hesitate. At fifteen, he'd already put a stop to her motherly hugs so seeing this side of David surprised Fern.

"He's asleep in Dale's room."

Oh. She hadn't thought he'd go there, but understood his need. They weren't coping well. They needed to "adult", but both of them were breaking in half. Fern knew this but hoped they understood sometimes breaking down led to healing. *Or so I hope.* She prayed it would be in their case but she had a suspicion she might drown in the muck of this change.

"Rose called. She's bringing supper. Duncan's back," he said.

Rose picked up the tea and took a tentative sip. Sweet. Not her type, but David watched her closely so she forced the hot liquid down. "This is lovely," she lied, pasting a faint smile on her face. "Where did Duncan go?"

David slouched down in the bed and ran a hand through his messy hair. "He went with Rose to meet with the minister this morning to help with the arrangements."

"Oh, I forgot he said he'd do that."

"Mom, are you okay?"

Nope. Rose forced herself to take another sip thinking how best to respond. "Not really."

"Me neither."

Rose put the mug down and pulled David in for a hug. Within seconds, they were crying.

"I'm mad at him," he said through his tears, his voice cracking; a reminder he teetered on the cusp of manhood.

"Me too," admitted Fern.

"Why did this have to happen?"

"Oh, honey, there's no why to this. It was a stupid accident and we're never going to be the same without him. But we can get through this," said Fern.

She had to believe. Fern kept preaching that reasoning to herself, sensing the falsehood of it. Fern reached around David for the box of tissues. She handed a pile to him and they each blew their noses.

"I'm exhausted. Would you think me a bad mom if I stayed in bed until Auntie Rose gets here?"

"No. Can I join you?"

Fern untucked the blankets on Craig's side of the bed. Her six-foot-one son got his lanky frame under the covers. "I set the girls up with snacks and they're watching a movie," he said, sounding older than she liked.

"Bless you," said Fern.

She pulled David closer and relished the smell of him. Dale used to smell like this - male teenage sweat with a hint of Axe body spray from yesterday. David hadn't showered and his wavy hair had a life of its own. Fern had always liked his wild hair. She ran her hands through his strands, half expecting him to shift away. Instead, his breathing calmed like it used to do when she tried to get him to nap as a toddler. Within a few minutes, sleep claimed him. She suspected he, like everyone else in their house, hadn't slept in days.

When Fern woke again, she felt suffocated. Thermal heat came from bodies. They nestled leeched to her other side; up against her sweaty back, were Allie and Ella. She rolled over slightly and noticed Ella, as usual, half out of the blankets. She always ran hot, whereas Allie's head was cocooned under the heavy blankets. Her hair would be plastered to her head with sweat, but Allie, the fierce one, was afraid of the dark. To avoid this, she kept the blanket over her head to keep all the scary monsters away. Fern knew this. Craig knew it. They had discussed it at length when the twins were younger because Allie slept exactly like how Dale had as a child. Fern's breath caught in her chest and an instant heavy feeling invaded her. This is what her life would be from now on. Comparing. Always comparing what she'd had to now. How life had been to this...existing.

David, still asleep on her other side, had thrown a skinny

arm across his head. For a moment, Fern tried to savour the sight of her three children piled into the bed like crisscross matchsticks. The smell of sweet and savoury meatballs permeated the air. Rose quiet as a mouse, had come into the house, armed with dinner. Fern raised her head to see the alarm clock: six o'clock. Where had the day gone? The girls were still in their PJ's. Under the blankets, the scratch of David's denim pants scraped her bare leg. Even fully clothed, in sleep, he looked angelic. She stared at them, wishing to freeze them in time, knowing awake their grief would worm into her.

At the moment, she had to pee and brush her teeth. When had she last brushed them or showered? It had been at the cottage. The cottage, when everything had been right in the world. The cottage, which felt like a million years ago, when only four days has passed. The cottage where she'd given into illicit passion, and now paid the ultimate price. Rose would surely slap her if Fern voiced her thoughts, but she couldn't help it. She didn't regret what happened with Sean, but crossing over the line made her realize she would have to own up. Her husband deserved the truth. However, even Fern knew today wouldn't be it because putting one foot in front of the other was a task she could barely manage.

With mother monkey-like expertise, she gingerly climbed out of the bed while her children slept; oblivious they were losing their source of heat. At the door to the adjoining bathroom, she had to grip the doorframe. She turned her head and looked at her sleepy children. She adored them but honestly didn't know them. A lesson she'd learned since Dale's death.

Fern peed, her bladder thanking her. She turned on the shower and waited until hot water streamed from its jet. Then she shed her rancid clothing and stepped inside. She tingled with pleasure for the feel of hot water sluicing over her achy body. She took a deep breath in and set about with the soap. She'd made it through most of the day. A victory of sorts. But all victories come with a price. The one she'd extracted from Willow hadn't been nearly so steep as it should have been, but still it had cut deeply for her sister. Not to her heart, but Fern and Willow weren't cut from the same family cloth. They didn't share the family burdens to care or the longing to partake in each other's lives. Fern understood that now more than ever. Willow had Lily and neither she or Rose could compete. They were the two peas in a pod, shaped in the womb with their own secrets. Fern shivered, recalling the last few pages in Lily's scribbler Rose had found. Some secrets did have the ability to shake you to your core. Who would have thought Lily capable and complicit? Certainly not Willow. Fern cranked the water hotter.

With Lily gone, Willow wasn't interested in her or Rose. At one time the knowledge had made Fern sad. No longer. She'd buried Willow years ago in her own way after the "incident" as her sister dared to refer to it. Funny how a word could change the entire meaning of a situation. Fern thought of an incident as something small and insignificant. Having her sister try to choke her to death had been anything but a tiny blip of a bad day. Even with Willow's sort of apology, the brutality of the act had traumatized Fern deeply.

It had been an awakening to the real Willow for Fern. Afterward, she'd spent days with the painkillers and heating pad giving her comfort as she re-examined her childhood with Willow. She hadn't known her sister. Maybe the decade gap was to blame, but Fern knew that wasn't quite true. The blame lay with Willow. She hadn't wanted to know either Fern or Rose. It had always been Willow and Lily, and Willow's way or no way. They'd all dropped their lives to come to Willow's rescue when she screwed up and even then, she never gave thanks for their help. Why should she? She expected it as the entitled one. She didn't need a crown but wanted the benefits. But Willow had been surprised this time. She hadn't expected Fern to insist or ask for the one thing Willow wanted most from their family – the ancestral land. Most certainly, Fern had shocked herself by leaving Willow with Lily's parting gift.

Fern had pulled in a big favour by asking her lawyer friend to handle things in an expedient manner. The entire transaction had taken less than an hour. Willow had met her at the lawyer's office, four blocks from the hospital, and hadn't said a word as she signed all the papers. Only once the transaction finished had she faced Fern to say thank you. She was thankful for Dale's liver, but Fern recognized her sister's hard expression. She wasn't happy she'd been forced into a corner. Fern knew all about it and savoured her sense of victory. Yes, it had cost her, in more ways than she'd ever let on to anyone. Maybe she'd pay with her soul at the end of her life, but Fern had mustered her courage and forced Willow to give up something to save her daughter. For once in Fern's life, she wanted Willow to give up something she cared deeply for. Most people wouldn't have thought twice, but Willow had asked for time to think about the request. It had been telling to Fern. She half expected Willow to refuse, but when she called, she said she'd meet Fern at the lawyer's office. The win felt better than a million dollars.

Fern shampooed her hair. The smell of eucalyptus and lemon filled the bathroom as the tears fell. She couldn't fight with her emotions. They would have the best of her as she tried to believe in Rose's mantra; they'd get through this. She'd get through this. Not whole. A piece had been carved from her heart forever and it would never mend. No one would understand. She got it. They, her children, and even Craig would all experience the grief of Dale's death in their own ways.

Shutting off the shower, Fern dried off and put on the bathrobe hanging on the back of the door. She opened the bathroom door and tiptoed out of the bedroom. The children were still asleep. A miracle of sorts. They'd probably be up all night but she didn't want them awake.

"Tea's on the stove," said Rose, when Fern entered the kitchen.

"How long have you been here?"

Rose turned off the TV. "About two hours. All is set for Tuesday's service. You okay?"

Fern poured a dollop of milk into a mug and stirred the tea before pouring it into her cup. She indulged in a long drink before moving to sit by her sister. "I'll make it. Where's Craig?"

"He came out when I got here and I think he's back in Dale's room. Have you two spoken?"

"Not about what I think you're referring to. I'm not ready to deal with it. Let's get through this for now."

Rose nodded. "Supper is ready. Listen, Sean called me."

Fern clicked on the TV. The sound a low background noise, essential. "I can't deal with him right now."

"I told him what you're going through. He wanted me to let you know he's there if you need him for anything and more importantly, he'll understand if you tell him to back off," said Rose, hugging a pillow for warmth.

The house felt cold. Obviously, no one had turned up the furnace. Fern reached out and captured her sister's hand. "Thank you. Thank you for all you've done." She fought the tears, and tried for composure.

Rose sniffled and patted her hand. "It's the least I could do. The minister sounded nice. It's a woman. She sounded young, but I liked the tone of her voice. It's not one you knew."

Fern choked on a laugh. "I think the last time we went to church had to be six years ago. Thank you for organizing it."

Her sister leaned forward. "What do you want me to tell Sean?"

Fern swallowed another hot mouthful of tea. What did she want her sister to convey to Sean? *I love him. I need him. I can't do this now. I'm a horrible person for wanting your arms around me.* "Tell him I need time."

"I will. Listen, I've left everything on the stove. Rice is in the casserole dish in the oven with the meatballs and the girls made chocolate chip cookies for you all. I'm going to go home and get some sleep myself."

Fern rose up from the sofa when Rose did. They hugged. The type of sisterly hug you didn't want to end. The type of sisterly hug to magically comfort and soothe.

"Thank you, again, Rose. I'm so glad you're in my life."

Rose had tears in her eyes and the tip of her nose had turned red. "I would do anything for you."

Fern pulled back to look at her sister. "I know. I'm not sure how the next few days are going to go, but…"

"Fern I'm here for you. Anything. You ask and it's done. Take your time. One day at a time. It's our saying we use with Mom."

"Mom, I miss her."

Rose understood what she meant. "Me too. I'm glad Harold came with me so we could tell her together. She cried. It broke my heart. I'm hopeful she understood."

"I'm going to visit with her soon. Maybe after …"

Fern couldn't finish her sentence. Saying funeral felt like a commitment to the end for Dale.

"I think it would be good. She's still our mother and you know, she might surprise you."

Surprises could be good or bad. Wisely, Fern refrained from stating such. She nodded instead. Rose picked up the jacket she'd draped over a chair and then left. Gone but not gone.

Rose had washed the kitchen dishes and swept the floor, and the aroma of her supper she'd made with care and love for Fern's family filled the house. Willow had never once done something like this for either Fern or Rose. Even Lily when she came back from Australia had hosted a BBQ at her rental to celebrate the birth of Fern's third child. Maybe Willow had done this for Lily and she and Rose hadn't been in the loop. For a moment, Fern wondered about the significance of the act. Did it define a true sister? It had to go both ways. It wasn't defined by blood or parenthood. Sisterhood's definition: care and love. With hugs when you were down. With cookies when you needed a smile. With a drink when you confessed you'd gained weight. With a meal when life had gone to shit. That underscored what sisterhood meant.

Pledge and pine. *I will never be able to smell it without thinking of Dale's funeral.* People piled into the church like stunned salmon. Standing room only, said Rose. To many people Fern didn't know but who obviously had a connection to Dale.

It should be pouring with dark clouds all day. Fern ached for the day to play out like such in her head, but she'd awoken to a blistering hot, sunny day – a new record for late October. A day Dale would have loved. She fought to add the past-tense to her sentences and felt frustrated. As a kid, this would have been the type of day he'd skip out the house in the early morning to play with the neighbourhood pack of children until forced in late at night. They'd all scramble into her house for a lunch of grilled cheese sandwiches with carrot sticks. They'd pop in again like a crazy mob for the stash of homemade cookies they knew she'd have on hand in the late afternoon. Always, Fern would check up and down the street for them, catching glimpses of them running across the road for hide and seek or lying like sardines in the hammock tied to the two front trees in her yard. She had prayed for rain, but as usual her lack of faith tested her resolve to believe in a higher purpose.

Fern peeked through the church's side door and wished she hadn't. Her wonderful neighbours filled the pews and they had formed a circle around her family in the last few days. Their kindness had surprised her. Her house was full of lasagnas, meatballs, cards and flowers. Such warmth from her neighbours felt overwhelming but she was so grateful. She'd known most of them for over a decade but their kindness was still a welcome surprise.

The two rows behind the family's reserved pews were filled with family and cousins from the Eastern Shore. Fern spied Kelly, who obviously had been looking for her as she gave a tentative wave while wiping silent tears away. The tears came then in a gush, forcing Fern to run into the old washroom.

The click of determined heels followed her. "You okay?" asked Rose.

Fern shook her head. "Can't do it."

Rose ripped off a sheet of paper towels, wet it under the tap and handed it to her. "Take all the time you need."

Fern hiccupped on another sob. "I can't do it," she repeated.

"You can and you will."

A tentative knock on the door and David's voice, "Mom, you okay?" forced Fern to get a grip. David had become overly concerned about her state of mind and it added to her worries.

Fern used the wet paper towel to cool down the back of her neck. She took a deep breath and unclenched her hands while looking at herself in the old, cracked mirror.

"I'm fine, honey. Be right out." *Lying, yet another sin to add to my list.*

"Okay, just checking," he answered.

She waited until the sound of his new leather-soled shoes faded before sighing and collapsing on the toilet. The shoes had been Dale's and David's feet didn't quite fill them. He, however, had been determined to wear them. It had saddened and thrilled her at the same time, the mix of emotions something she had to learn to cope with. He had insisted on stepping literally in his big brother's shoes.

Rose leaned close. "He'll be okay."

"I know. He's been clingy in the last few days. I'm worried about him and he's worried about me," said Fern, forcing a chuckle. "Kelly and her family are sitting directly behind us."

Rose pulled her in for a light hug and helped to straighten her suit jacket. "Of course, they are. They're more like family than friends. You ready?"

"This is going to be so hard."

Rose had tears in her eyes as she looked earnestly at Fern and gripped her hands. "Yes. Yes, it is."

The truth hit Fern like a nail on a coffin.

"But Fern, we're going to hold you up. We're going to be there for you and the family. So much so, you're going to get sick of us."

"Never," said Fern, leaning in for a much-needed hug.

Linked arm in arm, they left the washroom. She nodded at Craig and he urged all the silent children together. The oppressive sound of the church organ echoed loudly in the side room. In a line of sorts with the minister leading them, they solemnly walked into the church. The twins held hands and Duncan took up the rear. Craig sat on one side of her and Rose. Fern was thankful she'd taken the Ativan her sister had offered her. She wasn't sleeping well and knew today would be especially hard.

When the minister started speaking, Fern prayed for guidance to simply get through the next hour. She didn't want to break down in front of everyone. She had to be strong for her children, who were not coping well. *Who would cope well?* Craig reached over for her hand and she gave it a squeeze. They weren't doing well, but today they had to put their issues aside.

She had always liked St. Peter's church. The décor was old but not ancient. When the children were young, they'd had an active children's service. She'd stepped in to help first in the nursery and then with the children's activities. One year, Dale had snagged Joseph in the Christmas play and had walked off the stage. He had broken his arm. Fern hadn't known he'd broken it at the time as he jumped up, smiled and even took a bow before leaping back up to the stage to continue. Tucking him into bed that night, he'd mentioned his arm hurt. A trip to the emergency room and six hours later, he wore his first cast with pride. Ten minutes later, all his siblings had scrawled their names on it. Dale had been a trooper. He never wanted to worry her, hence why he hadn't said anything about his arm until much later. As the young minister droned on, Fern realized why he never mentioned keeping his relationship with Scarlett. Once again, in his own way, he'd been protecting her.

When the rap music at the end started to play, Fern felt relief. She knew this song. It was Classified's *The Day Doesn't Die* and had been one of Dale's favourites. She looked over at Duncan. Tears streamed down his cheeks, but he cracked a smile in her direction when she mouthed, "thank you." In the end, they were the first to exit the church for the reception inside the hall, which Rose had arranged.

Fern should have pleaded with someone she wasn't up to the reception. She wasn't herself. Not like anyone expected much of her. They simply offered condolences, but their eyes spoke volumes. People said a thousand things with visual cues. They didn't need to speak because pity, sadness and relief were easily conveyed. Fern knew the feeling. She'd sat in a church hall sipping lukewarm tea and eating egg sandwiches with those eyes bearing witness to a family's grief. It had been a cousin's son's funeral, who had overdosed. Fern vividly remembered being grateful it wasn't her family.

Another woman gave her a crushing hug and Fern prayed for more strength. She wanted to slink away, curl up somewhere and never get up again. That wasn't living. She'd get through this. Dale would expect her to. Sad, she thought so little of herself.

Chapter 34

Sean

Sean had always thought funerals were made for cloudy days. It seemed wrong the October sun would herald one last hurrah to beam its rays on the cars packed tightly in the church lot, making them appear sparkly and new. He slunk into a rear pew a minute before Fern and her family walked in looking solely at their feet.

Fern clutched Rose's hand and Sean wished she held his own appendage. He yearned to be the one to comfort her. This separation when they hadn't had a chance to talk about what had happened between them killed him. However, he knew his pain didn't equate to hers and vowed not to add to her burden. Knowing Fern, she shouldered the blame. Sean worried about her mental state. He didn't want her to think their time had anything to do with Dale's death. They were two different things entirely, but having grown up with Fern, he knew that's not how her intricate mind and heart would work. She could reason the felling of a tree in the woods had ramifications for hundreds of years. Over the years, he had started to see the patterns of her thinking linking things together.

If Fern hadn't ended things two months before high school graduation, would he have been spurred to join the RCMP? Probably not. His choice back then hadn't been the natural path he would have chosen. Fern said she wanted out of their small community, citing she wanted more out of life. Sean had never sought more, but when his father's drinking started to get out of hand, leaving became the only option. As a lark, he had applied with his buddy Joel to the RCMP. Joel had always had his heart set on a career of service. It hadn't surprised Sean when Joel easily passed the tests and got accepted. Sean received his acceptance letter in the mail a week later. If things with his father were more on an even footing, he might have found a different career on the Eastern Shore. With Fern out of his life, he'd grasped the opportunity to leave and for over fifteen years he'd stayed away from the place of his birth.

Two years before his marriage finally broke, the last link tying him to the Shore had been his father dying and leaving him the property. He had come back East to settle the estate, thinking he'd sell the property. Once he set foot on the land, his priorities changed. He hadn't realized how much he missed being by the lake or the sea until the second week in the house when he'd finally been able to relax. He'd held a small funeral for his father, but instead of selling the property he'd told his wife he needed time before making a big decision.

This funeral felt nothing like the one he'd held for his father. After all, his father had died at the age of seventy-nine, four months shy of turning the big eighty. How he'd lived that long had mystified Sean as the man drank a quart of vodka daily. Sadly, fate worked mysteriously. Dale's funeral felt oppressive in its sadness for a life on the cusp of living to be snuffed out so senselessly in the blink of an eye. Falling asleep at the wheel seemed an unendurable way to die. One minute alive to the fun of the world; and Sean suspected the two young people going on adrenaline from the concert had certainly enjoyed themselves, and then in a blink, the pull of sleep casting one into eternal slumber and the other left fighting for her life.

Looking back, he'd known coming back to the Shore to bury his father had been more than one simple act. He'd known his marriage had expired long before she acknowledged the affair. He had gone so far as to introduce himself to the local RCMP officers in Musquodoboit Harbour all those years ago. While he hadn't thought much about it at the time, he didn't hesitate to take their business cards. Two years later when he had reached out, he'd discovered an opening would soon be coming as one of the officers planned to retire. Sean hadn't hesitated. Paperwork moved like molasses with the RCMP, but within nine months he had the offer, which came with a slight reduction in pay, but to him worth every cent.

The young people sitting in the pew in front of Sean had obviously known Dale. Two teenage girls cried openly and the three boys had a hard time keeping it together. By the end of the service, Sean had tears in his eyes. He suspected Fern barely held it together. When people dispersed to munch on food in the hall, Sean silently left. He wasn't sure what he'd hoped for, but Fern hadn't looked anywhere except at the front of the church or her children sitting next to her. He felt like the unwelcomed guest not to be acknowledged. With a heavy heart, Sean got back into his car. He'd text Rose later to let her know he planned to wait for Fern. If he had any hope for a life with Fern, Sean knew he'd have to give her time to grieve, even though being without her made him feel like he was the one slowly dying.

Chapter 35

Fern

"You're being too hard on yourself."

Fern groaned into the pillow. She clenched her already shut eyes and inhaled the sweaty, stale cushion she clutched like a useless lifeline.

"Nothing you could have done would have changed the outcome."

Rolling over, Fern forced her crusty eyes open and surveyed the ceiling. "Stop it." She resisted the urge to turn her head to the left side, which is where Lily's voice originated from. "You have no idea how I feel."

Lily sighed. Fern hated she observed such.

"I know you've lost a part of yourself. Trust me, I get it."

The words, shockingly prophetic, forced Fern to sit up straighter in the bed; her back dug uncomfortably into the headboard. Turning her head, there Lily stood, a presence and reminder of all Fern had lost. Lily belonged to another realm or Fern's crazy subconscious. Often, she wondered if the later were true.

"Lily, I can't do it. I can't go on."

"Yes, you can and you will. It will get easier."

That was what worried Fern. The death of a child should never get easy; never slide into the conscious thick folds layered with mundane to-do-lists. *This pain should scrape and peel, flaking off pieces of me, leaving nothing behind but a skeleton.*

"Do you like to play the martyr?"

Lily's question seared Fern. "What are you talking about, Lily? Why would you ask that?"

"Grief is not assigned solely to you. We all grieve. We all lose things. We all hurt and those lucky ones, like you, love. You are beating yourself up because you can't face your feelings."

Fern wanted to hide back under the thick duvet. Instead, she let Lily's words trickle through her palpitating heart. She slipped her legs out from the warmth of the blanket and let them dangle over the side. The mess of clothes on the floor, which normally never happened, informed her how much she'd careened into self-absorption. That plus the two laundry hampers full of the twins' clean clothes, which days later still hadn't been folded. The energy to deal with the daily household chores suffocated Fern.

"How exactly do you want me to face my feelings? My son died."

"And once again you are not to blame," stated Lily.

This time, Fern looked away. Maybe she wanted that blame. It felt easier than thinking how unfair it all felt.

"It is unfair, but that's life. Now you must deal with it. Others need you and most importantly, you know Dale would want you to forgive yourself. You, again, did nothing wrong."

"But he did. He fell asleep. It was a stupid thing. He should have pulled over. And, now he's dead," yelled Fern, shocking herself fully. She had tried for days, which had turned into weeks, to bury her anger, but as a new blade of grass it continually pushed its way through. More than anything, Fern wanted it to go away. Grieving her son meant not being mad at him. Or so she told herself.

"It was an accident. You can't control fate. Live your life. That will honour Dale's life," said Lily.

"Is it wrong I'm mad at him for dying?"

"You're angry with him for keeping a secret from you."

Nodding, Fern knew her sister was right. "Why didn't he tell me?"

"I think you know the answer," said Lily.

"I would have been understanding."

Lily shook her head.

"Okay, I would have tried to be understanding," said Fern.

"Time heals in many ways."

"Your cryptic sentences are giving me a headache," said Fern, flexing her toes.

"You wish you could be understanding, and now, with enough time having passed, you probably are, but then...not so and you know it."

"Stop playing the big sister and I hate it when you're right."

"Fern, blaming yourself for loving someone isn't going to bring Dale back."

Fern looked at Lily. "Deep down, I get it, but I feel I must take blame."

"Why?"

Fern yanked the top duvet off her. "Because our entire family has fallen apart. I miss Willow. I miss what we had, what we could have had. I miss her kids. I miss you. Now this. The losses are killing me and somehow all of this feels like it's my fault."

"Taking the blame isn't going to change things."

"I wish I could explain it, but maybe that happiness I experienced with Sean caused this."

"Oh, because you were a bad wife, made a mistake, or is it because you dared to love?"

"Honestly, I don't know."

"Maybe you'll never know. You're making your own definition of what a bad wife is. Like I've been saying, you want to blame yourself. It's not going to change things. What's wrong with you being happy?"

Fern felt the tears well. How was it possible for her to continually cry? Surely, she'd used up all the liquid within her body. "I miss him so much. It's an ache that won't heal and I don't want it to mend. What if I start to forget him?"

"Fern, you could no more forget Dale than you did me. I am here because of your love."

Fern looked at Lily, her sister who never aged. "I miss you so much. I love that you visit me, but when you leave me…"

"I know. You're going to be okay."

Fern nodded. "Maybe."

"Some days *maybe* is all we need."

With those words, Lily faded away, but the sisterly conversation lingered and dug deep into Fern. Slowly, Fern got out of bed. She pulled the first laundry hamper up onto the bed and made quick work of folding the clothes.

One hamper complete, she repeated her actions with the second. Then she tackled her clothes on the floor. Only when her bedroom looked presentable did Fern take a deep breath. *Lily is right. My family needs me. I can do this. I will honour my son and yes, Lily, maybe is okay.*

Three weeks had passed since Dale's funeral. Fern's head always felt fuzzy. When she had a clear thought, something made her think of Dale and then it took a lot of energy to keep on track. She probably had walked a hundred kilometres around her neighbourhood since her son's death. Staying home was smothering. So many memories of Dale she couldn't process and worse, so many others needing her. Being selfish was new to Fern. She wished she could flip a switch to make her feel better, but nothing worked.

Is this how Willow felt with Lily's death?

After a late October heat wave, the afternoons were starting to cool. Fern knocked on her mother's apartment door. Wendy, her mother's favourite personal companion, opened the door. Fern smiled and breathed a sigh of relief. A short, compact woman with a warm inviting face, Wendy had grown up on the Eastern Shore and knew their family. The delicious aroma coming from her mother's small one-bedroom apartment meant Wendy had cooked one of her amazing meals. She glanced at the counter and saw a delicious looking casserole and, sure enough, a dozen oatmeal cookies graced a plate.

"You are spoiling my mother," said Fern to Wendy.

Wendy gave a tiny chuckle. "Spoiling is fun. You know I love to cook and it's only Eric and me so I have to share, or I'd get fat."

Fern smiled. Wendy didn't own an ounce of cellulite. "How is Eric?"

A beam of a proud mother's smile lit up Wendy's entire face as she tucked her hair behind her ears. "He got accepted into Halifax's police academy program. I'm so proud of him."

"Such wonderful news. From what you've told us, he'll ace it and it sounds perfect for him," said Fern, moving toward her mother.

"We've been looking at some photo albums," said Wendy. "I cleaned the bathroom and did the laundry. I did manage to get her to shower, but it took a lot of sweet talking. I made a list of groceries she needs soon." Wendy, handed her a note.

"I'm so happy you got her to shower. I'll get the groceries tomorrow. Mom, Wendy's getting ready to leave. Would you like to go for a drive?"

"Am I going to the doctor?" asked her mother.

Fern smiled at her mother's normal banter. She always thought Fern planned to take her for a doctor's visit. "No, Mom. Only a drive. Maybe we'll head to the public gardens so we can enjoy the flowers one last time."

"As long as it's no doctor's visit," said her mother, closing the album and picking up the green sweater she couldn't part with.

Fern longed to make the ugly sweater disappear, but didn't want to upset her mother. Textures had started to matter to Sylvia and if wearing a tattered old woollen green sweater made her mother happy, Fern would swallow her pride and help her into the blasted thing.

Fern reassured her mother and said a quick goodbye to Wendy. Five minutes later, they were in the car on their way to the gardens. Wendy was wonderful, thought Fern. They'd gone through a number of personal care workers. Fern had installed a nanny camera in her mother's living room, on the recommendation of a friend. A handful of the personal care workers had been useless and spent more time on their cell phones than talking to their mother and the few who had worked out usually left after a few months for a better paying job. Wendy had been the exception from day one. She'd been with the same private agency for over two years and had instantly hit it off with her mother. Wendy now visited Sylvia three times a week and continuing care workers came in twice a week. She and Rose tried to make up the other two days, usually rotating who would drop by to check on their mother.

The fates were on her side, thought Fern as she slid her car into a parking spot next to the popular Public Gardens. Linked arm in arm, Fern managed to steer her mother through the park paths. Friendly by nature, her mother wanted to chat with anyone who passed them. Fern forced herself to have patience.

"Want to get a cup of tea from the store?" asked Fern.

Her mother smiled. "When have I ever said no to tea?"

Hearing her mother chuckle, the sound so much like Rose, eased the muscles in Fern's shoulders and the worry taking her mother to the park dissipated.

Once they got their teas and an ice cream for her mother, Fern found them a shaded bench to sit on. Fern had to lead the conversations so she quickly found herself talking about the kids.

"Mom, Rose said she told you about Dale," said Fern, stumbling over her words.

Sylvia sipped her tea. She turned her head. "He's on one of his adventures, isn't he?"

Fern felt tears gather. She mused a sad smile. "Yeah, he most certainly is."

"Just like Lily, that one of yours. Home and then off again she was. Always planning for something else. Never content for the now," said Sylvia, as the vanilla ice cream slid down her cone.

"Well maybe. Had Lily always wanted to travel?"

"Oh yes. First off to Australia and then trekking all on her own throughout Europe and then off to Italy. Why? What was she looking for? You should ask her." Sylvia finished her ice cream and then turned her head toward Fern. She pursed her lips into a slight grimace. "She's gone, isn't she?"

Fern understood exactly what her mother meant. The lucid moment of memory often cut straight through the mind and heart. "Yeah, she is."

"And Dale?"

Fern felt a tear slip free. The look her mother gave her was priceless. She leaned toward Fern and hauled her in for a hug.

"I'm so sorry. I forgot. Forgive me."

There was nothing to forgive. It wasn't her mother's fault dementia was eating her memories. "It's okay, Mom."

"There is no greater hole in a mother's heart than losing a child," said Sylvia, further surprising Fern while reminding her this too they now had in common. "I was looking at Lily in the picture book today."

The identity of the album on her mother's lap was finally revealed. "I'll have to take a peek when we get back."

"She had been so unlike any of you. Nothing could keep her still. She wanted to be a pirate when she had been little and I think in her way she became a modern day one. Did you find the cat?"

It took Fern a few minutes to connect the dots. "You mean Buster?"

Sylvia picked up her cup of tea and took a sip. "Yes, that cat was always running off. Why she wanted a cat when she couldn't put down roots is ridiculous. I told her so. Will you tell her when we get back?"

Fern nodded. As fast as the ice cream melting in the cone,

lucidity evaporated. Dementia, a cruel mistress, clutched her mother tighter and tighter in its embrace. Buster had been Lily's cat she'd found two days after being home from Australia. The kitten had been abandoned in the woods, but Lily had caught the soft mews of life and tucked the feral thing inside her hoodie. Her parents had raised the kitten who liked to trek in the woods for sometimes weeks at a time before returning home half its size.

"Yes, Mom. I'll talk to her."

"Good. I need to pee," said her mother and instantly Fern regretted the outing. She hadn't brought a change a clothing and prayed none would be needed.

Fern helped to ease her mother up off the bench and at a turtle's crawl, they made their way to the public washroom. Fate this time laughed hysterically at her. Fern, so used to dealing with messes her Mom made, barely flinched. She threw the soiled underwear in the garbage and quickly proceeded back to her mother's apartment. Then with lots of laughter, she once again urged her mother into the shower to clean her off. She placed the soiled clothing in a bag to wash at her own place. With a second cup of tea, she settled her mother once again on the sofa.

"Want to look at the album, Mom?"

"That would be nice. I haven't looked at this one in a while," said Sylvia.

Fern didn't remind her mother she had been viewing the book an hour ago. Instead, she opened it and a few minutes later joined her mother on a walk down memory lane.

"I'm so impressed you kept up with a photo album for the twins. I found when I had the girls, I didn't have the energy anymore," said Fern.

"Well, I had to do something at night or I would have left your father."

A stark truth from her mother caused Fern to chuckle. "Dad and you didn't get along by then, did you?"

"Nope. He had always been a stubborn man, but we managed. Oh, look at this one. Why is this in here?" said Sylvia.

She held a photo of Lily, in her early twenties, looking wild with long wavy hair and tanned skin with the kitten draped across her shoulders.

"Oh, I took this. She'd been home about two weeks from Australia. I forgot about this. I gave it to her years later," said Fern, feeling sad. "She had already started to plan her next big adventure with her sights set on Italy."

"I remember this. She got mad at me because I wouldn't let her use the car to drive into the city to look for work. I told her to take the bus tomorrow and make calls today, but it wasn't how Lily worked. Lily liked to walk into a place and only if it felt right would she consider asking for employment."

"She had a special knack. I honestly don't believe she had to work hard to find a job. Work seemed to find her."

"You're right. I mean how she landed that job in Australia is uncanny. Luck was on Lily's side."

Fern wisely refrained from saying until the end. Lily dying in a freak boating accident certainly wasn't lucky.

"I don't think she liked being home. Always wanting more.

Not at all like Willow, who never wanted to leave," said Sylvia with a slight chuckle. "Those two were night and day but thick as thieves."

Her mother's statement was true. Could she say the same about her own twins? She handed the album back to her mother. "Well, it's time I got going."

"You off to work?" asked Sylvia.

Sometimes Fern wondered if her mother enjoyed playing her or if she did forget she stayed home. "Nope, home in time to get something on the table for supper."

"Home is good, but working is better. At least you've got a university degree so that's helpful. Not like in my day. My only choice had been secretarial school. I must say I loved to work and miss it. Give my love to the kids and Craig for me," said her mother, turning her attention back to the family photo album.

Fern nodded and promised she would and then got in her car. Today her mother had been motherly. Yes, she'd stumbled with her memory and had an accident, but she'd nailed her advice as surely as an arrow to Fern's heart. Fern chuckled to herself. The visit had turned out to be exactly what she needed.

Chapter 36

CRAIG

A month after Dale's funeral, Craig realized the life he'd had would never be the same for him or his family. He had known it, but accepting it felt like the equivalent of solving a Rubik's cube. No matter how he turned it he only got more frustrated. Today was no exception. The twins' laundry had piled so high in their room he'd caved and had done the washing. The task had been something his wife normally oversaw like a drill sergeant. The clothes had to be folded a certain way, or else. No longer. When he'd mentioned it to Fern, she'd stormed out of the house. It had become her usual method of escape. He wanted to tell her there was no escape, but knew enough to keep his mouth shut. Any little thing these days set Fern off, including asking for help with household tasks. He'd rather Fern angry than her tears, which seemed to condemn him. At the moment, she was taking another five-minute walk, which meant she'd be gone for hours.

"These don't smell right," said Ella, attempting to fold her own clothes.

Mid-afternoon and Ella held a smooshed peanut butter and jam sandwich in one hand. Had she'd made it herself? The normal routine of breakfast, lunch and supper had disappeared, but he told himself they were getting through the days. *That had to count for something. Right?* Her hands probably weren't clean and the clothes would be ruined but Craig suspected she took Allie's clothes.

"What are they supposed to smell like?"

"Sunshine and happiness," said Ella.

Craig took a whiff of a shirt. *Sunshine and happiness my ass.* "They're clean."

She wrinkled her tiny nose. "Mom makes them smell better."

Of course, she does. "Why don't you show me next time what Mom uses."

"Okay," she said, dropping a shirt Craig knew Allie loved into her pile. "You sure those are your clothes?"

She gave him a crafty look and his gut clenched. That look had been mastered by her big brother Dale. Craig had to blink back tears.

Naively, he had thought the days and weeks would get easier. The opposite had happened. His life had become more complicated and harder. He'd confessed his crime to Fern at the hospital and since then, an ice wall had formed between them. Craig wondered if he'd ever be able to chisel through. He couldn't push Fern. She cloaked herself in full mourning, which he understood. Craig had expected Fern to be mad when he'd told her about the gambling and losing it all. He got it. He hadn't anticipated being blocked out of her life. That's how it felt to him. She didn't want him in their bedroom, a big first for their marriage. Sure, they'd had their fights over the years where he'd gather blankets and try to make a bed on the sofa, but his wife had always dragged him back to the bedroom for them to talk it through. It certainly hadn't been easy, but they had done it, talked, and more importantly listened to each other. This felt different. Maybe the death of Dale overrode everything. Craig tried to accept her feelings but it rang hollow. Things had changed with his wife and he didn't understand it. Maybe they had moved beyond each other. It felt like a hurtful thought. Physically he knew his chest pains were anxiety-induced, but couldn't Fern see he needed to be comforted?

He had climbed into Dale's bed the first night when they'd finally come home from the hospital for good. He longed to wrap his arms around his wife. She, however, didn't want him near. He had given Fern space when he sought comfort. Dale's bed didn't offer a soothing balm to his heart and certainly not to his body. Never in his worst nightmares did he expect to lose a child. His nightmares always consisted of losing his job and his family. Part of his nightmare had come true, but Craig was a fighter and he'd get another job. But a child? He felt like he'd lost a limb. Falling apart wasn't an option.

"Why are you in Dale's room?" asked Ella, surprising him out of his own misery.

"Mommy says I hog the bed and she needs her sleep," he lied.

"She's sad. I'm sad. I miss Dale," said Ella with all the honesty of a child.

"Come here," said Craig.

Ella came into his arms and Craig's heart eased. "We all miss Dale and we're all sad."

"When I feel happy, I feel mad at myself," said Ella.

Her honesty undid him. *Why can't Fern be here to deal with this?* "I know how you feel. It's normal." *Is it?* "You know Dale would want you and us all to be happy. Your big brother loved you very much."

"He promised to take me and Allie to the store for a treat when he got back."

So, the kids had known but both Fern and I had been in the dark. A rush of anger at this newfound knowledge gripped Craig. He forced himself to breathe through it, realizing how stupid it was to be mad at his dead son.

Before Craig could formulate the proper response, Ella said, "Why did he leave us? Allie said God took him. God sucks. I want my brother back," she said, with tears in her eyes.

Craig knew he had seconds before she lost it. He understood. Distraction was key. "Listen Ella, let's ditch the clothes and go for a swim."

She jumped off his lap and smiled. "Can Allie come with us?"

Craig chuckled. "Of course. We can't leave her here alone. Go ask her to get her suit and grab the towels and sunscreen, okay?"

She nodded and darted out of the living room and a few seconds later he could hear the twins squealing. Life for the twins existed in the now. Not so much for Craig. He finished the laundry and gathered his own clothing. He thought of placing them in his bureau drawer, but on second thought placed them by the side of Dale's bed.

A pile of Dale's clean clothing sat on the floor. Craig placed his next to his son's. He couldn't deal with gathering it up and thankfully Fern wasn't interested in cleaning out his room. Dale's room had always been a vibrant mess. Fern and he had agreed early on not to interfere in this aspect of their children's lives. Their bedroom, their responsibility. They had been a united front.

Craig darted into his own room and found his swimming trunks. The weather was still warm for the end of October, but this would probably be the last swim for him and the girls.

Taking the girls for a swim warmed Craig's heart. He wished he could have their view of life. He knew they were grieving in their own way, but he liked how they embraced the joys discovered in everyday things. Like swimming. They had the lake all to themselves. The wind had picked up and the air got a bit nippy, but the water had been warm. On the way home, they stopped for burgers because in his heart Craig knew no home-cooked supper had become the new norm in his house.

At the end of the day, Fern had barely spoken two words to him. He didn't push her because deep down he was a coward and didn't want a confrontation. Craig went into Dale's room and stripped down to his underwear. He sat on the bed relishing the scent of Dale. How many more days would Dale's scent fill his room? Thoughts like this made his heart race. He took a sniff of the light blue sheets. They smelled. They probably hadn't been washed in months, but for once he felt grateful. He found solace with the scent of his son still lingering in his bedroom. He punched the pillow, trying to get it into the shape he wanted but no amount of manoeuvring worked. He could march into his bedroom and steal his pillow but thought better of it. He'd do it tomorrow when Fern went for another one of her walks. Walking had become her new exercise routine. He suspected the motion of movement soothed her brain. Sort of how jogging worked wonders on his joints while his brain did a tailspin into 'how did this become my life' mode.

Craig re-read the text he'd received after supper last night. His old friend from Toronto had sent him a message when he'd heard of Dale's death and Craig had gone against his instinct and called him. It had been good to hear Tom's voice. Tom had divorced about five years ago and whined he paid alimony up the ying-yang, but he sounded good. Craig had told him about losing his job and Tom said he'd put out feelers for him. Craig hadn't expected to get a text a few days later saying Bob Feanders, who owned one of the biggest insurance companies in Toronto, wanted to meet. Tom had assured him it wasn't a guarantee, but Craig knew he had to get his butt on a plane and make himself available. Dare he leave Fern to hold down the broken fort?

A soft knock at his closed door had him clicking off his cell.

"Come in," he said, feeling foolish. When had he ever said 'come in' to his wife?

Fern wore cute flannel striped PJs and stood by the threshold of the door with two pillows in her hands. "I thought you might want these."

So much for letting him back in the bedroom. "Thanks." He didn't want them. He wanted his wife back.

"Fern."

"Craig," she said.

They spoke in unison and both cracked a smile. "Go ahead," he urged, sitting up more in the bed.

"I...I need to speak with you," said his wife, whose eyes were looking everywhere but at him. She spied the mess of clothes on the floor and pursed her lips but didn't say anything.

He patted the side of the bed, inviting and hoping she'd sit beside him. Instead, she handed him the two pillows which he used to prop up his back. She closed the door but remained standing, giving him pause.

"I'm sorry," she said.

"Okay, for what?"

"For all of this," she said.

Craig knew what she meant. He shared a sense of blame in all of this too. "Fern, Dale's death isn't your fault. It was an accident."

"I didn't know him. Not really," said his wife, who finally sat on the bed beside him.

Craig wanted to take her hand in his, but refrained. She fidgeted with the loose threads on Dale's quilt. Something was up.

"Fern, do we actually know our children? They're individuals. We love them. We raise them and you've done a wonderful job of it."

"No, Craig. I've failed."

"Oh honey, you didn't fail. This was a terrible accident."

"No. You don't understand. I deserve to feel like this."

Craig yanked out a pillow from his back. "No one deserves this. You've done nothing wrong."

She looked at him and something in his gut twisted.

"I had an affair."

Craig's chest pain intensified. His throat seized up but he didn't speak. He didn't need to; his wife was speaking a mile a minute and it took all his concentration to follow her.

"I didn't mean for it to happen. I'm so sorry. Sean came to the cottage last summer and then when he showed up this summer it sort of happened."

Who the heck was Sean?

She must have sensed his confusion.

She twisted a thread free from the quilt. "Sean was the guy I dated in high school. He moved back home a number of years ago. He's the guy who brought me to the hospital."

The only person Craig could sort of see in his hazy brain was a RCMP officer. "The RCMP guy?"

She nodded. Craig noticed she wasn't crying and it surprised him because he certainly felt weepy. First his son dies and now this. *What the heck?*

"Say something," she urged.

Craig felt his heart skip a beat. His skin felt clammy. Maybe he'd finally have a heart attack.

"Why?"

She hung her head and Craig took great satisfaction in finally seeing tears well in his wife's eyes. His were full.

"I don't know. I haven't been happy in a long time and…"

"Fern, an affair. You slept with the guy. What were you thinking? I can't deal with this," said Craig, his voice hitched. He threw off the covers and stormed out of the bed. Visions of his wife naked in bed with another man hit him like a baseball bat to the gut.

Fern remained sitting on the bed. "I'm sorry."

"You should be. Fern, what were you thinking?"

She didn't respond. Craig picked up the clothes minutes ago he'd thrown on the floor. "You should have talked to me. I didn't know you weren't happy."

She raised her head and gave him a piercing look. "Yes, you did. I told you, but as usual you didn't listen."

"Don't you dare turn this back on me. I wasn't the one who slept with someone else."

Fern stood up. They faced each other. Craig yanked on his pants. "Do you love him?"

Craig expected her to immediately negate the notion. She tilted her head to the side and closed her eyes.

Craig's vision narrowed and his heart started to beat erratically. He pulled his shirt over his head and stuffed his feet into his smelly gym socks.

Fern took a step back. "Craig, it's complicated."

Craig got right in her face. "There is nothing complicated about it. You slept with this guy because you wanted to. Admit it."

"Fine. I admit it," she said, with more balls than he expected.

"I'm leaving," said Craig, through clenched teeth.

"Where are you going?"

"Out!" Craig stormed out of the bedroom. He grabbed his coat and keys and took great pleasure in slamming the front door.

After an hour driving around, he started to calm down. He drove into the city and pulled into a bar. He needed a drink. The bartender thankfully wasn't chatty. He ordered a double whisky sour and tossed it back.

His cell buzzed. Automatically he looked at the number, expecting it to be Fern begging him to come home. Instead, he stared at Tom's number.

"Hello," said Craig.

"Sorry, man, for calling late. Any chance you can catch a flight tomorrow for Toronto?"

"Ah, sure, why?"

"Bob's joining me tomorrow night at the Rotary meeting."

Craig didn't know Tom volunteered with the Rotary Club. It must be how he knew Bob. Lately it felt like Craig didn't know anything. He certainly never expected his wife to sleep with someone else. Thinking about it made him angry.

"Did you hear me?" asked Tom.

"Sure. Not a problem. I'll book an early flight and give you a call once I land."

"Perfect. I've got a good feeling about this," said Tom, trying to lighten the mood.

Craig felt glad someone had a good feeling because he felt like dirt. Maybe a trip to Toronto would be helpful. Maybe the time apart from Fern would do them both a measure of good. He couldn't bear seeing her. When he closed his eyes, he envisioned his wife naked with a man and it made him want to punch something. Preferably the man, but hitting an RCMP officer was out of the question.

"Want another one?" asked the bartender.

Craig shook his head. "Nope. I'm good."

He laid down a twenty. A few minutes later he headed home. Fern had turned on the outdoor light. A thoughtful gesture. He snuck inside, careful not to wake anyone. He went to Dale's room and used his iPhone to book a 6 a.m. flight to Toronto. Then he slowly opened what had been his bedroom door, expecting to see Fern asleep. She wasn't in the room. He breathed a sigh of relief. She was probably with one of the twins. Craig turned on the light, grabbed his travel suitcase from the top shelf in the closet and started packing. Within thirty minutes, he was all set. Already, two in the morning, Craig knew he wouldn't be able to sleep. He placed his stuff by the front door and went downstairs to the rec room to watch

TV. He'd leave the house by 4:30 a.m., which was a few hours away but before he left, he'd write Fern a note.

He might be angry at her but he didn't want to add to her worry. She had spoken the truth. He'd known she had been unhappy and he'd done nothing to help. Did it make him a bad husband? Who knew? In all honesty, he'd thought it had been a phase. The last thing on earth he'd thought his wife capable of was to climb into bed with another man. Fern felt she didn't know her children. Well, with sudden insight, Craig knew for a certainty he didn't know his wife.

Chapter 37

Rose

Rose felt swamped with juggling her hectic life and trying to find that elusive work-life balance. The only thing she didn't need help with turned out to be her ever faithful, loving husband. Something had shifted between them. They now clicked on a scale she would never have imagined.

She came home from the cottage to a house transformed. Beautiful ceiling moulding had been installed, the dishwasher broken for two years, fixed and the big surprise turned out to be a new washroom in the rec room. A transformative change in their relationship and house had happened. He hadn't had a drink in weeks and had been attending AA meetings weekly. Twice a week he made supper and he'd begun making sandwiches for the girls the night before for their lunches. Would it be pressing her luck if she asked him to fix the leaky upstairs bathroom faucet? Rose didn't want to jinx things, so she refrained from asking. Today, she'd come home and stepped inside the house to the smell of spaghetti sauce and meatballs: a Harold specialty. When she'd gone upstairs to freshen up, voilà the tap had been fixed. Harold must have come home early and fixed it. It felt to Rose that he had tuned into her again. The stuff in the house needing his attention for years was being taken care of without her whining about it.

Rose cried tears of joy only to instantly feel guilty. Her good fortune had come about because of Dale's death. Turning on the tap, she used a washcloth to clean her face and then made her way to the kitchen.

"Dinner will be ready in about ten minutes. The girls are upstairs working on homework." Harold flipped the meatballs on the cookie tray before placing them back in the hot oven. Only then did he look up. "What's the matter?"

Rose walked up to him. "I need a hug."

Harold's arms were as hard as steel as they hauled her close to him. Rose tried to absorb his strength. "Harold, I love you."

He smiled down at her with a twinkle in his eyes she was staring to appreciate all over again. "I'll show you how much I love you later tonight," he said, his voice husky with mischief.

Rose punched his shoulder. "Stop it. I'm feeling guilty."

"Oh darlin', not again. We talked about this. We, and most importantly you, are allowed to be happy and it's all guilt free."

"But it's because of Dale," she said with a stutter.

"And is it so bad? Out of all that happened, some goodness

came our way. We rediscovered each other. I think Dale would like it."

Rose tried to absorb Harold's reasoning, but it fell flat. Guilt had always been an ingrained Siteman trait. Must be part of some ancient Scottish heritage gene which got switched on when good things came their way. Did Willow or Lily have thoughts like this? Fern did, but then again, Fern had a weird sixth sense about things.

Rose remembered the day before Lily's death. Fern had come over and the two of them were planning a thrift store run with the kids in tow.

"I keep having this weird dream about Lily," Fern had said, as she sorted through a bin of clothing. It was late August and they were already on the hunt for sweaters and winter gear for the kids. "She's flying a weird kite and then loses it and the next thing I know she's the one flying and I'm yelling at her to come back but she's laughing and won't listen and then I can't see her. Two nights in a row, it's weird."

The hairs on Rose's arm had stood up, as electricity skated along her skin. She had made eye contact with her sister, who had given her one of those 'I have a feeling something is going to happen' eye stares and instantly Rose's gut had twisted.

She said something flippant, not wanting Fern's "feelings" to ruin the day. Even as they laughed and shopped, took the kids to a playground to wrestle off their energy, Fern's uneasy feeling kept snapping back into Rose. She'd dashed into the house with bags of clothing, dumped everything and immediately called Lily, who had answered on the fourth ring. The relief Rose had felt had been buckling. She'd told Lily about Fern's dream and they had laughed at their crazy sister, comparing her to their grandmother in their favourite 'let's make fun of the eldest sister' in a loving way. Lily had told Rose about her plans to go boating with friends the next day and they'd talked a few minutes about the list Lily was making in trying to determine which new country to visit. Rose had pushed Fern's strange dream to the side, praying her sister's premonition of something bad happening to Lily would dissipate. She should have known better. The next day, late afternoon, the minute Rose heard over the radio there had been a boating collision with multiple casualties on the Eastern Shore, she knew to her core Lily would be one of them. Not two minutes later, Fern called her, crying on the phone, begging if she had more information. Ten minutes later, Rose had the confirmation she'd been dreading. Three people had lost their lives in the freak accident and Lily had been one of them.

Fern as usual had been right. Lily had left them for good this time; the warning dream a knife finely crafted to slice into her family. When Rose thought about Fern's strange ability, she shivered, thankful she hadn't inherited the "gift" as her grandmother liked to call it. Fern didn't consider it a gift; Rose knew first-hand. The feelings that sometimes came over her sister were crippling and having a sense of doom coming into your life had to be a horrible feeling when you thought about it. Plus, seeing your dead sister wasn't normal and Rose wanted nothing to do with experiencing any of that strangeness.

Rose recalled seeing that same strange look on her sister's

face. It had been the morning she'd found Fern bundled on the cottage porch a few days after Sean had come into her life. Rose, as usual, had diverted her sister and they'd gone fishing. Later when Sean had turned up decked out in his RCMP uniform, Rose had known with a certainty Fern's feeling had come to fruition. How sad nothing could stop this ethereal pull of fate's web that was connected to her sister.

"What was Fern doing today?"

Trust her hubby to divert her from her morbid thoughts. Rose smiled and brushed her hair out of her face. *Nice diversion.* She talked with her sister daily. They were closer now than ever and it felt good. Rose got a glass and filled it with tap water. "She had a job interview. Said it went well and will know within a week. I hope she gets this."

"Job interview?"

"Yeah, with a non-profit, which means little money, long hours but it's helping people – right up Fern's alley."

The oven timer went off. Craig pulled the meatballs out of the oven and gently tossed them into his spaghetti sauce. "Is she ready for such a commitment?"

"Yes, I think. Things aren't going great with her and Craig. I think getting out of the house will do her good."

"It's only been a few months. I worry it's too soon since Dale died."

Rose started to set the table. "Harold, staying home certainly isn't helping her or will change the fact Dale's dead. She's moping around the house all day when the kids are in school. She needs to do something. Plus earning a paycheck will boost her self-confidence."

"I guess. So, what's up with her and Craig anyway?"

"Wish I knew. He's been working in Toronto and paying the bills, but things don't look good. She doesn't want to talk about it."

"Well, you should stay out of it. She'll tell you when she needs you."

Holding the napkin holder in one hand, Rose looked at her husband. "When did you get so smart?"

"About the same time I convinced you to marry me," said Harold, not missing a beat as he placed the large bowl of spaghetti and meatballs in the middle of the table.

Rose laughed. "I did make you work for me, didn't I?"

Harold poured milk into the children's cups. "Best thing I could have ever worked at. You, Rose, are what keeps me going."

Rose had stopped flirting with Blair. She'd told him Harold and her had reconnected and he said she deserved happiness. They remained friends, but she no longer fantasized about him, which made working with Blair easier. In a way, Dale had saved her marriage. Tears threatened to take hold again, so Rose plopped herself down in her chair. Harold placed the milk by the girls' spots and stole a kiss from Rose. "I hope Fern gets a job."

"You might be right. Maybe it's what she needs," said Harold, moving to the foot of the stairs to call the kids for supper.

What she needs is to take control of her life and return Sean's calls. Rose hadn't pushed Fern, but she thought talking to Sean could help. Her sister was punishing herself. She believed she didn't deserve happiness. Rose understood. She hoped her sister allowed slivers of happiness to invade her life soon, because torturing herself for the death of Dale because she had an affair only made sense to Fern. Rose had tried to get her to see reason. Harold's keen insight startled Rose. Fern had to forgive herself first before beginning to live again. Rose bit into a meatball, savouring the taste.

The boys came up from the basement, arguing over who had been victorious from one of their online games. The girls ran into the dining room like they hadn't eaten in years. No hugs. They were all too big for public displays of affection. Rose missed it but couldn't ask for it. They were growing up and displays of affection dwindled with their age. They all said hi and dug into their meals. This felt normal. This was her life. No more tears tonight. She had her family here around the table and she'd count her blessings.

Chapter 38

Fern

Fern plopped down on the sofa and yanked off her sweater. A month into her job, she felt exhausted but happy. It shocked her. It had been over two months since Dale's death. Yes, she still counted time, days and sometimes hours, but in a way, she felt life moving on. She'd been nervous accepting the part-time work, but enjoyed helping the organization.

Mentally, Fern made a list of what needed to be done, a task she did daily. Tomorrow she had a doctor's appointment scheduled for her mother in the morning and then she had promised to call Craig in the afternoon. She wasn't looking forward to the discussion. Craig had come home last weekend and it had been awkward. He'd slept in Dale's room. Fern took her time cleaning out his room. On Monday night when Craig had gone back to Toronto, she knew her marriage had ended.

They hadn't tried to reconnect. Anger at her for the affair consumed Craig and Fern couldn't forgive him for not putting more into their marriage for years. Craig wanted them to attend marriage counselling, but it would only draw out the inevitable. The sacred vows of marriage had dissolved. Trust on both sides had evaporated. Her with having an affair with Sean and he with gambling all their savings away. The years had carved an insurmountable mountain between them and while Craig offered a half-hearted fight to bridge the gap, she felt it a futile gesture.

Craig wanted to fight for it, but Fern didn't. She had moved on. The state of her newfound employment enabled her independence. She enjoyed meeting new people. She had even gone out with the girls from the office last week for supper. It had been something she'd done all the time when she'd worked in Toronto. Since having the children and staying home, Fern couldn't remember the last time she'd gone out with a bunch of friends for a meal. It had been a fun time and one she planned to add to her roster more often.

The twins seemed to be handling Dale's death okay, if such a thing existed. It might be their age, or their unique bond, but after the first rough month, the girls were now back into the swing of their lives. David had the hardest time. Duncan, old enough to spend time out in the evenings with his friends, coped differently than David, who often was left alone. Tonight, she and David had a date. It was Friday night and she had two tickets to the new Star Wars movie. Duncan promised to be home by seven to watch the girls. It had surprised Fern when David had said he'd see the movie with her. Fern had thought for sure he'd rather go with his brother, but Duncan wasn't a Star Wars fan, much to Fern's chagrin.

Fern forced herself up from the sofa. Five o'clock and supper did not cook itself. Last weekend she'd taught the twins how to make eggs and KD. They had loved the lessons and Fern vowed to give them and David more freedom in the kitchen. David had surprised them last weekend by cooking up the sausages for supper. The nachos and sausages might not have been the healthiest of meals, but he won big brownie points that night. Food equated to fuel. Fern had made it a point to teach her children to cook and be more independent. She had to cope and they all seemed to like their newfound freedom. They were now doing their own laundry and cooking one meal a night. Duncan planned to make meatloaf tomorrow night and a new friend was joining them for supper. Fern suspected it might be the girl he had been chatting on his phone a lot with in the evenings.

It would be nice to see him with a girl. She worried about Duncan in a way she couldn't express. He had taken on the burden of ensuring the younger children had been okay when she and Craig had been useless, but Fern wasn't sure he'd been given the opportunity to grieve for his older brother. Dale had been the shadow, one he'd willingly looked up to, which had been good. Who did Duncan have now? Fern vowed not to read too much into things if he brought over a girl, but she'd view it as progress.

Tonight's feast was a favourite, pancake supper. Friday

breakfast night had always been a hit when the kids had been younger and it made life easier after a long day of work. Fern fixed up the homemade pancakes and added the chocolate chips to the pancakes for the girls. She cut up oranges and voilà, supper was served.

Duncan came through the front door and a gust of cold air followed him.

"How was your day?"

He smiled. Fern's heart dipped. She'd forgotten how cute he could be when his dimples showed. "I got in."

Fern filled up the kettle and placed it on the stove. "Got in?"

"To the overseas program. At the end of the school year, I'm off to Guatemala."

Fern dug out her favourite mug from the cupboard. She had to think fast. *Had they talked about it?*

"Remember, I told you Dale and I both applied."

Not really. "Sure."

"So, it's okay if I go?"

Every instinct said no. Fern poured the boiling water into the tea pot. She looked at Duncan. He needed this. She walked over to him and pulled him in for a hug. "I think it's great. What an experience you'll have."

"So, you're okay if I don't go to university right away?"

"Duncan, if you want to do this, I will support you." *And what exactly will you be doing?*

"But Dad won't. I talked to him on the weekend and he wasn't keen on it."

"Travelling is good. My sister, Lily, travelled a lot. Did you know after high school she did a gap year in Australia?"

"No, you never really talk about her," said Duncan, pouring a large glass of milk.

"Sorry, it's sometimes hard to talk about her. She stayed in Australia for a year, then came home to save up money for a trek around Europe and then was home again for a couple years and then off to Italy for two years. She didn't stay home long. Don't get any ideas, fella, because if I say yes to this, you'll leave me for good."

Duncan laughed. The sound was light and carefree; a reminder she hadn't heard it from him in months. "Mom. Get real. I'm only going to Guatemala and by then I'll figure out my life."

"Well, smarty pants, that's good, because I'm almost fifty and I'm still trying to figure out my own," said Fern, teasing her son.

Fern released her son and took out the milk from the fridge. "I think once you explain what you'll be doing, your father will understand."

"Can you tell him?"

The old Fern would have said yes. Instead, she gave the tea a stir and then poured it into her mug. The mug, which had a picture of a black kitten and the words "Have a Purrfect Day" had a small chip on the lip. Dale had given her the mug almost a decade ago as a birthday gift. It had been her favourite mug for years. One day it would crack completely, but until then, she'd keep it.

"I think it would be best if you talked to your dad about this on your own." Fern tried to get her children to be more independent and it meant letting them fight their own battles.

Duncan picked up the bowl and used the spatula to scrape out the remaining batter. "Yeah, you're probably right. It's weird he's not here."

Ah, the crux of the matter. When Craig had first left, she'd used the excuse he needed a job to support them. Now what to say? "Talk to him. He'll understand."

"Okay, but if he doesn't understand, will you talk to him then?"

Fern nodded. Duncan grinned again and then his smile died.

"What's the matter?"

He dropped the spatula into the bowl. "Dale and I were going to do this together. Maybe I shouldn't go."

"Duncan, if there's one thing I do know about your brother, it's that he'd want you to be happy. Go. Do his memory proud."

"You know I find myself talking to him?"

Fern smiled. "Yeah, I do too. I think it's good."

"For now. If he ever answers back, I'm going to kick his ass."

"Kick whose ass?" asked David, entering the kitchen.

Fern suspected he wore yesterday's outfit. She eyed her youngest son. "No one and don't say that word."

"Ass is not a bad word, Mom," said Duncan.

"It is in my books and mother knows best," said Fern, handing the boys their plates.

David grabbed four pancakes and poured a mountain of maple syrup over them. "You should hear the language from some of my friends. It's disgusting."

"You're disgusting. Enough with the syrup. Hand it over. Where are the girls? Are you and David still planning to see that lame movie tonight?" asked Duncan.

Fern yelled for the girls to join them for supper and yanked out the two tickets from her pocket. "Can't wait."

"Neither can I," mumbled David with a mouth full of food.

"I'm so glad I'm not a Star Wars fan," said Duncan.

Allie claimed the chair next to Duncan and Ella sat next to her. "Is Duncan babysitting us tonight?" she asked.

Fern sat down and helped herself to two pancakes. "Well, not sure how much babysitting is needed since you're both almost teenagers now, but yes, he's home and in charge. And we won't be late."

"Will you bring us home a pretzel?" asked Ella.

"No problem. Do you want one, Duncan?"

"Sure, sounds great. Do you think I should call Dad after supper?"

"Wait until closer to eight to give him a call," said Fern, taking a sip of her tea. "And tell everyone your great news."

Duncan grinned, and then launched into what had been his and Dale's plans to go to Guatemala and work for a year to help build schools and orphanages. It touched her to hear him talk about Dale. The twins soaked up all the information like sponges and David looked awestruck as Duncan told him some of the projects he'd be working on.

Her family was coping. They were making plans and it felt like a positive move in the right direction. They were able to talk about Dale without weeping; a huge move forward. Fern wanted them to talk about him. She didn't want the children to forget their big brother. They seemed to get it. Each day did get a little easier. Fern knew she'd never be whole again, but adaptation had become her new normal. She had to accept the chunk of herself torn apart from her being without a hint of warning and daily act like she wasn't in pain.

The façade of faking all was okay with her life was expected. Pretending was so much better than dealing with reality. Fern smiled as she stuffed a chocolate chip pancake into her mouth. She deserved an Oscar for her daily performance even if no one else noticed.

Chapter 39

Fern

Fern thanked her sister for having them all over to her house for Christmas dinner. The cramped house with so many people made it bearable. The girls were upstairs playing one of the new board games Allie got as a gift. All the boys, except Duncan were in the basement playing something online, which involved a lot of shouting and some cursing from them, Fern tried best to ignore.

"Want more wine?"

"Sure." Fern held out her glass so Rose could fill it up with more red wine.

"So how are you doing?"

"Not going to lie to you. This month has been especially tough."

Rose took a sip of her wine. "I can't even begin to imagine. I thought for sure Craig might join us."

"I asked him not to. I probably should have told you earlier but it's official, we're getting divorced."

Rose placed her wine glass on the nearby coffee table. "What? You're sure about this?"

Fern nodded. "Yes, I am. I feel relieved. We honestly drifted too far apart over the years and while Dale's death might have been the catalyst to make it a reality, you and I both know I haven't been happy for years."

"What about Sean?" asked Rose, giving her a pointed look.

"Oh, Rose, I can't even think about him at the moment. I'm still barely getting through each day." Fern reached out and grasped Rose's hand. "Anyway, don't say anything to the kids yet. I haven't told them. Actually, Craig's coming home next weekend and we're going to do it together as a united front."

Rose made a face. "You've got guts."

Fern released her sister's hand with a light squeeze. "Yeah, I think it will help. I don't want the kids to hate him or me because we're both responsible for the ending of this relationship. Craig isn't a bad person. That's the bottom line. We've moved on. They need to hear this from both of us." Fern reclaimed her wine and took a sip. "Is Harold still in the kitchen?"

Rose smiled. "Leave him. He enjoys cleaning up. You know it's been over eight years since Lily died and I still have days when I miss her so much I physically ache. The other day, I thought about the thrift store when you were telling me about a weird dream you had of her."

Fern sipped her wine. "You mean the time when you stole that beautiful woollen fisherman's sweater from me?"

"I had dibs on it first," said Rose, chuckling.

They each took a sip of wine, sobering up as they recalled the past.

"I hate what's happened to our family. First Lily, then Dad's sudden death, then this weird unsettling relationship with Willow, Mom's dementia and now Dale's death. When I think about it all, it makes me never want to get out of bed," confessed Fern.

"I hear you, but tragedy affects most families. We got our fill. I find myself thinking of the scribbler we found. Maybe it found us. I...it's sort of hard to reconcile Lily's thoughts with the Lily we knew."

"I think Lily had been more complicated than we thought. Mom made a comment a few months ago how she and Willow were night and day and she's right. Willow had been the homebody and Lily the wandering nomad. She didn't fit in on the Eastern Shore."

"But you didn't fit in, either. You left as soon as you could."

Fern smiled. "Yeah, you're right. Guess we had something in common after all. But don't forget I came back and wanted to be back."

"I don't think Lily ever wanted to be back, except for Christmas. She loved that holiday." A huge smile plastered Rose's face.

"Do you remember when she first got back from Australia and I told you about how heavy her second suitcase had been?"

Rose nodded.

"Well, I finally figured out why at Christmas. Her suitcase had gifts for all our kids. She had been excited seeing them open them," said Fern, with a sigh.

"Oh my gosh, you're right. She gave matching boomerangs to the boys and Toby's went straight through our neighbour's window. Minus twenty below zero and my rebels were outside playing in the yard in the snow throwing those stupid things," said Rose, chuckling.

"She gave kangaroo plushies to the girls and I had to put red nail polish on Allie's so you could tell them apart because the girls were going through their 'that's mine' phase," said Fern. "I'm trying to remember what she gave Willow's kids. Do you recall?"

Rose leaned back on the sofa. "Yes. She gave them those musical instruments. Remember how mad Willow was? I think Sam and Scarlett each got a didgeridoo and the two younger ones got clapsticks. I can't believe I totally forgot about those toys. Honestly, what had Lily been thinking?"

"They'd like to play musical instruments."

"Or she wanted to drive her twin insane," chimed Rose.

Fern laughed for real. "Yup, I think that might have been it. I forgot how loud those things could be. I removed the batteries from a few toys the kids loved for that reason alone."

"What mother hasn't, but those musical instruments didn't have batteries," laughed Rose. "I'm actually starting to feel sorry for Willow. How much have I had to drink?"

"Not enough," said Fern.

"I know you must have talked to Willow. How did it go?"

The mood in the living room instantly dropped a few degrees. Fern placed her wine on the table. "It's been hard for her. We had each other when Lily died, but I think losing Lily, her twin, cracked something in Willow that can't be repaired."

Rose nodded. "I get it, but I'll never forgive her for what she did. Please tell me you didn't forgive her."

Fern tucked her hair behind her ear. "I'd like to forgive her, but I'm not there yet. I think I understand her a bit more now, but I can't condone what she did."

Rose finished her wine. "Do you think our family can ever be reconciled?"

Fern reached out and took Rose's hands. "Time has a way of healing things we can't talk about. I'm hopeful someday it might come true but it's not going to happen overnight. Maybe baby steps, like my meeting and talking to Willow, are what's needed."

"Well, I'm not ready to chat with her. I'm still mad at her."

"Rose, staying mad isn't healthy for you. When I first discovered Dale and Scarlett were staying in touch, I had looked at my son lying on the bed hooked up to machines keeping him alive, and my anger at his secret felt sharper than his impending death. How sick."

"Fern, you didn't know what to think. Don't blame yourself for those thoughts."

"I do and did, but I also realized I couldn't stay mad at him and heal. I had to find a way to function in my new reality. To do it, I had to forgive him and slowly I'm forgiving myself. It's an uphill battle and some days I admit to finding myself back at the bottom of the hill, but since I've starting working again, learning to be independent, I'm rediscovering who I am. Better yet, I'm starting to like myself again."

"You're a likeable person. You're naturally kind and good. I'm more inclined to hold grudges like hostages and rarely am I able to let any go."

"I think if you examine yourself, you'll discover that's not the case. Your ex hurt you deeply but you never once complained about him to your sons."

"That's because he's still their blasted father," snapped Rose.

"Really? I believe it's because you're a good person at heart."

Harold walked into the room armed with another bottle of wine. "My wife has a heart of gold," he said, refilling both of their glasses and then darting back into the kitchen to finish up, but not before stealing a kiss from Rose.

"Things between the two of you are good," stated Fern, with a smile.

"Yeah, they are."

Fern patted her sister's leg. "I'm so glad. You deserve to be happy."

Rose laughed. The sound as usual travelled straight to Fern's heart. She smiled.

"It's exactly what Harold says," said Rose. "Listen, I know you don't want to talk about Sean but ..."

"Rose, I can't talk to him. Not yet. I'm not ready. I still feel..."

"Don't you dare feel guilty," said Rose, moving to look out the window. "Wow, it's starting to come down. So much for the sprinkle of snow they were calling for."

"Rose, I hate to put you in the middle, but can you tell Sean I need more time?"

Rose stood by the window, a hand on her hip. She looked so much like their mother for a moment Fern had to blink. Their family gathering wasn't complete and maybe it would never be again. Sylvia had been over during the day and Duncan had a few minutes ago agreed to drive her back to her apartment. Both Rose and Fern didn't want their mother to be alone on the special day and while the day had its tense moments, they'd survived. Sylvia loved being with her grandchildren and they all laughed when she got their names mixed up but so what? It's what families did to cope.

"Do you ever think about Scarlett?" asked Rose, still staring out the window.

Fern rose from the sofa to join her sister. They stood side by side, gazing at the hypnotizing snow. "Almost every day. I hope she's doing okay."

"She's had a few complications but..."

"She's alive," said Fern completing her sister's sentence. Sometimes the knowledge was a bitter pill. "How do you know?"

"She's been quite candid about her recovery on Facebook."

"Oh, I never thought to look and honestly, not sure I want to."

"Scarlett's not like her mother, so you don't have anything to worry about."

Fern looked at the floor. "It's not that. Her updates are reminders for me of Dale's sacrifices."

"Fern, you did good by donating his organs. You have to believe the choice you picked had been right. Dale would be happy," said Rose, empathically.

"I know, but understanding and hurting are two separate things. I'm not sure I can explain."

Rose gave her sister a small hug. "No need. I do get it. Listen I'm off until Tuesday. Want to come over for supper tomorrow? I do believe we cooked enough for an army."

"Can't. The kids and I are spending the day stocking food for the food bank's warehouse. David's idea of helping the community."

"You are becoming quite the benevolent family."

Rose moved from the window to pick up her wine. Fern followed suit. "Yeah, it's sort of strange, but I'm proud of how they're turning out."

"Grandma certainly would be. She had been a true volunteer believer."

"I confess I'm happy we're not volunteering at church suppers. I had enough of it growing up."

"I thought you always liked doing them."

Fern pulled her hair behind her neck. "Some of them. What I enjoyed had been my time with Gram."

"You and she always had a close bond."

Fern laughed. "I spent most of my weekends at her place because..."

"I remember. Things weren't great at home. Not an easy thing to forget."

And Gram understood the touch. Fern needed to change the subject. Thinking about their childhood made her sad. "I'm thinking of getting my hair cut."

Rose gasped. "I think it's a great idea. How short?"

"Not sure. Any advice?"

They talked about hair, make-up, and planning a girls night out. An hour later Fern and the kids hit the road for a slow drive home.

It wasn't the normal traditional Christmas their family had grown up with but change had been inevitable. Fern had to accept their new state.

Chapter 40

Fern

Summer had begun. The days were still crisp and a sweater a must have, but there were signs heat would follow soon. For Nova Scotians, it meant a lot. Winter had come about two weeks before Christmas with two snowstorms and hadn't let up until the beginning of May. Everyone complained and it seemed the weather had become the main topic on the talk shows and nightly news. They'd even made The National news for their new snow record. A record no one wanted, but liked to complain about, citing that they'd survived and it's how life existed on the East Coast. Secretly, Fern suspected a number of Nova Scotians enjoyed the new record as much as they complained about it.

Today, the late May morning sun, bright in its intensity, promised a day of paradise to enjoy outdoors. There were hints of flowers finally awakening from their frozen slumber. The air, tinged with fresh green grass and early daffodils, reclaimed lawns, making the air sweet smelling. Fern had a week off from work. It was Monday and it was going to be a hard day. She didn't look forward to it but the time had come for her to place Dale's ashes where they belonged. The girls were taking an art class at the Art Gallery of Nova Scotia for the professional development day the teachers were having.

So much had changed since last summer. If Fern thought about it, she got overwhelmed. Officially single, her divorce had gone through without a hitch. Craig had secured a new job in Toronto with higher pay fairly fast and he provided for the family. Fern suspected he'd met someone and she found it odd the notion didn't bother her. She was moving on and wanted Craig to find happiness. Her part-time job had become full-time and financially things were improving on the home front. After years of not earning a pay check, she took great pride in bringing one home now.

She pulled into Rose's driveway. Rose, as usual, was waiting on her stoop. She hopped down, but before she got into the car, Fern rolled down the window. "Where's your boots?"

"Where are we going?"

"You'll see," said Fern.

Rose went back inside and grabbed her boots. She shoved them in the back of the car as she shimmied into the passenger seat. "You are being Ms. Smug. What's with all the big secrecy?"

Tears welled in Fern's eyes. "I...Dale's ashes are in the back. I want to bury them."

Her sister shut up. She buckled in and with steely determination said, "Lead the way."

Fern felt grateful and chose to ignore the tears pooling in her sister's eyes. She wasn't up to chit-chat for the drive. Rose turned on the radio and immediately clicked the button until an oldies rock and roll station caught her attention. She turned onto the highway heading East with the song *"I Will Remember You"* by Sarah McLachlan filling the car. The tune, strangely fitting.

Rose glanced her way. "We're going to the land, aren't we?"

Fern nodded and wiped away a tear. "I want a part of him buried next to Dad."

Rose reached over and laid a hand on her jean-clad knee. "I think it's a perfect idea."

"Thank you," said Fern, gathering herself.

They continued the drive talking about safe subjects: new recipes, their jobs, Harold, the kids and people at work. At the start to the land's old country road, overgrown with grass and tree limbs trying to obscure the path the locals still used when they wanted to fish on the lake, Fern parked to the side. They replaced their shoes for rubber boots and Fern grabbed her backpack.

Rose eyed the large backpack. "Want me to take it?"

Fern pulled her cap down. Her chin quivered. "No. I'm good."

Rose pulled her in for a hug. "Come on. We can do this."

This was her sister she loved so much. When Fern's strength waned, Rose didn't hesitate to step up to the plate to lend what she needed. Today, Fern tried to gather her strength, breath it in deep, because with every step she took up the muddy path it felt like someone two hundred pounds overweight sat on her chest. Her fingers tingled and a dull ache took up residence in her lower back.

Halfway up the road, Rose turned and gave her a look. "You okay?"

"Not sure. This is harder than I thought. I didn't tell the kids I kept some of his ashes. Not even Craig knows."

"Oh, Fern. Why?"

"Not sure. I guess I wanted to keep a part of him with me."

"Dare I ask where you've kept it?"

Fern cracked a smile as she stood and stretched her back. "Underwear drawer."

"Figures. No one would dare go there. Did you ask Willow if it's okay for us to bury him here?"

Fern lifted her head and looked around at the trees. The white pines looked like a bug had infested them. More than half had brown needles. They were so close to the Atlantic Ocean, even a mile into the woods, the scent of salt clung like a soft blanket to the trees. Old man's beard blew in the slight breeze. "No. It's okay though."

"If you say so. Oh my, Fern, look at these bushes. These are all blueberry bushes lining the road. I am so coming back for these," said Rose, letting her hand reach out to caress a few of the plants. "We're going to make blueberry jam this summer. Okay, enough. We're moving like old women."

"We are old women," said Fern, with a chuckle.

"Nope. You might be old, but I'm not giving in. Hair dye, diets, waxing and working out, it's my motto."

"Waxing? You're nuts. I tried it once and it hurt way too much. No thank you."

"Yes, my darlin' it does, but it's worth it. Lasts a lot longer and Harold likes it."

"TMI, sis. TMI. I heard Harold's been helping Toby Baker build a cottage in the woods."

"Where on earth did you hear that?" asked Rose, picking up her stride.

Fern guessed her sister stored mental notes about the blackberry and raspberry bushes dotting the old road as she craned her neck this way and that.

"One of my co-workers' brothers was helping him clear the land and he mentioned who had helped with the construction of the cabin," said Fern.

Fern picked up her pace to keep up with her much more athletic sister. They finally crested the first large hill. Fern placed her hands on her knees; the pack on her back chafed and felt heavier with each step closer to the homestead. They both knew a puddle the size of a small lake would be at the bottom, hence the rubber boots. "Kelly might have also told me."

"Of course. Yeah. It's a project keeping Toby out of the house, if you ask me."

"What makes you think that?"

"His wife is pregnant and crazy," said Rose, flippantly.

"That's not nice to say, Rose. Pregnancy can change people. I'm sure you're exaggerating."

Rose stopped walking. "Nope. I'm not. Toby spilled the beans to Harold last week. Said he came home on Friday night after spending last weekend finalizing the baby's room and she'd wrecked the room. Harold said it had been the first time he'd heard more than a few words from Toby. Harold thinks their marriage is in real trouble."

"Do you know what happened?"

"She used a hammer to smash the crib to pieces and took a black marker to the fresh paint. I think Toby spent the weekend at the cabin."

"She needs help."

"Oh yeah, he knows it but she refuses to get help. I sort of feel sorry for him."

"You feeling sorry for a Baker? I knew the day would come."

Rose stuck out her tongue. "Don't even go there."

"I have no idea why you hold such a grudge against them. They're all a bit needy, but overall nice. And, you know, they'd drop anything to help anyone in the community."

"Fern, stop it. That teenage memory is burned into my brain and sorry, sis, but I'm not sharing."

Fern knew not to press. "Is there anything we can do to help him?"

"There goes that heart of yours. Fern, you can't fix everything. If Toby can't get her to go see a doctor, complete strangers suggesting it isn't going to help. It's why I don't mind Harold's out there helping him on weekends. They should be finished in a month. Harold's now helping Toby with a small shed for his tools. Harold said the cottage is cute. Yeah, I know.

His words, not mine. Toby made it for her. It's a big surprise for his wife, who if you ask me, doesn't deserve it."

"Well, I hope it helps, but if she destroyed the baby's room, my gut says it might not." Fern gingerly placed her foot on a large rock as she manoeuvred around the puddle.

They were quiet as they crested the last hill. The old house, over one hundred and sixty years old, greeted them. The meadow, a mess from the machines which had been used to clear a large path from the back of the property to the lake, looked diseased. The start of construction of a large barn sat to the right, while four cement foundations made it clear where the cabins would go. The place had changed, but parts stood rooted in time and Fern prayed with a sense of hope they'd be able to find the old cross marking their great-great uncle's grave. Beside his grave, a hand-painted stone marked their father's resting place and directly to the path to the lake stood the Lily memorabilia.

"I've missed this place," said Rose, taking Fern's hand.

"Me too," said Fern, giving her sister's hand a squeeze before letting it go to move toward the rundown shed. All the machines were gone and the quiet of the place felt comforting. She lifted the pretend lock and stepped inside. Fern found a shovel and together they made their way to the back of the property.

They walked past the outcrop of cedar trees which had been the height of their father when they were growing up and now were well over ten feet tall. It had been the place where they played pretend kitchen. Rose, four years younger than Fern, always acted the chef part and Fern her happy servant. They had spent hours of their childhood making pretend soups, pies and stews huddled among the cluster of trees, closeted away from prying adult eyes.

Rose spotted the old cross first. A great-great uncle had been buried there and next to him, their father's ashes had been placed in the earth. Fern had to work the rusty shovel into the still hard-crusted ground. Within a few minutes, she'd dug a deep hole. She pulled out a large Ziploc bag from her backpack. Inside were the remains of Dale, her first-born, her baby, her child. Today she had to finally let him go.

Rose stood as a silent witness. Fern couldn't look at her sister. She suspected Rose shed a stream of tears.

Forgive me for not knowing you, for not paying attention to who you were becoming. Fern let the tears fall. Gently she poured Dale's remains into the small space. Rose said a prayer as she took the empty bag from Fern.

Fern's shoulders shook with her tears.

"Let it all out, honey," said Rose.

Fern cried with true anguish; the sound animalistic in its agony. This hurt more than Dale's funeral, but it felt crucial to Fern being able to forgive herself and move on with her life. She knew there would be other moments like this, when she'd break down, but what she did today felt like a difficult healing step.

A number of minutes passed before Fern could get herself under control. She turned and looked at her sister. "I miss him so much."

Rose had tears streaming down her face. "Me too. I'm so

sorry this happened to you, to us." She handed Fern a tissue. They each blew their noses, the sound echoing in the forest.

Fern bent down to use her hands to pat the cold dirt over Dale's ashes. "This ache I feel will never heal."

Rose sat beside her and joined her in the task. "I think it's normal, Fern. I'm glad you brought him here. Do you remember when we brought the boys up here the summer when the ants swarmed?"

Fern patted the dirt flat as she placed a chunk of grass over the hole. "I remember you laughed so hard you wet your pants."

"I forgot about that incident. I remember the boys shrieked like mad while the girls quietly walked into the shed to wait it out. Dale freaked when the ants went up like a cloud. He and my Toby ran into the outhouse. They smelled like the outhouse the rest of the day," said Rose, trying hard not to laugh.

Fern hiccupped and then laughed. She couldn't help it. She'd forgotten that memory. As they patted more earth around the hole, they shared stories about what the kids had done over the years at the camp. They talked about Dale but they also spoke about the time the twins fell in the pond trying to catch tadpoles, how Harold thought he could fix the outhouse only to end up breaking it, how once the old stove had caught on fire and they'd had to smash off a part of the flue and haul it outside to stop it from burning down the house. They also talked about the times Willow had joined them with her kids. She recalled Scarlett slipping on the wet rocks by the lake only to fall head first into the lake and bash her forehead open. Rose and Fern had looked after Willow's children so she could take Scarlett to get stitches. The children shared the small beds, tucking their bodies in tight. Fern had been shocked when the latch opened in the middle of the night only to hear Willow and Scarlett sneak into her room. Fern hadn't hesitated. She'd lifted the covers and Willow and her daughter's cold bodies filled up the queen-sized bed. Willow said thank you and said Scarlett didn't want to miss any of the fun with her cousins.

"We certainly did have fun," said Rose.

"I do miss it and if I'm honest, I'm finding myself missing what we had with Willow as much as missing Lily," said Fern, wiping her hands on her jeans.

"When I think about the memories, I do too, but ..."

"But it's not enough," said Fern.

"Not when I know she has this and how she got it," said Rose, her voice sounding tight and sad.

When they finished, their faces were streaked with dirt and tears, but they were smiling.

"I have always loved this place," said Rose, casting her head up to look longingly at the old house.

"Me too. Rose. Listen, I've got to tell you something."

Rose stood up slowly to wipe her filthy hands on her jeans. "Go ahead."

Fern watched her sister stretch. She did the same. Her bones ached and her heart still felt heavy. "I did something not-so-nice."

Rose turned and looked at her. "What do you mean?"

Fern couldn't speak. She reached into the backpack and pulled out an envelope and handed it to her sister.

"What's this?" asked Rose, giving her a questing look.

"This is ours," said Fern, walking slowly away from the graveside down the hill to the old house. Her sister didn't follow. She stood anchored to the spot. Fern didn't give into temptation to watch her read the document. What she'd done couldn't be named. She'd extracted a price from Willow some would say she shouldn't have. Fern smiled and opened the front door to step inside the house. It smelled exactly the same as the cottage - musty, woodsy and full of family memories. Fern did not regret forcing her sister to choose. Everything came with a price and she'd forced Willow's hand. Fern would not let guilt eat this victory. She'd paid the ultimate price and would never forget it. Knowing it didn't make what she'd done any easier.

Chapter 41

Rose

I can't believe I'm doing this. Rose tugged on her purse strap and marshalled her thoughts as she opened the door to the café. She spotted Willow immediately looking serene but drained. *Good, she thought, she deserves sleepless nights.* Her sister gave a little wave with a tentative smile and immediately Rose felt guilty for thinking ill thoughts.

"She is your sister after all," said Harold, who had urged her to meet face-to-face with Willow, pointing out Fern had.

The shock of discovering Fern had pushed Willow to give up the land to save her daughter had at first made her euphoric. However, after listening to Fern talk about Willow's state of mind, slowly over the course of weeks, Rose had realized something: she missed her sister.

She walked into the small café off Portland Street in Dartmouth with mixed emotions. Rose ordered a black coffee. Armed with her cup, she sat at Willow's table.

"Two chats in so little time," said Willow, glibly.

Rose took a sip of coffee. "I did want to ask, how is Scarlett doing?"

Willow leaned back in her chair. "Good. She's resilient."

Is that code for she's on her own so I'm assuming she's okay? "I'm glad. What happened was a terrible accident."

"Accidents seem to like our family," said Willow, ripping off a piece of her cranberry muffin to eat.

"How's the muffin?"

"Dry and bland. Not like yours."

Rose felt her eyes widen. *Wow, a compliment.* "I glanced at their baked goods but they all looked overcooked."

"This had been the lesser of the evils," said Willow, finishing off the muffin with a grimace. "What can I say? Hunger called me."

Rose nodded. "I'm glad you and Fern worked out something."

"She finally told you. I guessed you jumped for joy."

"Actually, I'm not as happy as I thought I'd be. I'm sad we couldn't be more like sisters."

"As I said to Fern, you had each other and I had Lily."

But Lily's gone, so who do you have now? "Fern said she gave you Lily's scribbler we found at the cottage."

"She did. Makes for interesting reading material. How is the cottage?"

"Basically, the same. Do you remember the time Lily found a wasp's nest?"

Willow smiled. "She brought the thing in the house. How could I forget? We spent most of the day either killing wasps or putting toothpaste on stings the kids got. Scarlett had gotten the worst of the stings that day and Lily kept laughing at our antics."

"Dale didn't get stung. He refused to swat at them."

"Not sure I could have stood still. I hate bugs."

"At night, we drank your homemade beer and I still regret it."

Willow laughed. The sound surprised Rose. She hadn't heard it in such a long time, she'd forgotten how much she liked it and how much it reminded her of their mother.

"We all got sick that night. Thank goodness the kids had crashed by then. Fern ended up throwing up in the small bathroom sink because I claimed the toilet, you had the kitchen sink and Lily spent most of the night throwing up into the flowers off the porch. I can still picture it," said Rose, smiling.

"To this day, I won't touch the stuff," admitted Willow.

"Oh, I've had some good stuff since then, but I don't make it."

"I didn't make it. My hubby at the time did. I should have known better. He had always been useless," she said with a twinkle in her eye.

Rose felt herself relaxing. "Why did you leave him?"

"Easy, I thought I could change him, but I learned a hard lesson. I couldn't. We weren't suited for each other."

"But he adored you."

"Adoration isn't enough."

No truer words could have been spoken. "Mom would say he's your children's father."

"Yeah, she would and did. Trust me she loved him and when I told her I planned to leave him, she got mad at me. But it had been my marriage, not hers. I vowed after watching Mom and Dad fighting all the time, I would not live with negativity in my life. Rose, walking away had been brutal but I had to do it. I had to try to find myself."

"I hear you. I did the same with my ex." *But I didn't run home and make my parents buy me a house.* Rose took a sip of her bitter coffee to silence her thoughts. "So, what are you doing these days?"

Willow took a moment to look around the café. "You see those prints on the wall?"

Rose twisted in her chair to look at the large photographs displayed. There were eight black and white shots of up-close personal items, like a toothbrush next to pieces of crushed shells. The juxtaposing jarred the viewer. She liked them. She turned her attention back to Willow. "Are they yours?"

Willow nodded.

"I love them," said Rose, meaning it. "I had no idea you were into photography. These are really good."

"This is the second café to agree to display them. I took them with Lily's camera."

The knowledge sliced into Rose and she couldn't help but

sigh. "Well, let me tell you something, Willow, you are a better photographer than Lily."

"I'm getting there. I'm not sure if Fern told you, but after she died, I sort of spiralled out of control and I had to get help."

"She mentioned it. I'm sorry we weren't there for you."

"It wouldn't have helped. I resented you and Fern and honestly, I sort of still do. Anyway, I've been seeing a therapist. She's the one who suggested when I told her about Lily's camera, which I inherited, to take pictures," said Willow, with a sad chuckle, "I see the world through what had been her lens. It's helped me."

"I'm glad. I get why seeing Fern and I might not have been helpful. I think the decades separating us growing up displaced us as sisters."

"Maybe. Or maybe I'm messed up."

Rose reached across the table and placed her hand on Willow's. "You are not messed up and Fern and I aren't perfect. Our lives have been bumpy, maybe not like what you went through, but we had each other. I'm so sorry you felt you couldn't come to us and I am sad when I think about the rift separating us to this day."

"I think letting go of the land has been helpful for me. When Fern first demanded it, I had been shocked but after a couple of months, things got easier. When I started to pick up Lily's camera again and turn the images into what I wanted, I finally felt a sense of freedom. I think the land acted as my anchor I didn't see holding me down, until it got taken from me."

Rose nodded. "You know I get it. Listen, I have something for you."

"What?"

"A box of stuff from Lily's place. Harold found it when we were cleaning things out. I think you should have it. It's in the trunk of my car."

Willow turned her head but not before Rose saw the tears quickly gather.

"You sure?"

"Yeah, I am. I think she'd want you to have it."

Willow sniffled. "Thank you, Rose."

"No problem. Come on, let's get it. I've got to get to work."

They finished their coffee and walked outside. Fern opened the trunk and handed the medium-sized box into her sister's outstretched arms. She felt for the first time things between them might actually get mended.

"There's more scribblers in there. I think it's more journal entries from her. I couldn't read them," said Rose, feeling tears prick her eyes.

"Thanks again. You've surprised me."

Rose smiled. "Maybe we both surprised ourselves. If you need anything call me. You have my number now, so I think we should do more of this."

"More of what?"

"Talking and listening. I didn't know until today, I've missed you. It would be nice if you could join us at the cottage sometime. We did have lots of fun back in the day."

Willow silently cast a quick look into the box. "Maybe, someday. I'll think about it. Thanks again for this."

Should I hug her? Willow turned and walked away making the choice for her. Rose closed the trunk, got in the car and smiled. Then she called Fern, planning to let her know she'd done the unthinkable – talked to Willow. She highly suspected Fern would be pleased with her actions because she certainly was herself.

Chapter 42

Sean

Time had become Sean's enemy. Late summer and anxious for any word from Fern, he kept his days busy. He'd given Fern time. Rose had made certain of it and while he knew she had been correct, part of him hated it. He longed to comfort her, but Rose with her short text messages made it clear he had to stay out of their lives for a while. Fern had to cope with the death of her eldest son, Dale, and according to Rose, she and Craig were divorced. The knowledge pleased Sean, but he couldn't do anything with it.

Rose told him Fern would contact him when ready. *When would that be?* He had become obsessed with the seasons. Christmas had been his own kind of nightmare. He'd missed his daughters and had taken extra shifts to keep occupied. Lonely, the only person he wanted in his life was Fern. He'd ignored the pleas to join his office buddies for extra-curricular activities and instead poured himself into work and fixing his house.

Both his girls had come to Nova Scotia for a visit, which had surprised him, and while his eldest liked the improvements he'd made on the house, this province wasn't in their blood. They didn't feel the longing for the Atlantic, the desire to sit in a canoe for hours and paddle leisurely down a lake, the joy of hiking through the wet woods or picking sand dollars from the beaches. The knowledge made him even sadder, but what could he expect? His girls had grown up in Calgary. They had friends and his wife's family there and were more settled with their lives out West than any ties to the East.

Another Saturday and he planned a day of fishing. He pulled into Weaver's parking lot. Kelly was down at the dock giving instructions to George. She spied him and waved him over.

"This is for you," she said, handing him a note.

Sean opened the small folded piece of paper and his heart speed up.

"I'm at the cottage," Fern had written.

"Thought the note might make you happy," said Kelly with a saucy smile.

Sean grinned. "When did she get here?"

"Two days ago, and she's alone. George is taking more supplies to her."

"I'll do it," said Sean, feeling slightly anxious she hadn't tried to reach him on his phone and worried she had been on the island by herself.

George didn't hesitate. He loaded the last of the boxes into the motorboat and stepped back onto the wharf. Within a minute, Sean steered the boat to the island. Ten minutes later, he pulled alongside the familiar wharf. After tying the boat to the wharf, he made his way through the stone path to the cottage.

He knocked on the door. No answer. Sean knew where he'd find her. He made his way to the hammock and sure enough, there was Fern, sitting on the canvas giving small pushes with her feet to make the hammock swing.

"Fern," he said.

She turned her head and looked at him. She'd been crying. "I prayed you'd get my message."

Tempted to say she should have called, instead he moved to where she sat on the hammock. A photo album claimed her lap. She patted the side next to her and he sat down. Finally next to Fern, he longed to hold her but felt hesitant.

She wrung her hands and had a hard time looking at him.

"You okay?" he asked.

She turned and looked at him. Her eyes were full of tears. "I've missed you."

Sean wrapped an arm around her shoulders and brought her closer. "I've missed you so much."

"I'm sorry I never called. I couldn't. So much had happened."

"Fern, it's okay. I'm here now."

It took her a moment before she could speak. "Would you like to meet my son, Dale?"

Sean looked at the photo album. He smiled. "I'd love for you to tell me all about him."

Fern opened the book and took her time showing him pictures and telling him stories. Sometimes she cried openly and took a few minutes to gather herself. Sean didn't fight the tears forming in his own eyes. This was the Fern he loved. She had loved her boy with every breath and now he was gone. When Fern finished showing him the album, he pulled her up from the hammock and they walked silently back to the cottage. He led her pass the kitchen and into her bedroom. He cupped her face in his hands and kissed her tears away.

She melted into his arms and with tenderness and care, Sean removed her layers of clothing. Only when they were both naked did he look directly at her.

"Please don't leave me again," he said, voicing what he'd longed to say months earlier. Their separation had been hard on him, harder than he'd expected.

Fern kissed her love into him and only when they both needed oxygen did she answer. "Never. I need you in my life."

Sean smiled. "Good, because you're not getting rid of me again." He eased her down to the twin bed.

They took their time and the slow torture of their love-making made up for the agonizing months of separation. The woman he'd loved all his life was finally back in his world. Their journey hadn't been straight-forward and would certainly have its ups and downs, but for Sean, holding Fern in his arms meant finally finding peace and coming home.

Chapter 43

Fern

Sun streamed through the window. A glorious day beckoned. Fern smiled. She felt hot and sweaty. They had been at the cottage for the rest of the week, but after the first night in her twin bed, they had slept in Rose's bedroom. While the setting had felt strange to Fern, having Sean in her bed felt wonderful. Sean had proved to her many times during the night how much he'd missed her. She told him all about Dale and her children and even about Craig. He listened; a strength he'd always possessed. Fern tried not to be jealous when he talked about his girls and ex-wife. He probably felt the same when she talked about her family, but they weren't keeping secrets. She told him about the joy of working. He told her about what he'd done to his family's house and today he had planned for them to visit.

"Should we get up?" asked Sean, kissing her bare shoulder.

Fern grinned and wiggled her bottom against his not-so-subtle erection. "Well, something most certainly is up already." Fern felt certain she'd burned off a thousand calories over the past few days, thanks to their lovemaking.

He hauled her closer. "I think we need another half hour before we leave this bed."

Fern didn't complain when he rolled her over and kissed away all the years they'd been separated. An hour later and feeling like a teenager, she finally got out of bed. They were parting ways because Fern had to get back to her kids, but they'd promised to reconnect tomorrow night. The boat ride back to the mainland went too fast. Fern felt slightly anxious as she got in her car and waved goodbye to Sean, who started a new shift in a few hours.

Kelly came out from the canteen and Fern rolled down her window.

"How you doing, love?"

"Better," said Fern, trying hard not to grin and failing miserably.

Kelly winked and said, "I'm glad. It warms my heart to see you and Sean together again. He's one of the good ones."

"He certainly is. Thanks again for letting us use your boat for the week."

"I heard you got the land back," said Kelly, as she waved at a passing car.

"Did Rose call you?"

"Well, that's the thing, I've been meaning to speak with you about something."

Fern sat up straighter in the car. Kelly looked cagey, which wasn't like her. "About what?"

"Well, I know you and Willow aren't speaking but as much as it kills me to admit, Sam's been wonderful and helpful around here. George and him are friends and he's actually been living with us for the past six months. Guess he and his stepfather weren't getting along. I feel so bad. I planned to tell you and Rose after your weekend retreat but then..."

Then my son died. Fern placed her hand on Kelly's. "Kelly, I'm glad you're helping Sam. It's not his fault what happened with his mom. I honestly didn't know he needed help. I'm glad you could help and sort of mad at myself for not trying to keep in touch with her kids. They are after all my nieces and nephews. I should also tell you, both Rose and I have started talking to Willow again."

Kelly breathed a sigh of relief. "I'm pleased. I'm so glad you don't mind. Sam's a good kid. He and George are thinking of going into the landscaping business together."

Fern nodded. She tried to picture Sam but failed. The only image popping into her head was a short, skinny kid with a thatch of straight black hair. He hadn't looked like Willow, whereas Scarlett could be her mother's double.

Kelly straightened and looked up toward the back of the canteen.

"He's here, isn't he?"

Kelly leaned back down to the window. "Yeah, said he'd like to talk to you but I didn't want to ruin your day."

Fern smiled, unbuckled and then got out of her car. Kelly

waved and then the next thing Fern noticed was Sam walking toward her. The lanky teenager she remembered was gone. Born six months before Dale, he had the timid walk of a man trying to find his way. At well over six feet, a beard graced his face.

"I'm going to leave the two of you," announced Kelly, when Sam got within arm's reach.

"It's good to see you, Fern," said Sam, his voice more man than boy.

"You used to call me auntie," said Fern, stepping into his space to pull him in for a hug.

"I'm so sorry about Dale," he said, sniffling.

The next thing they knew, they were both hugging and crying, latching on to each other, trying to reconnect. Fern led Sam toward a deserted picnic table and they sat there, still holding hands.

Fern listened to Sam and felt even more ashamed at her actions. She might have been mad at her sister, but giving up seeing her nephews and nieces, not being connected to them in any way had been wrong. She learned Sam quit school, spent time on the street and only recently reconnected with George and his family. His mother didn't want him and he couldn't stand his stepfather. Fern's heart ached. If she'd known any of this, she'd have taken him in.

"I'm so sorry I wasn't there for you," said Fern, meaning it.

He wiped a tear away. "At the time when things with you and Mom were strained, we had no idea why. Years later, Scarlett and I found out. By then, Mom had pretty much left and I had a few hard years. Scarlett, as you know, kept in touch with Dale but I haven't seen Willow in two years now."

"That saddens me," said Fern, catching the fact he referred to his mother by name.

"Like you, I've had some issues with her. Things changed after Aunt Lily died."

"I'm coming to realize her death had a profound impact on Willow and our lives. I'm glad things are going good for you."

"Kelly's family is wonderful and George's been helpful."

Fern looked up at the canteen, noticing Kelly on the stoop. Fern waved at her and then George nodded and walked away. Kelly had been worried about how Fern would react to Sam but in her heart, Fern knew Kelly would take Sam under her motherly wing.

"Kelly's family is wonderful. I hear you and George might be opening up a landscaping business."

"It's our goal."

"You know Rose and I have the land. I'm guessing Scarlett told you. How is she doing?"

"She's coping. It's been hard on her. She and Dale were quite close. Willow told her you made her give up the land for Dale's liver. Is that true?"

A blush of embarrassment flushed Fern's face. "It's a bit more complicated."

"Well, good for you, auntie."

"Thanks. I think. I should have kept in contact with you all," said Fern.

"Families are weird," said Sam with a slight laugh. "I'm glad we reconnected and Scarlett would love to see you. She's living with a friend in Dartmouth."

This news shocked Fern. "I thought when she got discharged, she would be with her mom."

Sam laughed for real this time. "Maybe for a night, but that's long enough for Willow to do her motherly act. Scarlett got dropped at her apartment the next day."

"But she had been still recovering."

"My sister is pretty resilient, plus Kelly made her a ton of food George and I delivered, so trust me she's okay. Listen, I've got to get back to work. I'm helping George get the cabins ready this week. I hope we can stay in touch."

Fern reached into her purse and yanked out her cell. She shared her details with Sam and asked for Scarlett's information. Ten minutes later, she hit the road to home with a newfound sense of awe at Willow's children.

Three weeks later, Fern sat in Sean's pickup truck. She took a sip of the Tim's tea they'd picked up and felt anxious when they finally pulled into his family's old house. Immediately Fern noticed the differences. A new red tin roof graced the small three-bedroom home.

"Come on in," said Sean, helping her out of his truck.

His boyish charm was adorable. He held her hand and led her inside. They took off their boots and then Fern kept quiet as Sean gave her a tour of the place.

Only when seated in the living room did she notice the books lining the homemade bookshelves he'd created.

Sean ran a hand through his hair, blushing.

"I'm slowly reading them."

"Sean, please don't feel you have to read them to impress me."

He laughed. "Actually, it might have been the reason in the beginning, but turns out I like most of them. Thomas Hardy especially," he said picking up the book *Sons and Lovers*, a classic she'd read in high school.

Fern wrapped her hands around his middle. "That's because it's naughty."

"You should have told me in high school and I might have gotten a good grade on that paper."

"Oh, so it's my fault you got a D?"

"No, it's your fault it took me over twenty-five years to fight for you. I should never have let you go back then. I'm putting the place on the market in the spring."

"What?"

"I applied for a transfer to the Tantallon branch and I found out last week I got it. I want us to be closer and I figured you wouldn't want to uproot the kids."

He turned her so she rested in his arms and they gazed at each other.

Fern felt tears well in her eyes. "You don't have to relocate for me."

"I know, love, but I want to. You've been gone from my life too long and life is short. As much as I love this place, it's only a house. It's not a home without you, Fern. I love you and plan to tell you and show you daily." He grinned wickedly and gave her a wink.

Fern smiled and felt her heart expand. She'd weathered the storm. The love and peace settling inside of her she needed but she also knew it had more to do with her finding herself again. Maybe a part of the missing piece in her life had been the love Sean offered. Fern knew for a certainty she would never compromise again. She deserved to be loved. Sean showed her his willingness to move mountains for her. She would be grateful every day for his empathy, for the love of her children and her life.

Would roadblocks come again? Probably. Life challenged everyone and constantly changed. Having love and family in her life made it worth those agonizing minutes.

He brought her hand to his lips and kissed her knuckles.

"I love you too." She let him lead her to his bedroom and giggled when she spied the king-sized bed.

Sean, a man of his word, believed actions spoke louder. He used his lips, hands and body to show her how much he enjoyed loving her. Fern relished every second of it. Closer to fifty years of age, Sean made her feel like a teenager all over again.

She'd known since a young age beautiful things grew after a storm. The miracle of life did get tested. Letting herself love Sean was the reminder her new life was worth fighting for even when born from tragedy.

. . .

Fern was spending two night at the cottage on her own. She wanted to spruce up the place and also needed some quiet.

However, the roar of a motorboat meant Fern's day to herself at the cottage wasn't to be. For a moment, her heart and soul prayed it might be Sean. As the boat came closer, her heart lurched and sweat glided down her back. George steered the boat but his companion was none other than Scarlett. Fern wanted to run and hide inside the cottage and attempt to pretend she wasn't home, but she shelved that childish thought. Shelving emotions, thoughts and partitions of her life was her expertise. Walking toward the dock, she mustered her courage and waved at George. Expertly, he steered the motorboat up to the dock. Scarlett gingerly stepped onto the dock. *Fragile.* That adjective slammed into Fern. Gone was the confident, hyper-sleek girl she remembered. It wasn't lost on Fern how George watched as Scarlett slowly moved from the dock to the shore. Worry was a hard crease on George's normal smooth forehead. Once Scarlett was safe on the shore, he moved the motorboat slowly from the dock and then it was the two of them, Fern and Scarlett.

"I came to visit my brother and when I heard you were out here, I had to see you. I hope it's okay," said Scarlett , standing straight on the dock.

She is shockingly thin. Fern fidgeted with a loose string on her shirt, barely resisting the urge to haul her niece inside and get her settled on the sofa with blankets.

"Yes, of course. It's good to see you," said Fern, meaning it.

Scarlett smiled and slowly made her way to where Fern stood further up on the path.

"Come inside and I'll fix us something to drink," said Fern, amazed at herself.

"Fern, you have every right to be mad at me," said Scarlett, surprising the heck out of Fern for nailing exactly how Fern felt.

Fern didn't trust herself to speak. Instead, she went into the kitchen, added water to the kettle and tried to get a hold of her emotions.

"Fern, I can leave if this is too hard. I told George to come back in fifteen minutes if he doesn't get a text from me. I get it. It's okay," said Scarlett, standing in the kitchen like the unwanted guest she was, but Fern realized her anger wasn't completely directed at Scarlett. She still was miffed her son hadn't shared this secret with her.

"He should have told me you two kept in touch," said Fern.

"Yes, we should have."

"Not you, Scarlett. My son. It's him I'm mad at and that's sick."

"No, it's not. I tried to get him to tell you years ago, but he didn't want to upset you and then we simply left it. No harm done, we thought. How wrong we were. I still can't believe he's gone."

"You and me both. How are you doing?"

"I'm not going to lie. It's been rough."

I bet it has. However, as Fern looked at Scarlett, the knowledge she was alive because of her son eased something which had still been unmoored inside of Fern.

"I miss him," said Scarlett.

"I think I will always miss him. Where are you staying?"

"For the next little while with my brother. Kelly has a spare room and she thinks I should stay with them until I'm more myself."

"I think it's a good idea. Your mother…"

"Oh, we don't speak. Haven't really in years. I'm not a part of her life," said Scarlett as she eased herself into a kitchen chair.

Why did that statement make Fern sad?

"What about you and her?"

Fern poured the hot water from the kettle into a pot. "A bit. We talked in the hospital and I actually reached out to her about four months ago."

"How did that go?"

"Not as bad as I thought it might," said Fern, smiling. "Actually, she told me some things I didn't know."

"I bet," said Scarlett, with ice cutting through her voice.

"Did you know she had a nervous breakdown and checked herself into the hospital for help after Lily died," said Fern, pouring the tea into cups.

"You sure?"

Such trust. "Yeah, I am. It makes sense to me. She's still on medication, so I think it's helping her."

"Maybe."

Scarlett thanked her for the tea and took a small sip. "I

wondered if you had a memorial for Dale or are planning anything."

Fern took a deep breath in. "It's been on my mind lately, but I'm not sure. Did you have something in mind?"

Scarlett drank more of her tea. "No, not really, but I'd like to help if you do plan one."

"Thank you, Scarlett. I appreciate your offer. I'll talk to the children and get back to you on that. I think first though, they'd like to see you."

"Really?" asked Scarlett, clearly surprised.

"Yes. I'd like us to re-establish our relationship. I shouldn't have cut you and your brother out of our lives. It wasn't fair to you, and our children and most importantly, it wouldn't be fair to Dale's memory," said Fern, finishing her tea, amazed she wasn't crying.

Without thinking of her actions, Fern reached out and captured Scarlett's hand and gave it a squeeze. When she looked at Scarlett, she saw the tears pooling in her eyes. She knew she'd be a mirror image. For a long moment they simply sat there, connected by the touch of flesh sculpted through tragedy.

"Tell me about the times you went away," said Fern.

"You sure?"

"Yes," said Fern, finally releasing their tethered connection to lean back, needing the feel of the ancient wooden chair to ground her with the reality of the now.

For the next forty-five minutes, Fern listened, nodded, laughed and got teary-eyed a few other times, but mostly it was cathartic to hear Scarlett talk about her son, Dale. It was clear from the tone of Scarlett's voice and her facial expressions how much Dale meant to her, which was a balm to Fern.

When it was finally time for Scarlett to leave, Fern promised to get in touch with her and her brother soon. She wanted her children to get to know their cousins once again. They should be allowed to have a connection and it hadn't been right for her to slam the door shut on them simply because it made it easier to deal with Willow.

"Thank you once again, Scarlett, for coming here. It means a lot to me. I'll be in touch soon and we'll plan Dale's memorial together with the family."

Scarlett gave her a hung. "Thank you, auntie. That means a lot to me."

Fern fought the tears this time. *Auntie.* She hadn't been called such by Willow's children in what felt like forever. Gamely she squared her shoulders and returned Scarlett's hug. She helped her walk down the path and eased her into the motorboat.

"All good?" asked George.

"Yes," they answered in unison, causing them both to giggle and for George's face to ease into one of his relaxed smiles.

Fern waved as the boat slowly eased from the dock and then she stood on the wharf until the sound of the motor was a small rumble.

"I'm glad she came to visit."

Fern didn't need to turn around. She knew Lily would be behind her. Steadying her nerves, she slowly turned toward the house. Lily, in all her splendour, stood on the path.

"I had hoped you might show up," said Fern.

"I know. I'm not staying, but I wanted you to meet someone," said Lily, moving from the path to beach.

Before Fern saw the beach she heard it. The sound of someone skipping stones. Every nerve on her body tingled and her breath shallowed with anticipation and fear. Dare she follow? Her legs, leaden, moved slowly over the rocky path. There up ahead, she could see a stone completing four skips on the mirror calm lake. She knew to the marrow of her bones, Dale, her dead son, would be on the beach.

"I'm not ready," said Fern.

Lily stopped her ascent to the beach. "Yes, you are. It's time."

"No. I can't do this."

"You can and you will. One thing about you is your strength. It won't fail you now."

Fern swallowed. Her throat felt parched. If she left now, would he come back? Fear she could mess this up, or he'd leave, overrode her senses and automatically her limbs moved forward to the beach. There he stood. Her Dale. Looking exactly how he had the last time she'd seen him alive. Dressed in his ripped jeans he loved and a black shirt, he radiated youth.

"Good to see you, Mom," said Dale, sounding exactly the same.

His voice, his bearing, everything about him made it seem like he had simply returned from a day at work. The opposite clawed into Fern's subconscious.

"I can't believe it's you," she said, not bothering to wipe the tears sliding down her cheeks.

"We're not staying long. We've come to say goodbye."

Fern took in the entirety of the scene. Lily stood to one side of Dale, and she flashed back to the time she had first discovered her younger sister teaching Dale how to skip stones. It was at this beach. All week he'd been trying to master the art and no matter how often Fern tried to explain the trick, he couldn't catch on. He desperately wanted to because Duncan, his younger brother, had quickly grasped it and had managed to skip a stone twice. It was almost the end of the week at the homestead and Lily had said she'd pop over for the last night. By mid-afternoon, Fern had figured she'd ditched them for something more exciting and much to her surprise, when she'd gone looking for Dale she'd found Lily carefully showing him how to flick his wrist and voilà, he'd started skipping stones. Fern had been so happy for Dale but also because Lily hadn't erased her sisters out of her busy social calendar. They'd had a beautiful last day at the cottage and the memory, buried deep, eased into Fern.

Then Dale's words penetrated her logical mind. This was it. Both Lily and Dale were saying goodbye for good. This would be the last time she'd see them. An ache welled within her.

"I don't want to let you go."

"I know, but I want to go," said Dale.

Lily placed a hand on his shoulder. Fern slapped a hand over her mouth, trying to stop the anguished cry.

"I waited for him. I wanted to be the one to walk with him on the next journey," said Lily.

Fern crumpled to her knees; the beach stones dug into her flesh and she didn't care. "Thank you, Lily," said Fern, her voice muffled while her heart, which she'd thought broken, started to splinter. Lily, however, was right. It was time for them. She had to be the one to let them both go. It was selfish of her to keep them tethered to her. *Dale and Lily deserve to be free and happy and even if it kills me, I will let them go.*

Then before she knew what was happening, both Lily and Dale were hauling her up from the ground, engulfing her in a mammoth hug. The heat of their embrace felt glorious.

Fern looked up into her son's eyes. Everything about him screamed he was alive. Fern knew the mirage wouldn't and couldn't last.

"Goodbye, Mom," said Dale.

She nodded. There was no way she could say those words to her son. Every part of her wanted to hold him forever. Fern knew it was selfish. He came to say goodbye and she had to be the brave one and let him go.

"Goodbye, sis."

Fern instinctively tightened her grip on them, trying with her might to absorb how they felt while burning the scene into her brain. She wanted to remember this moment for a lifetime and while she knew it would never be enough, *maybe* it could be okay.

Fern cleared her throat, finally finding her voice. "I love you both so much."

"We know," said Dale, smiling at her. "It's time for us to go. Don't be sad. I'm ready."

"We're ready," said Lily, capturing Dale's hand in hers, as she playfully tousled his hair.

Fern's chin wavered. She was a blubbering mess. With a nod, like she'd see them again tomorrow, she watched the two people she loved walk for good out of her life. One minute they were there like two ordinary people holding hands on the beach and then in a blink of an eye, gone.

Fern knew she'd been given a gift. Lily had after all these years waited because she'd known what would befall her family. That sacrifice made Fern love her sister even more. A peace she had never felt before settled through her and unbelievably she found herself smiling. Dale would not be alone as he started his new journey and the knowledge made it easier for her to make her way back up to the cottage. She had a phone call to make. For once, the no cell phone rule would be thrown out the window. Rose deserved to know exactly what had happened today because most certainly the majestic spiritual magic of the family cottage had truly come to life.

Epilogue

Out of the blue, Willow had called Rose and told her partially what she'd discovered. Something had happened to Lily in Italy. Rose had urged her to continue to investigate. Two days later, Fern had called and they'd had a civil conversation, which made Willow smile. A day later, Rose and Fern had shown up at her apartment with an envelope full of cash. They were the ones who had urged her take a trip to Italy to find out more information. Now, armed with a ticket to Verona, Italy, Willow was finally leaving Nova Scotia.

For the last time, she turned the key in the lock to her apartment. She never wanted to see the muddy brown four-storey building in Dartmouth again. It had been a place she'd slept in for the past two years. It had never been home. Willow had made sure of that. Home had been something she'd left when she'd walked away from her husband and children. She knew now she'd needed professional help, but at the time, leaving had been the only way to keep breathing. The choice, like all choices, had consequences. Her children, thanks to her exit, had their own abandonment issues. Motherhood hadn't been instinctive to Willow. She'd chalked that up to being a young mother with a terrible partner. The sad reality was she'd often felt like giving her life to her children meant placing her life on hold. Even back then, it hadn't been fair. Not anymore, she thought, as the taxi drew up to the curb.

"Where to?" asked the driver.

"The airport," replied Willow, hoping it wasn't a chatty drive.

"Looks like a nice day for a trip. Where you heading?"

"Italy," said Willow, turning her head out the window, hoping he'd get the hint.

"You'll love it. The people are very friendly," said the driver, who went on to explain the time he and his wife went to Rome a few years ago.

Willow nodded but didn't add to the conversation. The drive felt endless and fast all at once.

She paid the driver and for the first time in her life, stepped inside the Halifax International Airport. The place teamed with all walks of people. She smelled fast food from the nearby cafeteria area and something else. Willow smelled a zest of life coming from the people as they hustled their way through the place to their next destination and it gave her a bounce to her step.

I can do this. I am doing this.

Taking charge for once to do something out of the ordinary felt exhilarating. She'd even mustered the nerve to call Sam and Scarlett to tell them her plans. Both had been surprised at first but in the end excited for her adventure. She'd promised to tell them all about it when she returned, but some lies enabled others to live happy lives. She'd learned Scarlett was staying with Sam and both were living with Kelly, and none of it upset her. Years ago, she would have probably attacked Kelly on the street if she'd seen her, but all those emotions, thanks to the blessed pills, were bottled up tight where they belonged so she could function in the real world.

The shock of Rose, out of all her sisters, being selfless had knocked Willow off kilter. For years she'd hardened herself against her two older sisters. Maybe time was nature's bandage. *Or maybe letting the ancestral land go is enabling me to breathe.*

At first, when Fern had stated her demands for Scarlett, she'd been fuming, but now, months later, she felt nothing but relief. She had finally ended her relationship with her boyfriend, and realized she should have walked away years ago. Being on her own for the first time in years should have scared Willow. Instead, she felt like she had a new lease on life. One she wasn't going to ignore. This was her time.

Willow hadn't bothered with a suitcase. Instead, she had shoved a few outfits into a large backpack, thinking Lily would have been proud of her. Normally a clothes horse with enough shoes to fill her own closet, she'd stepped into her twin's sneakers and gone with the basics. She planned to follow the journey her twin had undertaken all those years ago in Italy – the city which had changed Lily for good.

Willow knew in her heart both Rose and Fern hadn't noticed Lily's change when she'd come back from Italy. Her twin had had a knack for being the life of the party and telling everyone what a great adventure she'd had. Willow had seen through the façade and noticed the cracks. She'd tried to talk to Lily, but her sister had continually brushed her off. After reading her diary of sorts, Willow slowly started to understand the Lily she'd known; the one who had shared a womb with her, who as it turned out had been a deceiver. *Maybe we aren't so dissimilar after all.*

She'd told Rose and Fern she'd be the one to venture to Italy, but she hadn't mentioned she had no plans to return to the province. There was nothing left for her in Nova Scotia and for once she was going to be the adventurous sister.

After learning the real reason why Italy had changed Lily, Willow had planned her escape. Thanks to her two sisters who had come through for her in the end, she now had the means to follow through. Years ago, Willow would have bent in half with her discovery and probably spiralled out of control, but not anymore. She had a therapist she saw regularly and medication she took religiously. She never wanted to get to that dark place again and if it meant having checks and balances in place to cope, so be it. The thought she could now reach out to both Rose and Fern did lighten her load.

The Heart of Family

There had been four scribblers in total from the box Rose had found containing some of Lily's stuff. Clutched in her hand was one of the scribblers. She'd cried for hours while trying to get through them. The tattered blue one had been the last one she'd read. Willow watched out the window as the plane took off. Her first flight, and Willow should have been excited. Instead, she felt sad and angry. She hadn't told Fern or Rose what she'd discovered. Willow, the type of person who needed to see to believe, wanted proof. Hence why she sat with clammy hands on the plane, flying the skies to a destination she'd never longed to visit. Adventure had been Lily's thing. Staying home had suited Willow, but not anymore.

August 23, 2013

She has dark tufts of hair and the bluest eyes I've ever seen. The birth was easy compared to this. I'm so sorry, little one. The nurses want me to give you a name, but it hurts, for I can't keep you. I promised to give you up. It's the right decision. It was all a mistake what happened and I'm the fool who thought it could be more. I'm so sorry, little one. Why can't you be screaming your head off like the baby in the next room? It would make my task easier. Instead, you stare at me with a calmness I find unsettling; like you know you must gaze at me while you can.

What can I tell you about myself? Here is all you need to know. I love to travel and want to see the world and I love my twin sister, Willow, like I do you, with an instinct nestled and tied to my heart.

The nurse came in again. She said I can't leave the room until you are named. Such a daunting task, to leave you, but it had been the deal I had to make. Only I didn't know what it meant until you became real. Even when you grew big inside of me, I thought it would be a simple thing – give you up. How stupid and naïve I've been all my life. Now, I understand why Willow kept Sam and Scarlett. She too had options and I used to laugh at her for not choosing what I thought I'd pick. Now, I know this option will kill me.

I want to give you a ridiculous name, grace you with something laughable, but that's the anger in me speaking. I kiss your head, inhaling and memorizing the smell of you, wishing I could bottle it with me.

I turn as the nurse comes to stand at the door. I want to shout at her to leave, but know the time has come. I hand her the form and she looks at it and then graces me with a smile.

I turn my head to the wall, my arms now free as my entire body fills instantly with the ache of missing you.

I named you Speranza, my little one. Hope in English, but I know Italy will be your world so thought it best to start you on the right footing. You, my little one are my hope and dreams even though you will never know me, or feel the Atlantic Ocean spray on your face or come to know your cousins who I love with all my heart. This wasn't an easy choice but for you it's the best I can offer. Please don't be mad at me. I love you with all my heart, but there are some deals one can never escape from and this is the best I could do.

Willow read the page again before closing it. She'd had no idea Lily had a child, but she certainly planned to find out what had happened. She owed it to her twin, and to her family and nothing would to stop her.... Read an excerpt from book two of the Saga of the Shores series, **The Spirit of Family**.... Eric's eyes had grown accustomed to the dark. He knew the time was near and from habit over the years, didn't need to check his watch. He eased open the door of his pickup truck and gently closed it. It felt sacrilegious to let it slam shut. His right hand held a bundle of black-eyed Susans and he had a dishcloth and two water bottles in his backpack. He leisurely strolled down the road. The moon shone like a lighthouse, its beacon of light bright in its intensity as it graced the small Atlantic harbour. With the last hoorays of summer ending, the chill of the night was welcomed. When he got to the spot he couldn't erase from his brain, he knelt down and tipped out the decayed bouquet, which sat in a cheap plastic vase, letting the brown, clumpy sediment water from the bottom get absorbed into the dirt on the side of the road. He took the two plastic bottles out of his pack and using one, scrubbed the larger vase clean. Task accomplished, he ensured the rotten flowers were pushed further into the ditch, filled the container with clean water and placed the new flowers in the vase to carefully erect it by the wooden guardrail.

Thank you for the flowers and you remembered these are my favourite, said Sally.

Eric smiled. Sally's voice had been silent for a long time and for a while he'd thought he wouldn't hear her childlike cadence again. He wasn't sure if it was good or bad, for Sally's voice was the only sound Eric heard as clear as day.

Eric didn't hesitate. Using his hands, he signed, "I thought you might like the flowers. You remember when we stole a bunch from Mr. Smithers?"

Sally laughed. *How could I forget? I got grounded for ruining my sneakers because of the stupid mud I fell into.*

Eric ached to turn his head to see if she'd be by his side, but breaking the magic of the night made him fearful. Illusion often felt more real and solid and tonight Eric ached to hold tight to his memories.

"You only fell in the mud because you went to the right of the path, not the left," he signed.

Wrong. You got your rights and lefts mixed up. You're the reason why I fell in the mud.

"I did tap you on your shoulder and pointed in the right direction."

I had no idea what you were doing. One minute you tapped me and then you were running ahead of me. It's totally your fault I got grounded.

"You should have seen the mud?"

Oh, you've got to be kidding me. Seen the mud. You're mad. You told me you knew the paths in the garden.

"I did, which is why I tapped you to follow me," said Eric,

smiling, his body relaxing with the easy banter he'd missed so much.

The flowers are really lovely. Who knew you'd become a romantic?

"I was always romantic. I was simply broke when we were teenagers," signed Eric, realizing time had no meaning to the depths of his sorrow. "I miss you."

Sally sighed. *I thought if I left you alone, you'd move on.*

It took more willpower than normal for Eric not to turn and look for the sound of the voice coming from his left side. "My decision, not yours. Plus, I could say the same to you."

Sally chuckled. *Not sure it works the same. You do need to forget about me.*

"Never. Can't. Sally, you wove your way into my life from the get-go."

I don't want you to waste your life on what we had.

A slight gust of wind shuffled the bouquet. For a second, it looked as if a hand was brushing the top of their petals. They'd had the same argument at least twice a year since Sally's death. It was familiar and sad at the same time.

"I'm not wasting my life. I've moved on. I haven't stopped living."

Have you met anyone?

"Countless women are in my rotation," signed Eric, smiling.

Countless. I'm impressed. I didn't know so many women liked a man with grease under his fingernails.

Sally was right about the grease under his fingernails, but it made his heart flutter. She's always loved examining the differences of their hands. Hers were tiny, pale and always clean. Every few days, she'd have a new hue of fingernail polish to show off. His were callused from tinkering in the garage and usually layers of grease had embedded themselves in his palms' crevices and under his nails. He'd scrub them in an attempt to get them clean, but always failed at the task. "It's the new trend. Women like men who work with their hands."

I remember your hands and would agree with your assessment. How's the garage?

"Busy. Very busy. I'm thinking of hiring someone to help," signed Eric, glad they'd switched from the painful memory-filled topic of what had been.

You should. All work and no play makes Eric boring day-to-day. She came back.

Eric didn't need to ask who? Kim had arrived a day ago after supper with a knock at her mother's door, totally out of the blue. His father had been having supper, as usual, with Margaret. According to his father, Kim had looked lost and shaken, but Eric had yet to see her. Eric wondered if Sally's voice graced him tonight because Kim was back on the Shore.

"You said she'd come back, so guess you were right," said Eric, the chill etching deeper into his bones. Next month he'd wear his winter boots. He wiggled his toes in his sneakers and wished he'd thought to wear a hat.

She shouldn't have left. I think I made her leave.

"Sally, don't be silly. She left, like they all do, looking for greener pastures."

It freaked her out, hearing my voice, but I couldn't leave her. Did you ever talk to her?

Eric shook his head. He'd tried once to mention to Kim about Sally speaking to him, but by the time he'd mustered his courage and attempted to write out the words in his notebook, she'd left. It wasn't like he could corner her at the high school and confront her with what was happening to him. Back then, she'd been living her own version of trial by public prosecution, which Eric surmised was a living nightmare. They weren't in each other's company a lot. Margaret had only started inviting Eric with his father for supper at her place when Kim went away to university. Those homecooked meals were a treat. While Eric could reassemble a small engine in record time and discern within ten minutes what was wrong with a vehicle, he could barely cook mac and cheese.

"No. I never spoke to her about you."

Why?

"Honestly, I'm not sure she'd believe me."

Make her believe. She can't leave this time. She's needed here.

"What do you mean?"

It means Kim belongs on the Shore, like us. She's a survivor.

It was on the tip of his fingers to sign, "But you're not. You're dead." Instead, Eric refrained. Illusion over reality, he reminded his brain.

"I'm not sure how long she's staying," said Eric.

We have to do everything in our power to make her realize this is her home.

"Is it?"

It was subtle, the soft touch of ghost-like fingers on his rough cheek, but everything in Eric froze. The sensation, a first.

This is her home, my home, your home. This place is part of you, her and me. She came home because she's hurting. Our job is to ensure she finds the faith to love the Shore.

"You're out to ensure she stays. Causing mischief as usual," said Eric, leaning his head into the ghostly hand.

It's what friends do. Plus, someone has to stick around to save you guys. You need me.

Eric laughed and quickly signed. "You've got that right."

Later, Eric got back in his truck and cranked the heat. He drove the rest of the way down the East Jeddore Road, parked and then opened the door to the house he'd lived in for over thirty-five years with his father. For the past decade, it had been the two bachelors, ever since his mother had been relocated into a long-term care home in Musquodoboit Harbour. Even before her vacating the home, she'd been absent for most of his adult life. Diagnosed with early on-set dementia, he'd been the one to make tea, clean the house and ensure, when his father had been away on duty, she'd at least been clothed. They had help with trusted neighbours, but Eric had always felt they'd pitied him for two reasons: his mother's illness and him being deaf.

While he was two years older than Sally, they'd been good friends since elementary days. It helped she lived two doors from him in a mini-home perched close to the ocean. She'd asked him to teach her and Kim sign language and she'd mastered it like a pro. Kim had enjoyed the uniqueness of the language, but Sally had incorporated it into her daily life. Their lives had diverged a bit during junior high when Eric got busy with hockey, working part-time at the local gas station and helping with his mother's upkeep, but when he hit grade ten and she was in grade eight, they reclaimed their friendship. The summer of grade nine when Sally was about to start high school, their friendship turned into much more.

Eric wondered, as he slipped off his sneakers, hung up his jacket and gently closed and locked the front door to the house, where he'd be now if instead of moving their friendship up a notch all those years ago, they'd kept it as it had been. Would he have truly been able to move on?

His father peeked his head out of his bedroom door. "Glad you're home," he signed.

"Sorry, late night," signed Eric.

His father gave him a tired smile and nodded. "That time of the month, already?" he signed.

Eric returned his father's expression, nodding a, "Yes."

"I'll see them tomorrow. Bet they'll look great. You okay?" signed his father.

No. "Tired but okay," signed Eric.

"You know you don't have to keep doing this?" signed his father.

What's with the repetitive arguments tonight? thought Eric. "My issue, not yours," signed Eric, hardening his expression.

His father gave a curt nod and then finally went back into

his room. Ten minutes later, Eric laid in his own bed, replaying the conversation he'd had with Sally over and over in his mind, trying without success to make sense of the night. Exhausted, Eric realized illusion made him sad. He wanted to move on, but couldn't. He wanted what he knew he couldn't have – Sally back in his life.

About Renee Field

Renee Field grew up next to the Atlantic Ocean in Nova Scotia, Canada. She is a multi-genre author who enjoys writing romance, young adult, women's fiction and speculative fiction. Her first romance novel, Rapture, received an EPPIE Award for Best Paranormal/Fantasy Romance for an e-book. The EPPIE is the longest-standing, most-inclusive e-book awards and are run by the Electronic Publishing Industry Coalition. She has published books with Ellora's Cave and HQN Spice Briefs.

Under her pen name, Renee Pace, she writes realistic nitty gritty novels where teenagers come of age and edgy dark teen paranormal novels with strong female characters. Her first young adult novel, Off Leash, was a semi-finalist in the 2011 Amazon Breakthrough Novel Contest and has been in the Top 100 Amazon Paid ranking for Best Coming of Age story numerous times. The Amazon Breakthrough Novel Award (ABNA) was a contest sponsored by Amazon.com, Penguin Group, Hewlett Packard, CreateSpace and BookSurge to publish and promote a manuscript by an unknown or unpublished author.

When not writing, she's an active community volunteer. Renee is a member of Romance Writers of Atlantic Canada.

Check out Renee's books at www.reneefield.com

Follow her:

facebook.com/ReneeFieldRomanceAuthor
twitter.com/ReneePField
instagram.com/field.renee
tiktok.com/@reneefieldwriter

Manufactured by Amazon.ca
Bolton, ON